The Rovan Ruins
(Book 11 of the PIT Series)
by Michael McCloskey

ISBN: 978-1719419680

Learn more about Michael McCloskey's works at www.squidlord.com

Cover art by Stephan Martiniere
Edited by Stephen "Shoe" Shoemaker

Chapter 1

Telisa walked out onto her favorite balcony. A vast blue sky beckoned beyond the rubbery Celaran rail, but it was not real sky: it was an illusion created inside the huge space habitat. The Terrans called the habitat Blackhab after the troublesome Blackvines they had discovered here while hunting the Trilisk.

The dark green Celaran house floated a stone's throw from similar ones where the other PIT team members lived. Now that Telisa knew so much about the Celarans, she could see their personality in everything around her: the bright sky, the circular windows, and the flexible cord that served her as a balcony rail, which was a roosting point for Celarans. The only thing missing the first time the PIT team had explored this place was the giant vines, but now the Celarans had started tens of thousands of the plants growing on the interior surface of the habitat.

She heard footsteps in the house behind her. The light, erratic cadence did not belong to Magnus. A part of her went on heightened alert, but she would rely upon her incredible reflexes in the unlikely event of an attack.

Sounds like Marcant.

A house service informed her of Marcant's arrival, validating her guess. A tiny hope struggled to rise within her. Was he here to tell her of success?

"I'm outside," Telisa called aloud. It felt comfortable and quaint to yell instead of sending a pointer.

Wouldn't want to ruin this place's charm.

"Ah, there you are," Marcant said. He walked out next to her. Had he really found her without the help of the house or was he playing along with her old-fashioned facade?

"Do we have them back?" Telisa asked, skipping all niceties.

"No," Marcant said.

Of course not. Our fallen friends are still gone.

"It's not like you to make a social call, Marcant," she said lightly, disguising her disappointment.

"I thought you might want to know that a Celaran probe has discovered alien ruins," Marcant said.

"Really?"

Marcant retreated into the shade of the doorway, out of the light. Telisa supposed the habitat's artificial starlight was uncomfortable on his pale skin. He did not have to worry about getting a tan—melanin formation was easily controlled with a pill.

"Of course really. Looks like dozens of sites across a planet with breathable atmosphere, gravity just heavy enough it would have made Siobhan grumble, and best of all—not water dwellers. No thrashing around underwater waiting for the next oxygen crisis."

He mentions Siobhan so easily. It doesn't bother Marcant as much that she's gone because he's a simulationist. As far as he's concerned, she simply exited into the next reality on the stack.

"You're selling this hard," Telisa said.

In truth, she was already hooked. She was not built for sitting around waiting for artifacts to be reverse engineered and data secrets to be unraveled. It had only been a couple of weeks, but she craved action.

Magnus walked out onto the balcony.

"What's up?" he asked.

"We have a mission!" Telisa said.

"Really?"

Telisa laughed at his identical response.

"The Celarans know about another extinct alien civilization. We can go check it out."

"What about our missing people?" Magnus asked.

"The Celarans are working on it," Marcant said. "We've shared everything we know. I think they'll crack it, eventually." He sounded confident.

"And the AI?" Magnus asked.

The Trilisk AI had started functioning again once they left Quarus Cora, where they used it against another Trilisk artifact, almost destroying the moon on which the struggle had taken place. Since then, the Celarans had been making use of the powerful alien artifact to re-establish themselves at Blackhab.

"We leave it here," Telisa told him. "It came from their planet. They deserve it. It's just what they need to get themselves set up here."

"We could use it where we're going. It could be dangerous," Magnus said, doing his usual devil's advocate act.

Telisa laughed. It would be very dangerous, no doubt.

"We'll use it to stock ourselves up with supplies, robots, attendants... everything," she assured him.

"Is everyone in, then? Lee, Maxsym, Arakaki... Barrai?" Magnus asked.

"We'll see. Maxsym is the only one I could imagine saying no. He has so much on his plate he could probably work here for twenty years without looking up."

"Good," Magnus said.

"Get your robot parts together," she said. "We'll need a new army of them."

Magnus's mood lifted even further. He smiled.

Such an easy man to please.

"That's true! We don't have Shiny's watchdogs to fall back on anymore," he said.

"Team, something's afoot!" she said on the PIT channel, having a little fun. "Meet me next shift, over on the *Sharplight*."

Everyone acknowledged eagerly, even Maxsym. Telisa could tell they were all ready to go on another adventure.

***

Telisa arrived twenty minutes early on the *Sharplight*, but she found Marcant already waiting in the designated meeting room.

"I don't suppose with all that's happened you've had a chance to work out anything about shielding the AI," she said.

"I have news. I see how the Trilisk control host bodies!"

"That's great!"

"...Oh, no, it's not *that* wonderful. I don't know how to *fix* it."

"Uhm. So you understand the problem now, but a solution eludes you."

"Yep. Those bodies are set up to make their EM state remotely readable and settable. The same thing that makes them ideally suited for remote installation and removal of other consciousnesses is what makes them controllable."

"But I've had my consciousness moved around, even from my original body."

"I think Trilisks can do the swap at close range such as, say, in a Trilisk column, with any mind at all. But these host bodies are set up to be receptive at much longer ranges."

As we found out the first time we visited Blackhab.

The other members started to walk in. Magnus, Arakaki, and Lee showed up within a few minutes of each other. Maxsym was the last to arrive. He had fully recovered from his poisoning episode resulting from GNI's attempted espionage.

Telisa saw no reason to delay the news to the team members who had not already heard.

"Marcant brought an interesting development to my attention: The Celarans have passed along news of alien ruins to explore," she told them. "It looks like a race we've never seen. If you're game, I say let's take a look."

Telisa sent them a starmap pointer and let them look over the location information provided by the Celarans.

"It's a long way out!" Arakaki said.

"It always is," Magnus said.

"The planet has multiple sites with alien constructs, on the surface and extending below ground. There were also a handful of satellites in decaying orbits when this information was taken. Before anyone asks, the tunnels are pretty large, so we wouldn't be crawling around on our hands and knees... or sending attendants into ratholes."

"If you're in, think about what supplies you'll need," Magnus said. "We should draw up lists and try to fulfill our needs here before we leave the umbrella of the Trilisk AI."

"What? Why would we leave that behind?" Arakaki interjected.

"That was the next announcement. It's from their planet, and they need it. There's more of them, too."

Telisa paused. No one disagreed with her, though she could tell everyone wanted to bring it along. That did not surprise her—she felt it herself. The AI was amazing and it made life easier even though it was hard to use it to procure complex physical items.

"Those of you who are in, let's plan on leaving in two days. Hit me with your questions," Telisa finished.

"What ships are we taking?" asked Arakaki rapidly.

Enthusiasm!

"I think we'll leave our Terran *Iridar* behind for Caden and Siobhan just in case any of the Celarans can get copies out of that column."

Maybe even Imanol... Cilreth...

"Maxsym really likes to use the Vovokan *Iridar* for research, right?" Marcant asked. "Are we leaving that one behind for him?"

Eyes turned toward Maxsym.

"I'm coming along," Maxsym said. "And yes, I'd prefer to be in the other *Iridar* as always."

Telisa smiled.

"Maxsym has one or two adventurous bones in his body after all!" she said.

"Some of the ruins are underground?" asked Magnus. "Did the Celarans check against Vovokan signatures? Do they even know what Vovokan ruins would look like?"

"I don't think they checked, but I gave the data a cursory look-over and I don't think this is a dead Vovokan colony," Telisa said.

"Thank you for leaving the Trilisk artifact on this vine," Lee said through their links. "However, as a sunny day can turn dark, we should warn my friends: Shiny may learn of the vine's amazing sap and come for a slurp of his own, or even try to drain it dry. He could steal the artifact and take it home to his own vine."

"I'm hoping that with a Trilisk AI of his own, he'll decide it's not worth the risk," Telisa said. "But you're right Lee. We have to remind Cynan and the others that it has to be guarded carefully. And if Shiny comes for it by force rather than by stealth, they may even have to use the AI to defend themselves."

"One last thing: I'm inviting Barrai to officially join the team and come along on this exploration. Some of you already know she is... formidable."

Maxsym was not phased, but Marcant looked like he was going to groan. His sparring sessions had not been going well. He would just have to improve.

Chapter 2

Magnus watched Telisa bounce into the mess, brimming with even more energy than her host body usually provided. The new opportunity had her fired up. He drank in the sight of her.

So alive... vibrant... driven.

He suddenly wondered if she aged in the host body as he did. It would likely become obvious in another few years. He vowed to appreciate what he had.

If the skew between our ages becomes too great, we might be able to use a Trilisk column to give us bodies of the same age... any age. It's theoretically immortality.

The entire team had been busy praying up supplies and moving back over to the *Sharplight* for their voyage. Telisa was the most focused and enthusiastic of all of them.

"Do me a favor and get Barrai on the PIT team today," Telisa said, sitting next to him and starting in on a plate with four sandwiches.

"She's going to accept our offer, I assume," Magnus said.

"Unless you can talk her out of it. Try to scare her, Magnus. We don't need her death on our conscience."

Magnus almost told her she was being overly dramatic. It only took a moment of recalling their long list of dead friends to decide she was not.

"I will. I'll warn her and tell her to think it over."

Telisa nodded, her mouth full of food.

"How much should I tell her?"

"Mmm. Be vague about the AI, as usual. You can tell her how I knocked her flat if you want."

Magnus nodded.

"Does she resent you? Is that why I'm doing this?" he asked.

Telisa shook her head.

"No. If she's that sensitive, we don't want her on the team anyway."

"Right," Magnus agreed. "We'll know soon enough. Integrate her with our training schedule and see if she can mesh with the team."

Telisa mashed another half-sandwich into her mouth and stood.

"Finishing preparations," she explained to him through her link while she chewed.

He nodded and watched her rush out with the last sandwich in her hands. Magnus checked Barrai's schedule. He decided it was possible she would come through soon, so he took his time.

Barrai strode into the mess five minutes later. No one else was on a schedule to be looking for food at that time, so they were alone. Barrai came up to where Magnus sat and lifted one leg over the bench, sitting sideways to face him.

"Hello, Lieutenant," Magnus said. "Actually, are you still in the Space Force?"

"I am, though I take my orders only from you now. Or anyone on the PIT team, I mean."

"I could call you Barrai if you don't mind. We don't really go by ranks around here as I'm sure you noticed."

"Sure, okay."

"I wanted to talk to you about the PIT team. You've already worked closely with us, but we could extend you a formal spot if you're interested."

As if we do anything formally.

"I am! Are we going to do another truth check?"

"No, that won't be necessary. Today is more about what you want to do. There's something you need to consider before joining us. Everyone on the PIT team dies."

Barrai's eyes widened for just a moment, then her face froze.

She's waiting for me to say if I'm joking.

"You make it sound so appealing," Barrai said.

"I'm serious. Work with us for long enough, and you'll meet your end. Make sure this kind of life is worth it for you."

Barrai paused.

"I'll say yes, but I have a condition."

"Yes, I'll spar with you," he said.

"Then count me in!"

Magnus suppressed a smile. Barrai was nothing if not predictable.

"Take more time and think about, say, getting eaten alive by an alien predator, or... dying in a meaningless accident as we arrive at a new world."

"I guess you're this grim because of 'those who have gone before'."

Magnus recognized the Space Force line about the sacrifices that allowed Terrans to become a starfaring species.

"That's right. This is more dangerous than keeping the *Sharplight* in top shape. Which you would still be doing, by the way."

"I have the spare cycles. That's part of why I always want to work out with new people. It's something I can do to push myself—and absorb a lot of hours in training."

"Yes, we'll be doing intense training that helps with the tedium of long trips. Anything you'd like to ask me?"

"I've picked up what I could, but I'm having a hard time separating the rumors from reality. For example, what skills is each person on the team known for?"

Magnus paused.

What an excellent question.

"Caden was our best with advanced weaponry. Siobhan was really useful for setting up working systems on the ground in record time. They were both learning all about Celaran technologies."

"It's terrible what happened. They were heroes."

"Yes, they were. But what we want from you is to help us discover new things, not die in combat against aliens or frontier gangs."

She nodded.

"Maxsym is a xenobiologist. One of the best. He's also good at tossing out theories the rest of us may not have considered. I've seen him solve a problem in five minutes that stumped other people for days. Marcant is great at bringing computing power to bear on complex problems. Arakaki is a military scout, ex-UED. She has combat experience. I guess I do, too."

Magnus took a moment to consider Lee.

"Lee is brave and adventurous... for a Celaran. She's newish, but we hope having an alien on the team will bring in new perspectives, and she's fluent with advanced Celaran tech, not to mention that she can fly. She set us up with advanced cloaking that's integrated with Terran link technology."

Magnus stopped, thinking he was done.

"And Telisa?"

Magnus blinked.

"Who?"

Barrai laughed.

"What does Telisa bring? Leadership?"

"Inspiration. Energy. Yes, leadership. She has a formal education in alien studies, and she can hold her own in a fight."

"*Hold her own?* She kicked my ass so hard it still hurts. How did she defeat me?" Barrai asked. "I thought I was fast, but..."

"She cheated."

"Really? How?"

"Alien technology," Magnus said.

"I don't suppose she would give me another go without it."

"Sorry. It's built-in."

"Ah. Well, thanks for telling me. Makes my ego feel a little less bruised."

"Having an ego is good as long as it's not getting in the way of teamwork," he said.

Barrai nodded. "I get what you're saying. It won't."

"Okay. Think about it, and if you're still in, we'll fill you in with more details."

"So what you have planned isn't another military operation," Barrai guessed.

"That's right. We're going exploring. Our primary mission type."

"Yet your team is half combat specialists, and the rest are training to become one."

"Well, things never seem to go smoothly," Magnus admitted.

Nothing is ever easy.

"Team, we're leaving in an hour," Telisa sent them on the PIT channel.

"Here we go!" Barrai said.

Magnus nodded.

"Here we go," he echoed.

***

A day later, the team gathered in a meeting lounge for their first in-transit training session. Magnus sat down next to Marcant and prepared to join their shared virtual environ. Everyone was present except Telisa.

"Seven of us on the roster," Marcant said.

"At least for now, until the lovebirds rejoin us," Maxsym said.

"And Imanol and Cilreth," Marcant added. "Just think... there will be eleven people on the PIT team if we can get them back."

It was wishful thinking to leave an Iridar behind for Caden and Siobhan, Magnus thought. *Trilisk artifacts have eluded Terran understanding for decades.*

"Do we really want Imanol back?" Arakaki said.

Barrai gave her a look of horror.

Everyone laughed, causing Barrai more confusion.

"Imanol made Marcant look like a charming social butterfly," Magnus told Barrai privately. "But he was a solid team member."

Barrai smiled and nodded to him. They turned their attention to Telisa as she arrived.

"We're going for broke. We have no idea what to train for yet," Telisa told them. "All we have to do is get used to the new team configuration."

She said it mildly enough, but Marcant's mouth tightened and Maxsym shifted uncomfortably. Arakaki looked down for a moment. It was a polite way to say 'get used to our new team member and the loss of the old ones'.

Telisa initialized a scenario generator to create a new challenge for the team. They all joined the virtual environment.

They found themselves in a blue forest of straight spines growing from soft soil. Magnus stood next to Telisa. He noted that Marcant was missing a second before the mission directive went out: "Find your missing team member in the vicinity."

And, of course, expect trouble!

They got to work.

***

Magnus disengaged from the last scenario of their training session. He had been shot, stabbed, and eaten by a huge living mass of rocklike material. The team successfully negotiated about forty percent of the challenges, mostly the easy ones at the start of the session.

Barrai smiled at Magnus.

"That was instructive," she said. "Space Force training is a little more... structured. Or, maybe I should say: predictable."

"I imagine so," Magnus said. "It's been a while since I served."

"You owe me a sparring match," she said, changing the subject.

"I do."

"Got time?"

"I'll meet you there in five," Magnus said.

Barrai smiled and hurried off to change. Magnus left at a more leisurely pace. He mulled over what he had heard from the others. Apparently Barrai possessed elite speed and great stand-up prowess. His own speed was above average, but he doubted he could match hers, so he decided to cover and try out her ground skills. If she dominated him, so be it. He would try his best and learn whatever tricks she had.

He strode into the workout room and saw Barrai throwing a series of punches at a heavybag. His own body felt stiff from the hours of VR, so he ran around the perimeter a few times to get his blood pumping, then started to stretch.

After ten minutes, he met her out on the floor.

Barrai attacked boldly. Magnus circled and fended off her jabs, waiting to counter. Barrai mixed in rapid kicks and combinations. Magnus knew what to do in the face of her superior speed because he often faced Telisa's superhuman abilities. He covered as best he could, sacrificing cover of his trunk to protect his head while circling and retreating.

Barrai launched another assault, drawing his guard high, then low, then high again. Magnus tried to take a low hit while protecting his head, but she connected with his temple anyway.

Expecting her to capitalize on her advantage, Magnus threw himself for her legs. Barrai sprawled furiously to avoid the takedown. Magnus used his superior strength to throw her back, apparently victorious, but she went with the momentum and rolled aside before Magnus could establish himself atop her.

Barrai, elated by her close escape, returned to the attack without missing a beat. She kicked him in the side, connecting solidly. Then she launched a fist at his face, but he covered and dipped his head. He used her sudden confidence against her, sweeping her lead leg as she pressed. This time Magnus managed to get hold of her leg and pull her in. She punched him smartly before he established control of the mount.

Now Magnus began a methodical assault. She planted a knee to stop him, but he passed her guard and managed to control her. Barrai punched the side of his head a few times, but Magnus trapped the arm and forced her to tap.

They stood back up. Despite the success, Magnus felt he was the worse for wear compared to his opponent. They were both in great shape. As the battle continued, Barrai landed many blows. Magnus managed to take the Space Force officer down two more times, but as expected, he was taking a beating on the stand-up.

Magnus knew that if she were his size, they would be roughly equal in a roll. She had physical advantages of her own; his arms and legs did not have the quick snap that hers did, and probably never would. Her legs were longer than his. He could not respond to her speed, but he was solid enough to take a shot as he positioned himself for strong counters, which usually involved trying to grapple. On the ground, he had a clear advantage. He knew many techniques, and when necessary, he could capitalize on his greater mass to overcome her in close calls.

They stopped at the end of a ten minute round.

"You're good," Barrai said, breathing hard.

She's being gracious.

"You too," he said. "You're too fast for me. Let's set up a regular time for this."

"Sounds good."

The workout continued. Magnus held his own more and more as they fought on; Barrai's lightning speed slowed a little more than his own. In the end, they agreed to call it a draw, but Magnus felt that Barrai had proven herself to be superior—though by a narrow margin.

They showered in their undersheers, each in a niche attached to the workout center. On the way out, they stopped to clasp hands and clap each other on the back.

"Good first day. Glad to have you here," Magnus said.

She smiled.

"See you for VR in two shifts."

Magnus went back to his quarters, dropped some pseudo-VR gear off, and sought out Telisa in her room. He found her in a lotus position, eyes closed. He supposed she was absorbing input from her link rather than meditating.

"How did the sparring with Barrai go?" Telisa asked. She unfolded her legs and regarded him.

"She's fast. Got some good shots in."

"So who's top dog?"

"I think I held my own. Judging from today, I'd say she's better at stand up and I have the edge on the ground."

"Mmmm."

Magnus flopped into the sleep web. She was in one of her thoughtful moods, so he just lay there for a few minutes, resting.

"The training was weird today," Telisa said.

Because Caden and Siobhan are gone.

"I felt it, too. We lost two friends and then added Barrai. It feels off, but—"

"I know. In two weeks it'll be the new normal."

Am I so predictable? I guess so.

"One of the dangers of relying on an older man for advice," Magnus said. "Eventually, he starts to recycle all his old stories."

"Repetition isn't always bad," she said, rolling under the sleep web. Magnus slipped his arms through the netting, wrapped them around her, and kissed her.

No. Not at all.

Chapter 3

Arakaki woke up in the middle of a sleep shift. She sat up naked in her sleep web. Her hand traveled up her torso and felt for the armor sliver.

It was not around her neck.

She told the room service to turn on a low light source. The room came into view. She spotted her necklace on a wall by the shower tube. The fragment of armor was held fast in a small ring that let her remove it when she wanted to chew on it.

I took that off three days ago.

Thinking of her ex only brought the weakest, most distant sense of loss.

'Bout time you got over him.

Weeks of training had brought the new teams closer together. Typically they operated in three pairs—Telisa and Magnus, Marcant and Maxsym, and Barrai and Arakaki. Lee, as the only one who could fly, was logically the odd Celaran out, so she functioned as a scout more than anything.

Arakaki checked the ship's status. As expected, the team had arrived above at their destination as Arakaki slept: a small system with only four planets, one rocky cinder close to a yellow star, one in the habitable zone, and two gas giants.

Marcant and Telisa had dispatched a small army of attendants to take the first surveys of the planet below. Arakaki took a few peeks at the progress. The planet was green, covered in vegetation that was not fundamentally different than Terran plants. She saw vast fields of something similar to grassland. There were stubby 'trees': meter-high masses of tough, gray growth that served as central hubs for dozens or hundreds of long green streamers like bright blades of grass that went on for meters.

Arakaki paced about aimlessly for a minute, watching the video feeds in her PV. She slowly realized there was a reason she was still naked. She had not slept with anyone incarnate in a long time...

What are you going to do? Invite Maxsym in here?

Of all the crew, Arakaki figured Barrai or Maxsym would give her the least entanglement in a sex partner, and she narrowly favored men, so Maxsym would be her best choice.

Magnus would really hit the spot, but he's not interested. Should I settle? Ug. Does Maxsym even like women? I wish Caden...

Thinking of Caden made her feel sad. She lost the inclination to ask Maxsym over. She would have herself yet another virtual romp later, unless work prevented it. They were at the new planet, after all.

"So this is it," Magnus said on the team channel. His tone indicated he was summing up the place as the rest of them must be doing.

"The third planet of the Rovatick Ailia System," Telisa said.

"So what should we call them—the Ticks?" Magnus asked playfully.

"The Rovans," Telisa said. "For now, at least."

"The problem with 'for now' is that we'll get used to it and the name will stick," Magnus said.

"Rovans isn't bad. Sounds familiar, even," Marcant said.

"Because of the Romans," Maxsym said with certainty.

"The who?" Magnus asked.

"An archaism," Telisa answered for Maxsym. Arakaki imagined his frustrated look.

"It doesn't appear to be dangerous down there," Barrai said.

Arakaki snorted. She did not have her feed configured to send the judgemental sound through, so she responded more diplomatically.

"That just means the attendants haven't found the bad places yet," she said. "Trust me: it's dangerous."

"I'm picking up a few dozen artificial satellites in varied orbits," Barrai said. "Nothing large, and there are no course changes in response to our arrival."

"Keep watching them. We'll leave them alone until we know more," Telisa said. "If nothing else, we'll have a few alien satellites to examine."

"How does the microbiology panel look?" Telisa asked.

"The quick analyses look okay," Maxsym responded. "There are a couple of micros that can eat us, but nothing we shouldn't be able to handle. The chemical screen is similar. A few poisonous compounds here and there. Not worse than your typical life-supporting planet."

A couple of microscopic things that can eat us. Nice.

Arakaki smiled. She wondered if Barrai was still eager to get down there in light of that news.

"Barrai. Your training has been coming along. Do you want to make landfall with us?" Telisa asked.

"What? I'm a city girl. You go rattle around in the weeds without me," Barrai responded. "Now, if you find some hi-tech ruins you go right ahead and call me. I'd love to see alien spaceships!"

Arakaki raised an eyebrow. She had expected a nervous, 'yes'. The straightforward pass was not nearly as fun.

"That's weird. Marcant is coming and Barrai turned us down," Magnus said privately to Telisa and Arakaki.

"Marcant's been training with us longer. Besides, he's a simulationist, remember? He thinks if he dies out here, he just wakes up in some other reality," Arakaki said.

"Okay, but if we get ourselves into trouble, you're going to suit up and come save us," Telisa told Barrai.

"Got it."

Arakaki slid into her Momma Veer and looked over her arsenal. Judging from the density of vegetation, she would not need any long-range rifles, so she selected her favorite UED submachine gun and a laser pistol. She had a new breaker claw and a cloaking device, both produced by Celarans, and a pack with food and medical supplies. Two more packs held miscellaneous gear like smart ropes and tents for any base camp they might set up.

Arakaki grabbed everything and set off.

***

Arakaki stood in a small clearing behind the team's shuttle, breathing heavily.

"This stuff is tough, almost like rope," Marcant said.

She looked over at her pale teammate. He held a heavy cutting tool—not an ultrasharp—and stood atop mounds of the green streamers.

"This is much more passable for an attendant. I didn't realize how difficult it would be for us," Telisa remarked.

"It's easy for me!" Lee exclaimed, darting by at high speed.

"Show off!" Marcant called after her.

Arakaki did not mind the extra work. Behind all that foliage were alien ruins. There would soon be something to break the initial grind.

She walked up to the edge of their clearing and examined the vegetation again from the open cross section that exposed everything below the streamers. Dead brown leaves hung from the trunks below the long green ones. It reminded her of the dead frond stumps on a palm tree below the new growth.

When danger comes—we won't see it coming.

"Are you going to shoot something?" Magnus asked. Arakaki looked over and realized he had addressed the question to her. She had her weapon pointed toward the wall of plants.

"I expect I will, sooner or later," she said coolly.

Marcant took her meaning and looked at the streamer trees with new respect. He took a step back toward the middle of the clearing.

Maxsym barely heard her. Oblivious to any danger, the biologist was on his hands and knees at the edge of the plants, examining first the streamers, then the cuts in the larger trunks, then grabbing tiny life forms and putting them into sample containers. He had brought no less than four bulging packs of equipment from the ship, which lay all around him. Three of them were opened with equipment spilling out to make room for the new samples.

Where Maxsym goes, the base camp follows.

"So did you drop us in the middle of a random jungle?" Magnus asked Telisa mildly.

"No! We have ruins to check out, forty meters in that direction," Telisa said. She sent along a pointer.

"Cleared by attendants, I assume," Marcant said.

"Nope. The attendants were blocked by set of ceramic doors leading into a low hill that could be a buried building," Telisa said.

Marcant's face pinched for a moment. Then he shook his head.

"Let's start hacking," Marcant said.

"Not the kind of hacking you're used to," Arakaki said.

"Unnecessary," Magnus announced with an air of grandeur.

Arakaki turned with the others to stare. Magnus stood aside and pointed behind them toward the shuttle. Six long, thin legs emerged from an unloaded crate, lifting out an insectoid robot. The robot scuttled forward and unfolded four arms, which held up four sharp blades.

"This will do the cutting for us," Magnus said. "We'll watch it in operation and note any adjustments needed in the design."

"Nice!" Marcant said, putting away his machete. "Are they...?"

"Ultrasharps? Yes. For your own safety, stand back."

The team withdrew to allow the machine to pass. It attacked the foliage, smoothly cutting a path in the direction Telisa's map indicated. The whirring and chopping noise receded as the machine worked its way deeper into the vegetation. Marcant and Maxsym nodded appreciatively.

"Oh, look how narrow a path it cuts," Telisa nitpicked, but she could not keep a straight face. Magnus smiled back at her.

It bothered Arakaki a little to see them having so much fun, but she shook off her jealousy. It was a sunny day on a beautiful planet, and they were on a new adventure. It could have been another training simulation, but the knowledge it was real made all the difference.

The team walked in behind the machine once it had made its way thirty meters. Everyone stared to the sides at the plant structures that had been revealed. An occasional insectoid creature crawled among the streamers, never larger than her finger. Most of them were eating the plants. She assumed the ones not doing so were hunting the others.

The robot stopped cutting and turned to the right. Then it cleared away more streamers until it could halt out of their way. A concrete or ceramic terrace lay beyond. At the far side, massive doors were set against a black frame in the hillside. The portal was perhaps six meters wide and over two meters tall. Dirt and streamers covered the rest of the structure, which had either been consumed by soil and overgrowth or had been partially underground all along.

They must have been giants.

"A cave entrance?"

"An underground building," Telisa corrected. "What could be more fun than finding out what's inside?"

Attendants moved forward to scout the way for them but stopped short when they encountered the doors.

"How old do you suppose this place is?" Arakaki asked. She scanned the doors and their frame for sensor or weapon ports.

"I would say about..." Marcant paused. "...three hundred years. Could be as much as... well, a thousand years."

No time at all on a galactic scale.

"Based upon what kind of scan?" Maxsym asked eagerly.

"I was just using my attendants' observations," Marcant said.

Maxsym stopped as if doing the same.

"I'll watch for predators underleaf," Lee said. "I'd rather not go into that dark root pit!"

"Good idea," Telisa said. "Keep pinging us. I want to know if our signals will get out from down there, or if we need to maintain a chain of attendants to keep in contact with the surface."

"The door has no manual mechanism I can see," Magnus said.

"Perhaps it locks from the inside," Maxsym suggested.

"The cutting robot might—" began Arakaki.

"No." Magnus interrupted. "Even if it worked, it would ruin those blades."

"Blow it open?" asked Marcant.

"We have tools for this back by the shuttle," Arakaki said.

"I'll swing by and drop off what you need!" Lee said excitedly.

She has enough enthusiasm for three PIT members.

"Bond cutter, please," Telisa said.

"There are two robots patrolling around the shuttle," Lee observed. "I see they're part of our vine."

"Yes, they're guards," Magnus said. "I've got two more coming this way. They might be able to help us pry something open."

Arakaki watched everything happen through the attendant network. Lee swooped down to find a tool among their extra packs while two six-legged robots plodded toward the team through the tunnel cut in the vegetation. Attendants piped in views from inside the nest of streamers around them.

The robots arrived and positioned themselves to the left and right at the edge of the terrace. The machines each had two weapon mounts: a laser on the head, and a grenade launcher on the torso.

Lee arrived suddenly, diving out of the sky and slowing at the last moment. She deposited a metal frame with a mobile arm holding a sophisticated cutter. Arakaki remained alert while Telisa and Magnus affixed the cutter to the door. They stood back as the device scanned the door and started to slice through the tough ceramic with an energy beam.

Arakaki did not watch the cutting; she kept her eyes on the forest. Experience had taught her to look where the rest of the team was not. A barely audible whine told her the device was working.

The largest creature the attendants had found was a one-meter-long serpent about a quarter of a kilometer away. It moved slowly among the streamers. Its body was colored to look like a long streamer itself, green with a single white line down the center, mimicking the fold in the center of the plant's blades. She saw something that looked like a mouth on one end. There were four eyes atop each end, placed in a square configuration. It moved remarkably like a Terran snake. Arakaki supposed that made sense given its form.

Arakaki heard a clanking sound and the whine stopped.

"Finally," Marcant said.

"Attendants first, robots second," Telisa ordered.

Arakaki approved. She did not want to be the first one to step into that place, three hundred years old or not. She had seen too many people die doing things like that. Arakaki was aware that Telisa had additional reasons for the procedure: as a xenoarchaeologist, she wanted the attendants to scan everything before the team disturbed it. That way, the team would have a virtual reconstruction of the ruins' current state which could be studied for contextual clues about the Rovans.

Arakaki turned to look at the open doorway. Darkness beckoned beyond the opening.

The soldier robots marched in, accompanied by four attendants. Telisa entered next. Magnus followed Telisa, then Marcant, then Maxsym. Arakaki scanned the vegetation one last time, noting Lee in the sky overhead, before entering last.

At first she perceived it to be pitch black inside. Arakaki took a careful sniff of the air. It smelled musty and metallic. Arakaki thought of the place as a bunker, though to an alien it might have been anything; a pleasant summer home, a kid's playhouse, or a water pumping station. She wondered if it had been a safe place. Had it somehow failed to protect the inhabitants? Was that why Rovans no longer lived here?

She turned on her weapon's light and swept the area. Four thick pedestals rose from the floor. She supposed they had once held something... perhaps tabletops. The floor was not clean. She saw bits of gray and brown material that could have been rotted clothes or personal possessions. The far side of the room, 30 meters distant, had a squarish opening leading into a dark, wide corridor. She checked the wall next to her. It had many panels of various shapes and sizes that she guessed to be the covers to wall cabinets or bins.

"Kind of anticlimactic," Marcant said. "Are these bins? Let's open one."

Arakaki was ahead of them. She raised her weapon with her right hand and tried the panel's edge with her left. It did not budge.

"Try that tab on the bottom edge," Telisa said from somewhere. Arakaki thought they were opening another bin on the other side. She swept her light to the bottom of the panel and found a tab.

When she pushed up on the tab, the cover rose. She pushed it on up to open the bin. The panel seemed to bend back into the wall at the top as she lifted it. The inside was cluttered with several items of various colors and shapes, but before focusing on them, she swept the entire container with her light to make sure nothing moved. A fuzzy green mass lay in one corner. Arakaki's beam lingered on it for a moment, until she decided it was an object and not a living creature.

About twenty hand-sized cylinders bent into L-shapes were scattered around two clear, rectangular containers filled with rotted bits of black material. She saw a smaller box and two metal shapes that she guessed were tools. Dozens of tiny beads of gray matter, little nails or screws, and emblems or jewelry lay around and atop it all. She nudged the fuzzy green thing with the barrel of her weapon. It yielded and flopped to one side like a piece of garish party clothing.

She heard others rummaging around from across the room.

"It's full of... all kinds of stuff," Magnus said.

"This one, too," Marcant said.

"Stuff? These are *alien artifacts*!" Telisa said, exasperated.

Telisa had grabbed an orange object from a bin. It looked like a rubber planter. The outside was covered in studs made of the same soft material as the body. There were several others in the bin.

"What are these? Ideas?"

"Containers," Magnus said.

"Toys," Marcant said.

"Shoes," Arakaki guessed.

"Shoes? Hey, they could be shoes," Telisa said. She counted them. "This bin has two sets of four in orange and green."

"Okay guys. There's a lot of stuff—artifacts—here. Look for something we can recognize," Magnus suggested.

Arakaki shined her light on the objects in her bin again. A familiar shape caught her eye.

"Aha!" she said. She brought out a cylindrical object with fins and a pointy end.

She held it up for the others. "I know what this is."

Marcant took a step back. "Possible ordnance."

Arakaki nodded. "True." She placed the rocket back into the bin. "We can have a robot pick it up for examination later."

"Here's something," Maxsym said. He held up a coil of red and yellow rope.

"Rope! So there are a few things we can recognize. They aren't completely alien," Arakaki said.

"It doesn't bend," Maxsym observed. He shook the rope, but the coil did not flex.

"Even better—powered down smart rope," Telisa said. "We can search through it for the controller and learn about their cybernetics."

"And their energy storage," Marcant said excitedly. "If this does turn out to be a smart rope, we'll be able to compare their tech capabilities to our own."

Marcant held a shiny emblem or symbol in his Veer-gloved hand.

"I think I have... badges? Or markers..."

"These cylinders could be anything," Maxsym said, looking deeper into Marcant's bin. "Anything. This is kind of fun, but dangerous, too. They could be like sticks of explosive, or poison. We could all be dead in sixty seconds."

"That's the spirit!" Arakaki drawled.

Arakaki saw more bins along the walls. She took out a knife and held it before her as she opened another for a quick look.

"Looks like a lot of smaller containers. There must be a lot of stuff here... I mean, artifacts."

"Okay, let's finish exploring and come back here," Telisa said. "Maybe we can get more context to help us figure out these items. Such as, what a Rovan looks like."

"Searching for dead bodies?" asked Maxsym in an oddly hopeful way.

"Well I hope they're not merely sleeping," Marcant said.

"I think we should leave an attendant behind to scan and catalog all these items. It could screen for poisons and explosives," Arakaki suggested.

"Yes," Telisa said. "The attendants can scan it all and Magnus's robots can carry it back. The items that aren't clearly dangerous can be loaded onto the shuttle and taken back to *Sharplight* for careful study. I bet Adair is great at figuring out what artifacts do."

"And the items that *are* deemed dangerous?" Marcant asked.

"We'll set up a camp here somewhere. Maybe even in this room, actually," Telisa said, looking around again. "It has the space. We would need more light, of course. Magnus, have the robots put in lights, run a line outside, and hook up a few solar panels."

Everyone put the artifacts back into their bins. There was only one exit from the room, the one Arakaki had spotted early on, leading the opposite direction from the door they had forced.

The attendants had mapped the whole place while the team examined the items. Arakaki loaded their map. It displayed fourteen rooms. The place was at least as big as their old *Iridar*. The map had confusing narrow lines running in parallel groups between the larger rooms. Maxsym beat her to the question.

"What are all those... open pipes connecting everything?" he asked.

"We can examine some just ahead here," Telisa said. She pointed toward the dark corridor. The opening was wide enough for four people to walk side by side. Telisa led the way down the corridor.

After only fifteen or twenty meters, their lights revealed four round openings sitting near the floor on the right side. Each was about a third of a meter in diameter, and about a meter apart.

"That's creepy," Marcant said.

"Not helpful," Telisa replied.

"The complex is riddled with these. Are they vents or what?" asked Magnus.

"Those could be to bring in water," Maxsym theorized. "Maybe these creatures were amphibious. This could have filled the lower part of the floor with water."

Arakaki knelt before one of the pipes and shined her weapon's light into it. The inner surface was coated with dirt and peeling flakes of gray material. Her gut did not like what she saw. Instinct warned that danger would arrive from the dark opening.

Is that paint? Or the remains of whatever used to flow here?

"I'll take a—" Arakaki started, then she saw that Maxsym had already placed several of the flakes into a tube. "Never mind."

They continued down the corridor into another room. Long, curving shapes rose from the floor that she thought must be alien remains—an analogue of bones. The shortest pieces were straight, about the length of her forearm. The longest piece she saw was over a meter long. They were wrapped in black hide.

She knelt to rap on one with a knuckle. It was softer than ceramic, like a resin.

"These things are not mechanical as far as I can tell," Marcant said.

Maxsym moved in to examine one of the objects with a sampling device. "From the looks of these scans... if these are bones, the aliens form them in ways unique to our experience," he said. "I'll take a sample just in case."

"It's furniture," Telisa said.

Arakaki looked at the shapes in a new light. She decided Telisa might well be correct. The material she had thought of as alien hide or skin was probably the remains of whatever softer materials may have been wrapped around the structural components. Exactly what kind of things might have lounged on those strange curves, she could not guess, though they may have been large—or would dozens of smaller things have played atop each piece?

As they descended, the complex became dirtier. A rupture in one of the tunnels had allowed plant roots and a flood of mud to enter a room, destroying it.

They clambered over the roots and mud. A few more low-tech-looking items lay on the floor: a mud-streaked cone-shaped thing the size of her hand and a broken cup or container. Everyone eagerly moved on.

Soon they entered another large room. The remains of furniture or equipment were arrayed against black-streaked walls of gray. Ten of the pipe openings were placed near the floor, five on one wall and five on another.

The team spread out to search through the debris. Arakaki felt like she was looking through a disaster site for survivors. She lifted up a square piece of carbon mesh to uncover an oval frame a half-meter long. Complex machinery lay inside the frame. It looked like a gruesome cross section of an android head.

"Something here..." Arakaki said. The others came to look.

"I have no idea what that is, but it looks to be in good condition," Telisa said. She carefully brought it out of the garbage surrounding it and held it up. The frame had several round holes in its side and a smooth underside.

"It looks unfinished," Magnus said.

"A work in progress?" Marcant guessed.

"Or maybe a repair in progress," Magnus said, putting the artifact into a pack.

The team did not find anything else that looked interesting in the room, at least nothing intact that they felt warranted investigation. Telisa led the way down a gentle incline.

Arakaki half expected to see a huge alien corpse. She wondered what the Rovans had looked like. If Maxsym's theory was right, maybe they would find an enormous salamander-thing.

Their lights revealed another room, about twenty meters on a side. Three of the walls held low alcoves that were only half as high as the ceiling of four meters. The alcoves were about six meters long, with a maroon coloration. The bottom of each alcove was filled with an irregular gray material. An eight-legged table or stage sat less than a half meter high at one end of the room. Black spirals the size of a Terran forearm lay across the top—perhaps twenty of them.

"Beds," Magnus said, looking at the alcoves. He sounded confident of his guess.

Arakaki supposed he might be right, but there was not enough to go on.

Maxsym stopped near the spirals. He pointed a scanner at them and paused.

"This is a complex material," he said. "But homogenous. Probably a food item."

"You can say that already?" Telisa asked.

"It's a polysaccharide," Maxsym explained. "Chemical energy. I see the repetitive bonds suitable for digestion by low-temperature processes with enzymes... nothing weird here, just hydrogen, carbon, oxygen, calcium, chlorine... I think it's food."

"Alien spaghetti," Marcant said. "Any takers?"

"That's it for the big rooms," Arakaki summarized.

"No bodies," Maxsym said, finally looking away from the table.

"You said something about not having to crawl around on our hands and knees?" Marcant said, indicating one of the open pipes.

"We won't be," Telisa said. "But the part I said about not sending attendants into ratholes was apparently incorrect. Sorry, no refunds available."

"There's something important to note here," Marcant said. "You see this room, this one, and this one on the map? According to the attendant's data, these rooms are only accessible via the small tunnels. There are no larger corridors leading there."

"What's in those rooms?" Magnus asked. He stared at the wall blankly, accessing the map.

Arakaki brought up imagery of the inaccessible rooms the attendants had collected. One of the rooms was empty, though the walls had strange rows of small niches on them like staggered shelves with smooth depressions instead of rectangular storage holes. Another room held a stockpile of the black spiral material, Maxsym's theorized food source. The third room was filled with a perplexing maze of closed pipes that ran through several larger boxes. Rigid groups of even smaller pipes or conductors connected it all, often running in diagonal pathways. Arakaki guessed it might be the nerve center of the building, or at least a heating or cooling unit.

They marched back up to the first room and paused. Magnus's machines had installed four light bars in the corners, illuminating the room comfortably. Two of Magnus's robots were loading artifacts into cargo containers.

"What are your initial impressions?" Telisa asked the team.

The others traded looks. Arakaki waited one second, and when no one else spoke up, she said, "They were small, or at least some of them were. They used those narrow tunnels. The water theory is wrong because these small tunnels connect three different levels. The water would completely flood the lower levels but leave this level dry. Besides, there are so many redundant tubes without any valves or caps. Why would they need that for water? Any one of those pipes could carry enough water to quickly flood these rooms."

"Perhaps they *were* partially aquatic," Maxsym said. "Or maybe only their young were aquatic. The lower levels could have been completely flooded while this level remained only partially underwater. Multiple tubes are to allow multiple individuals to be swimming back and forth at the same time."

"The easiest explanation is that they simply had pets," Marcant said. "There are only a couple of rooms that are only accessible via the pipes. Maybe the pets slept there."

"The design is very pet-centric, wouldn't you say?" Telisa asked.

"Yes. But they're aliens," Arakaki said. "The amount they were willing to design their houses around their pets is different than how much Terrans do so."

Marcant's eyebrows jumped and he became more animated.

"Or, the pets could have been artificial. Servants, like our attendants. Or like Magnus's robots."

"Magnus?" Telisa prompted.

Magnus's lips compressed. Arakaki figured he did not like being put on the spot.

"I think that there were large individuals moving in these wider tunnels, and small individuals moved through the pipes. The pipes weren't for the young, because there would be a continuum of sizes, not just two. I think there may have been different genders with different final sizes. Or maybe a large one lived in here, like an ant queen, and the smaller ones were like worker ants, crawling through the tunnels and supporting it."

A lot of great guesses. But only guesses.

"Your turn," Magnus said to Telisa.

"I don't have much to add. We've observed there are two sizes of tunnels. That means, either the Rovans fit into the smallest sized tunnels, and they were all small, or, there were two sizes of... *things* that lived here. We have a good array of possibilities: at least two genders of different sizes, or perhaps young that go through a transformation into adulthood, or a kind of asymmetric system where the small ones were pets or servants of the large ones... I suppose we have to at least consider the possibility that the large ones served the small ones too. The large ones might have been the 'pets'. And yes, the pets might have been robots, but, with pipes being such a fundamental component of the entire place, and the redundancy, I'd have to say this started in their distant past."

"It's too bad we didn't learn more," Arakaki said. She had been looking forward to discovering what the Rovans had looked like. She knew Maxsym must have been even more eager to know.

"This is a big win," Telisa said. "Marcant has a rope he can check for controllers, Maxsym has a lot of samples to check for traces of the creatures long gone, and we have a ton of artifacts to pore over. I'm encouraged."

Arakaki knew Telisa was right. The job took patience. With all the aliens dead or gone, the process of learning would be slower.

"We'll stay here tonight. Get this room cleaned up. Lee, I won't ask you to come down here with us if it makes you uncomfortable, but if you don't, you should stay in the shuttle."

"Yes! I would stay on a familiar vine during an alien night. The shuttle will keep me safe, I think."

"I'll join Lee in the shuttle," Marcant said. "I'm not a fan of camping in dilapidated bunkers."

Telisa nodded. "Suit yourself."

The robots finished scanning and photographing the artifacts. The cutting robot cleared away room for a small camp beside the shuttle, but Telisa decided to move the equipment into the bunker with the team.

Arakaki kept a sharp eye on the video feeds from above ground and below while Marcant, Magnus, and Telisa argued over whether the scans had discovered anything dangerous about any of the artifacts. The item of most contention was the missile-shaped object.

"This is propellant," Magnus was saying, referring to networked scan results they examined in their PVs.

"It's a missile, yes, but without a warhead, it's not too dangerous to take back to the ship," Marcant argued.

"We don't really understand the payload, though," Telisa said. "Until we know what it is, we can leave it in a container outside."

"What if we cut it open and remove the payload?"

"Not in here," Telisa said.

"I'll have a robot do it in an isolated location," Magnus offered.

"Fine," Telisa said.

The team got the camp straightened out by the time the sun outside started to set. Their landfall had been only ten hours ago. The full day on the planet lasted about seventeen hours. Everyone stayed busy. The day had been short, so they all remained wide awake and eager to learn more.

Arakaki remained vigilant. She paid less attention to the artifacts, though she pondered one here and there while focused on the attendant feeds. As a result, she was the first to notice changes in the feeds.

"Something's happening outside!" Arakaki transmitted. "A strong wind is rising through the leaves or vines or whatever those things are."

"Be careful, there might be a kind of storm coming in," Telisa transmitted. "Can the *Sharplight* see anything? If there's a major weather event, maybe Lee and Marcant need to come in here."

"Nightfall has brought an uptick in wind, but there's no precipitation in your area," Adair reported from a geostationary position on the *Sharplight*.

"Life forms are moving in," Arakaki snapped. "Dozens of them!"

"Wait. Are we under attack?" Marcant asked incredulously.

"If we are, they're in for a surprise," Telisa said.

"Animals, I believe," Arakaki said. "Six-legged creatures, approximately 300 kilograms each. No signs of any tools or weapons."

"Let's investigate in person," Telisa said.

The others hesitated.

"Yes I know it's dangerous. I'm doing it anyway. Join or stay as you please, but activate your stealth if you're coming."

Telisa rushed for the door. Suddenly she had a stunner in her hand. Magnus followed her immediately. They dropped out of sight.

"You going?" Marcant asked Arakaki, but she had already started for the door. Maxsym was not far behind. They flipped on their stealth spheres.

As they approached the doors, Arakaki saw green streamers reaching for the dusk sky. The tightly packed miasma of impossibly long leaves around the terrace had untangled itself. A stiff breeze blew up the slope, causing the leaves to flap upward in long strands that rose five meters into the air.

What the hell?

Arakaki aimed her weapon across the terrace as she reached the doors. The last few steps made the tiny hairs on her neck stand on end. She emerged into the cool, windy night. A gorgeous array of stars twinkled in the sky straight overhead, moving Arakaki despite the ominous activity in the area. The cool air caressed her hands and face.

"It's beautiful, if alarming," Telisa said.

Arakaki listened for sounds from the animals, but all she heard was the sound of the wind flapping the long streamers. The leaves that had made passage impossible before were now well clear of the ground, leaving only the trunks of the plants. The tough black trunks were spaced about three meters apart from each other and clear of obstructions except for an occasional stiff brown leaf that had stubbornly refused to rise in the wind.

"I had no idea the leaf-things were so pliant!" Telisa exclaimed.

"There might be a biomechanical process that has allowed these leaves to untangle and flap like this,"

Maxsym said. "We should take another sample of one in this state."

Lee darted down out of the sky. Arakaki automatically tracked the sudden movement with the barrel of her weapon for a second before dropping it. Arakaki cursed the speed of Lee's appearance. The alien often unwittingly tested Arakaki's response to a sudden threat, attenuating her response. She was glad that her weapon had Lee on a no-target list, so that if Arakaki did have to fire, at least it would not hit her.

I'm surprised Lee was brave enough to come out.

"Dark and windy day, it's like this all across the slope!" Lee said. She activated her stealth unit and darted around the clearing.

"Stay clear of those strands," Magnus advised, though it looked to Arakaki that Lee was already afraid to fly near them.

Another, more focused rustling noise emerged from the vegetation.

"What's that sound? Something coming through the weeds!"

Magnus's tactical ghost pulled the rifle off its back. Arakaki tried to identify the source direction of the new sound, but it seemed to come from all over. The attendant feeds showed some of the six-legged creatures wandering closer. They did not appear to be charging at the team.

"How could anything make any progress through that mess?" Telisa hissed.

The wind rose another notch. The rustling sound changed, became smoother.

It's like the wind before a thunderstorm.

A deep grunting sound came from their left. The team's weapons pivoted as quickly as Lee fled the clearing.

An ugly beast became visible in the team's lights. It had a warty brown exterior that looked like the mangy coat of an old Earth mammal. Arakaki could not find eyes, ears or nose on the beast. She looked for natural weaponry. The thing had large bony hooks a third of the way up each of its six legs, but it was using one of them to pull at the tree trunks in a way which explained the formation.

The creature grabbed one of the dead streamers in a forward-facing maw and ripped it off the trunk. Its mouthparts worked furiously, drawing in the streamer and grinding it up with surprising ease.

"They're the reason the lowest half meter is clear below these plants," Telisa observed.

"So fascinating," Maxsym said. "If I could get a sample—"

"Don't disturb them," Telisa ordered. "At least not now."

The PIT team stood in the windy night on an alien planet beyond the frontier and watched the six-legged cows eat grass.

Chapter 4

Maxsym sighed. The robot had become stuck in the tunnel again. He indignantly sent three attendants to try to ram it loose.

If they break another of those tubes, I'll scream.

Maxsym took a deep breath. His discovery of colorful spirals in the suspected food storage room, accessible only by the attendants through the small tunnels had occupied his entire day. The attendants were transporting him samples now, though it seemed the laws of physics had conspired against him since the beginning. The rest of the PIT team worked nearby, either inside the complex with him, or close by outside.

Magnus came up to Maxsym in the brightly lit main room where they had set up their first camp.

"You've been working hard. Tell me something about the Rovans," Magnus said.

"They liked to play with their food," Maxsym said.

"Oh?"

Maxsym pointed toward a small tube entrance down the corridor.

"It's coming our way now," he said. They walked over to the corridor together.

A tube about a quarter a meter long emerged from the pipe, followed by an attendant. Maxsym picked the tube up and showed it to Magnus.

The cylinder was mostly clear, but the interior held swirls of bright color frozen in place. The object was light but very stiff.

"This is more of the suspected food substance," Maxsym said. "I don't know if the coloration is purely for aesthetics or if there are flavor elements involved. Chemical analysis may provide enough for me to guess, but of course I won't know for sure; any contaminant may provide both a color change and a taste difference to aliens."

"So do you think this is all they ate? There's no other kind of food in there?" Magnus asked.

"There is no other kind of food here," Maxsym agreed. "However, it could be an emergency store, so we can't conclude it was all they ate. It's entirely possible it would be like aliens going into one of our bunkers, finding the non-perishable rations and concluding that was the only food we ate."

Magnus nodded. "Makes sense. Knowing that they ate this, though, does bring us a step closer to figuring out what they were like. They were carbon-based lifeforms that needed an external source of calories as we do."

Maxsym smiled.

"Ah, assumptions."

Telisa heard Maxsym's statement and came over to listen.

"What? I thought my statement was pretty much based on the facts," Magnus said.

"Well, first off, we theorized there may have been two sizes of organisms living here. So the food might have been for one type of creature but not the other. Secondly, maybe these creatures normally made food inside their bodies as plants do, but they only needed these food supplies when down here in the bunker, deprived of starlight."

"Do you at least agree with the carbon-based part?" Magnus asked.

"Highly likely, yes. But keep in mind we don't know if the flora and fauna out there are native to this world, or brought from the alien's home system."

"Keep up the good work, Maxsym, we're lucky to have you here," Telisa said.

"Another discovery," Maxsym said before she could turn away. "As you know, these pipes have tiny ridges along the whole interior—likely a design choice—but their lower surfaces also have micro-patterns on them."

"Clues of the long-gone inhabitants."

"Yes. I'd say this is a wear pattern caused by small feet. Furthermore, they're directional."

He sent a pointer out. It showed a diagram of the complex. The pipes were always arrayed in pairs; there were either two, four, or six pipes between any two rooms. Exactly half of each bank of pipes were colored blue, the other half green.

"*Something* used them for one-way travel. Always allocated equally each direction."

"And the big corridors?" Magnus asked.

"They saw less traffic, I think," Maxsym said. "And it was chaotic. No real directionality. I'd say there was no clear pattern of movement in the large rooms or the greater corridors. I can, however, lend evidence to Arakaki's theory about those artifacts being shoes. The large corridors have traces of the same material all over their floors."

"Amazing observations, Maxsym!" Telisa said.

"Well, I... thank you."

Suddenly Arakaki was at his side.

"Maxsym! You came through for me and my shoe theory!" Arakaki said. She slapped him on the shoulder in comradely fashion. Maxsym smiled back at her.

Is she acting... a bit differently?

Arakaki kept smiling at him.

She's staring at me.

"If you... have any more theories, I'd love to hear them. Maybe I can find evidence for more of your suppositions," he offered.

"Great! Let's get together soon and chat," she said. She looked him in the eye for one more long second, then turned away.

Yes. Something different.

"Are you making progress as well?" Maxsym asked Telisa, looking across a long table. Telisa and Magnus had a variety of the artifacts lying across it. Some of the pieces had been disassembled or cut open.

"I found a clue," Telisa said.

"Tell me," Maxsym prompted.

Telisa picked up a small missile-shaped object and a cylinder. Maxsym thought he recognized the objects from the bins. She rotated the objects for a moment then held them out in each hand. Maxsym looked closely at the artifacts. Each had two parallel ridges or rails on its surface, each less than a half-centimeter wide and perhaps ten centimeters long.

"I've seen that, too!" Maxsym said excitedly. Magnus stepped closer to look with them.

Maxsym showed them a flat gray case he had found in the tunnels. It had two of the rails on one face, placed about five centimeters apart.

"What does it mean?" Maxsym asked.

"Mounts. These items were designed to be attached via a universal mount," Magnus said.

Maxsym looked more closely at the rails. Slender pieces of metal hidden on the inside of the ridge looked like they might work to lock the item in place.

"Interesting," he said. It was a small clue, but something to work from nonetheless.

"Maxsym, given DNA or the Rovan equivalent thereof—" Telisa started.

"I could use simulations to produce a wealth of theories regarding their molecular processes," Maxsym finished. "However, I'm afraid this place was once too clean and has been derelict for too long. I haven't found any usable samples. If I did, we would still have to be very cautious, because of the contamination from outside."

"There are a lot of ruins on this planet. Surely, somewhere, they had samples. Blood, tissue, whatever. We need to find a medical facility," Magnus said.

Telisa nodded. She spoke on the PIT channel. "I think we've learned enough here. Tomorrow, we go search elsewhere. We'll take the artifacts with us for continued study, of course."

"We should go out to watch the dusk breeze again," Arakaki said.

"It might be dangerous," Telisa said.

"Then we do it for Siobhan," Magnus said. "And have fun doing it."

"For Siobhan, then," Telisa conceded. "But we're not starting a habit of doing dangerous things in her memory. Besides, she's not really gone. Shiny probably has other Siobhans out there somewhere."

"And we may get one back ourselves," said Magnus.

Chapter 5

"Heads up. On the ball, jelly-brain," Adair said to Marcant. "Your time to shine."

Marcant blinked and focused on the input from his eyes. He stood outside the alien bunker amid the grassland. The last bit of equipment had been loaded into the shuttle. Telisa stood in the middle of the group. She looked ready to make an announcement.

"You all have access to the data we've collected on the planet. Where do we go next?" Telisa asked the assembled team.

Marcant already had a vote in mind. He spoke up quickly.

"I've analyzed these locations and found a spaceport," he summarized. He sent a pointer highlighting a spot on their shared map among the dozens of ruin sites that had been discovered by attendants and orbital scans.

"Nice! Let's visit that vine!" Lee said.

"I like the sound of that," Barrai chimed in on the team channel from far above the planet.

Everyone nodded.

"An alien starship would be great on many levels," agreed Telisa. "Top of the line alien tech, plus clues about what they looked like and how they lived. Let's go."

The team piled into the shuttle in good time. Arakaki interfaced with the navigation computer and told it to bring them to Marcant's destination. They lifted off without incident and accelerated toward the Rovan spaceport.

Marcant's link calculated that they would arrive in fifteen minutes, as the alien facility was on the same continent as the bunker. Some oddity of the planet's tectonics had produced fourteen continents surrounded by a global ocean. The search had discovered Rovan ruins on only five of the continents, so Marcant believed it could not be the aliens' homeworld.

"Be careful," Telisa said. "A spaceport could have had defenses. Especially if it was a war that killed them or drove them away from this planet."

"Copy that," Arakaki said. She told the shuttle to go in cautiously.

The gentle jostling of the ride steadied. Marcant poked around the shuttle interfaces, curious. The shuttle had slowed and put more energy into reserve as a result of Arakaki's new directive. An extra in-depth diagnostic on the defensive countermeasures had been launched and reported full readiness. The shuttle would now interpret a wider range of unknown phenomena as possible attacks and respond swiftly with countermeasures and course reversal.

"Of course, we can't really be prepared for an attack of unknown means from unknown sources," Adair said privately.

"You're not satisfied with the configuration? Should I ask—"

"The team should split up and use two or three shuttles."

"Overly paranoid," Marcant said.

"Famous last words. Or, more accurately, last words never heard or repeated since—"

"Right, because they died. I got it."

Marcant resumed watching their progress. They reached the suspected spaceport and descended in a spiral pattern from five kilometers up. Ten openings were visible on the planet's surface, ranging from 100 meters to 400 meters in diameter. They were each presumed to be landing and takeoff lanes for spacecraft with gravity spinners. The shuttle aligned with one of the openings as it continued its descent.

Marcant watched a feed from the side of the shuttle as they passed ground level. He felt anxiety rise as the star's light faded and the planet swallowed them.

"I don't think you'll be trapped there," Adair offered. "There are many ways out, both to the sky and passages to ancient transportation systems."

"It's instinctual," Marcant replied, to himself as much as Adair. "Fear of a strange, dark place."

The shuttle reached the bottom and settled on a thick spinner plate. Arakaki snapped on more lights to add to the illumination from its running lights.

The suspected spaceport was wide open around them. Huge pillars supported a vast sheet of metal or ceramic above, presumably to secure the rock against the stray forces of gravity spinners. Dead plant streamers and dirt littered the floor. A deep blackness waited beyond the range of the shuttle's lights.

"Reminds me of Vovok, just a little," Telisa commented.

"Yes, except dirtier," Magnus said.

If Vovok is like this, then I'm glad I never went there, Marcant thought.

"Let's hit it," Telisa said. The shuttle door opened and everyone piled out eagerly, except for Marcant, who was happy to go last.

The team fanned out. They felt the floor and checked the ceiling with lights. Attendants ventured out into the darkness in all directions. Lee flew around in circles but did not leave the vicinity of the group.

"Lee is even more afraid than you, jelly-brain," Adair said privately.

"The Celarans are remarkably intelligent," Marcant replied.

He waited.

"Found something. Over here," Telisa said. She led them away from the shuttle to a spot flagged by one of the forward attendants.

Their lights probed ahead. A square stack of dusty containers sat next to a pillar. Magnus and Arakaki each took a side and moved around to check the back with calm military precision.

Telisa and Maxsym walked right up to the stack. They brushed off one of the containers and cooperated to take it down from the stack and set it on the floor.

Telisa used her strong hands to crack one open. They lifted the lid. Even Marcant shuffled forward to get a quick glimpse inside.

Dozens of shiny disks lay within, reflecting the lights from their weapons. Telisa took one out. It was a little larger than her hand and about 3 cm thick.

"Metal," Maxsym commented.

"If these containers are all like that one, there must be 10,000 of them here," Magnus said, looking over the other containers.

Marcant looked through the data collected from Adair's attendant floating nearby.

"More," Marcant said. "Scans indicate they contain a complex fluid."

"Food? Drink?" asked Arakaki.

"I don't think so," Maxsym said. The xenobiologist must have been looking at his own scans in his PV. "Though I admit I'm not certain. I suppose it could be a recreational drink rather than an energy source. Something that made Rovans drunk or otherwise chemically affected."

"The rails are here again," Magnus pointed out. Marcant picked up a disk of his own and flipped it over. The underside had the same rails as most of the other small Rovan artifacts.

"Another attachable item. It's their way. We need to find something that mates with these rails."

"A common robot attachment?" Telisa guessed.

Marcant nodded. "That would be the first thing I would suspect."

"Or these vine hangers could have been part machine like Cynan," Lee suggested.

"Could these be fuel disks?" asked Magnus.

"I don't think so, probably for the same reason Maxsym said it's not food: the energy density is too low," Marcant said.

Maxsym nodded.

"Take a couple for study. Otherwise, time to move on," Telisa said.

"The attendants haven't seen anything spaceship-like," Arakaki said. Over a square kilometer of the dark space around them had already been scanned by the floating devices.

Marcant had to agree. The spaceport was too empty.

Telisa led them to the next area of interest, a small metal enclosure nestled next to a pillar. The entire area was dusty and eerily silent. The sound of their footfalls crushing the occasional dry streamer echoed off the ceiling. Marcant could actually hear the faint rustle of air from Lee as she flew by.

The enclosure had only the now-familiar tubes entering and exiting it. Telisa sent an attendant inside.

Magnus and Arakaki remained vigilant while the rest of them eagerly watched the feed from inside the enclosure.

The inside was mostly empty and unlit. A long tube the size of a chemical fire extinguisher was held to the wall by two straps. The attendant flew close. Attachment rails were visible on its side.

"Another disappointment," Marcant said.

"This is a good find," Telisa said. "Now we know the rails attach to the smaller things that traveled through the pipes."

"Not at all," Maxsym said. "That thing's diameter is barely smaller than the pipes. It would only fit out by itself."

"Meaning... that it could not be attached to something and still fit out," Telisa finished.

"Correct."

"So it means the opposite?" Arakaki asked.

"Not at all," Maxsym repeated.

"Right," Marcant agreed. "We can't conclude the rails are not for the smaller inhabitants, either. They could still have connected the tube *after* removing it from this room."

"It shows that the tube was only accessible by small creatures or robots."

"So Marcant is correct. This is a boring vine!" Lee sent as she flew in a lazy circle around the great pillar.

"Of course I'm correct," Marcant said.

"I've got your back," Adair said to Marcant privately. "I won't point out you were the one who suggested this place," Adair said.

"Onwards," Telisa said. They walked past the pillar and on through the darkness in a new direction. Marcant trudged along near the rear of the group.

After a five minute walk, they came to a new sight: A dark gray building that stretched from floor to ceiling. Circular portals of clear material had been set into its walls, each about 10 meters apart.

"Windows! That means they had eyes!" Lee trilled.

"Not guaranteed, but yes, I suppose they most likely did have eyes," Maxsym agreed.

Those could be for robots to see out, Marcant thought. He did not really believe that, though, so he did not voice the possibility.

A set of double doors, similar to what they had seen at the bunker, lay wide open at the front.

Marcant chose to stay outside with Magnus and Arakaki. He tried to remain as alert as they were, but there was little to see: refuse on the ground, the dull ceiling overhead, and several of the huge support pillars. He imagined some menace lurking behind one of the pillars. It helped.

The others emerged from building with an artifact. Telisa held it up for an attendant to scan. Marcant accessed the data.

"This, I can identify," Marcant said. "A laser."

"A weapon?" asked Telisa.

"A cutter, I think, judging from that aperture," Magnus said.

Marcant nodded. "I agree."

"We can compare it to our own and get an idea of how advanced the Rovans were," Telisa said happily.

"What if they were actually technologically *behind* Terrans?" Marcant asked Adair privately. "That would make these discoveries mundane."

"We could consider other interesting questions, like, how did they organize themselves, how did they conduct research, or even, how did they reproduce? You know, things like that," Adair said.

"Yes, I suppose. Or is whatever wiped them out a threat to us?"

"Ah! Yes, that's very interesting," Adair agreed.

"Are there any spaceships down here? I still don't see any on the map," Arakaki said.

"It's not looking good," Magnus answered.

"There's another artifact this way," Telisa said, pointing. Marcant saw it on the map. It was a nontrivial hike to the location.

He dug a glucosoda out of his pack and started to sip on it.

Telisa gave him a quick look. He knew it meant, *Fine, but stay alert.*

Marcant made quick work of the drink, collapsed the can, then put it back into his pack.

Ever since Imanol's accidental death, Marcant had felt a growing debt to the team that he wanted to repay with superior performance. Achaius's betrayal had brought that desire up another notch. Marcant now also strove to improve areas outside of his specialty, such as wandering through alien ruins while armed to the teeth.

Marcant checked the next site in an attendant recording before they arrived. A square hole perhaps five meters on a side had been cut through the floor. White cones stood around the perimeter as if in warning. The attendant had spotted a piece of equipment next to the hole: a cylindrical object with three fist-sized knobs on one end.

It looks remarkably similar to a Terran repair area. Bright cones to draw attention to the danger and a work area for the repair robots.

When they arrived, Marcant advanced carefully to take a look. His light dispelled the deep blackness of the hole, revealing a pit about eight meters deep. The bottom was cracked, dry dirt.

"So similar to a Terran work area!" Telisa said. "Another indication they had vision in some of the same wavelengths we do."

"The parallels here *are* striking. Cones are naturally stable in a planetary environment, so that seems natural enough of a design."

Telisa examined the artifact beside the pit.

"It looks like a hollow cylinder. I don't see any way a lid could attach or screw onto the opening," Telisa said. "It does have the rail on it, though."

They scanned the item and decided it did not look like any kind of explosive device. Telisa secured it and selected another site to visit in person.

"Next?" Arakaki said.

"Wait. There's one more thing here," Magnus said, pointing. Beyond the hole, a small object sat next to one of the pillars. Marcant had missed it in the darkness. They advanced on it until resolved into a squat shape that reminded him of a toad sitting under a mushroom.

"This is a funny shape," Arakaki commented. "Still, there's the connector rail on the top."

Marcant looked at the rail briefly, then saw a tiny circle on the surface of the artifact.

"It has a button on it, I think. Should I?" Marcant asked.

"No. Set it down over there on that gravity plate. We'll have a robot activate it."

"Smart jelly-brain," Adair commented from the peanut gallery that was the *Sharplight*.

Marcant picked the thing up. It weighed perhaps five kilograms. He put it on the raised area Telisa had indicated and stepped back ten paces. After a moment of thought, he backed off another ten. Magnus told one of his robots walking the perimeter of their lights to come over. The robot advanced steadily until it came within range and extended one of its feet's traction claws. It pressed the button.

A flourish of colorful light erupted from the device. The robot backed away.

The light settled on a pinkish hue and spread to a radius of three meters. Then tiny red dots rose from it like insects and started to fly around each other in playful circles.

"By the Five! It's so beautiful!" Telisa said.

"The most colorful thing we've seen on the planet," Marcant commented.

"Those could be dangerous. They could even be weapons!" Magnus said.

"Okay, I hear you," Telisa said. "If they come over here, activate your suit helmets and withdraw."

They watched the light display for several minutes. If the insect-things had any purpose, Marcant could not see it. Suddenly the light show was over. The device returned to dormancy.

The team shined their lights back on the device. The insect-things were gone.

"Where..." Magnus wondered.

"Attendant data shows the apparent flyers were only part of the light show. Illusions," Adair said.

Magnus sent a robot to pick the artifact back up.

"Ideas?"

"A toy," Magnus suggested.

"It could have been a complex communication we don't understand," Maxsym said.

"Yeah, like 'Don't park your spaceship here, there's a hole in the floor'," Marcant quipped.

"Where next?" Arakaki asked.

"Not far," Telisa said. She led them through the darkness again.

This time, they zeroed in on one of the pillars. At first, Marcant did not see anything interesting.

"Where is it?" he asked.

Telisa pointed. Near the floor, a black coil emerged from the column. They strode closer. Maxsym knelt at the end of the object.

"This one's easy. A hose for carrying liquid. Water, or fuel, or whatever."

"No rails I can see."

"Yeah, it's not as portable. One end is always connected to a pipe and you drag it somewhere nearby and use it."

Marcant looked where the other end met the pillar. A small flap had opened to allow the hose to connect.

"Look how that opens for the connection. All these columns could have this, or even more than one each and we never realized it."

"I think so. Attendants see these hairline cracks in some of the other pillars. This is common," Telisa said.

"There could be more than hose connections. Electrical connections or other services could be hidden away there, too," Arakaki said.

Marcant had already lost interest. He was ready to get back to the *Sharplight* and start cracking the codes of the Rovan artifacts. He managed to muster some excitement for it.

Another alien technology to add to my list! Just a while back I would have thought it impossible.

"What's wrong?" Telisa asked. Marcant glanced at her and saw she addressed Magnus, not him.

"The attendants have finished searching this level of the spaceport. There are no spacecraft that we can find," Magnus said.

Arakaki looked around with a frown. She settled her gaze on Marcant.

"Are you sure this is a—"

"Yes. Look at what the attendants have gathered," Marcant said. "Open lanes to the sky at regular intervals. These plates here at the bottom of each shaft. Look familiar?"

"Spinner plates," Telisa said.

"That's right. And there were major roads leading here. It all says 'spaceport' in big neon letters."

"Except there are no spacecraft here, Marcant," Arakaki said calmly.

"Those tiny cracks you found in the pillars... are there any around the landing plates? Maybe they're elevators that descend to store the spacecraft," Marcant said desperately.

"No cracks, and besides, the whole point of a spinner plate is that it's almost indestructible. Doesn't lend itself to being part of an elevator," Telisa said.

"It's not an engineering impossibility," Maxsym said.

"Look," Marcant said. "The Rovans died off. Well, I put forth to you that some escaped. In said spacecraft."

That shut everyone up for a second or two. Marcant luxuriated in the silence while he could.

"There's more missing than ships. Where are the rest of the Rovans? We haven't found any dead Rovans."

"Maybe there were enough spacecraft for them all," Adair said to the PIT team.

"This was no expedition. They had entire cities here," Magnus said.

"So? Maybe they still had enough ships. Maybe they were different than Terrans that way," Adair said to the team.

"It's also possible that they performed a longer term evacuation," Telisa said.

"Or perhaps Rovan bodies don't leave permanent remains," Maxsym jumped in. "They may have had degradable skeletons. Or no skeletons at all."

"There *is* a lot of dust on the floor..." Arakaki said.

"Make sure and wash your boots when you get back to the shuttle," Marcant said.

Chapter 6

Sarfal flew high over the knobby vine stumps that had no leaves. Their thin green strings hardly seemed adequate to Sarfal. It was such a sad forest. At least the star overhead was bright and warm.

I miss my vine.

Somewhere below, in the ruins beneath the overgrowth, the remains of a Rovan might lie hidden away in a container. The Rootpounder that Sarfal called Lifecollector wanted to find well-preserved Rovan remains. Given such flesh, the Rootpounder scientist hoped to tell them more about the creatures that had left these vines so long ago.

Sarfal had flown to four interesting spots logged by attendant surveys. As a flyer, Sarfal had been busy visiting places the Rootpounders found difficult to travel to given the twisted morass of streamers on the ground. The strange plants of the planet actually knotted themselves during the day and untwisted at night to flow in the breeze. Sarfal found the alien plants disturbing. The thought of getting tangled in their strings was terrifying.

A site of interest loomed. Sarfal lost altitude and zeroed in on the spot: A low building covered in the vegetation. An attendant had checked it and discovered the building had only one room. It had scanned and recorded everything; the results indicated there were possibly valuable artifacts within.

Sarfal asked the attendants nearby to re-check for predators. Even though they had encountered no dangerous native life, Sarfal would not blindly trust anything, especially in the creepy alien forest. An attendant slipped in through a crack in the ancient wall. The interior was cluttered, but no large life forms lurked within.

Sarfal gathered courage, then slipped into the single room. It railed against Sarfal's instincts to enter any cramped space preventing flight. Sarfal did not think any other Thrasar could have done it at all; but training with the Rootpounders had toughened Sarfal to many things.

In one corner, a pile of dirt and dusty artifacts sat atop a low table.

Sarfal's front-hand rod activated. A stream of charged air blew the dust away. Some of the rotted items crumbled away and joined the dirt. One artifact remained largely intact, a device half a meter long. It stood on eight legs, reminiscent of one of Grimfighter's robots. Instead of two distinct body segments, like the Rootpounder machines, this thing had only one body component: a smooth, relatively flat oval.

Sarfal did not want to touch it. Instead, Sarfal recruited four attendants to analyze the device for dangers while the Thrasar slipped back outside. Once safely distant, the attendants lifted the item and carried it outside.

The attendants found nothing dangerous, so Sarfal decided to help carry the find away. Sarfal's rear facing hand dipped down and grabbed one of the artifact's legs to assist the attendants. The awkward group then gained altitude and set course for camp.

The skies were clear. The alien planet had not yet shown any other weather pattern besides a notable rise in night winds. Sarfal and the attendants had only seen one type of alien flyer—a long, green insectoid thing that could jump and glide to distant vine-stumps. The creatures did not seem capable of attaining significant altitudes.

Sarfal circled down to the Rootpounder camp.

Palethinker saw Sarfal coming in and waved the Thrasar toward an empty examination table.

"I brought a new fruit to hang on the vine!" Sarfal announced brightly.

Sarfal brought the small robot to Palethinker and let him take it in his huge, five-fingered hands.

"This is superb!" Palethinker said. The Rootpounder set the device on the table next to an array of examination tools. He moved quickly (for an alien Rootpounder) which Sarfal had learned was a sure sign of excitement.

Sadfighter paced nearby, watching the forest. She was one of the offspring-carrying Rootpounders, which made Sarfal feel sorry for her. To serve the role of a vine for young still seemed a grotesque duty, though Sarfal had not yet seen any Rootpounder do so.

Sarfal suppressed another nightmarish image of young slithering inside the Rootpounder and feeding on internal fluids however it pleased. The Rootpounders had told her that the offspring stayed in a special chamber and got sap through a tube grown for the purpose. That helped a bit.

Palethinker was examining the eight-legged construct carefully. He had not yet even picked up one of his tools.

"Look at this," Palethinker said. Sarfal floated down closer to look. The Rootpounder pointed a single thick, short finger at a set of metal rails on the Rovan machine. "I think this mates to the Rovan artifacts we've found."

Why does Palethinker use our shared concept 'mates' to describe things that fit together? Oh, wait. Different types of Rootpounders do fit together, I guess... it's so much more elegant for a race to have only one form.

"You mean all the Rovan tools we've found under every leaf around here?"

"Yes! Exactly. You've found our first example of what all these things hook up with. These other artifacts can be mounted on this little robot."

"Then this was a carrier machine, used to move things around as necessary," Sarfal suggested.

"That's possible, though I think they did more than carry them around. Maybe all those things were employed by robots like this!"

Palethinker put a new item up on the Rootpounder's communication network. It quickly got the attention of the others.

"Great find!" Strongjumper said. "I'm going to send out the signature to our scout machines all over the planet. We need to find more of those!"

"The size is important," Lifecollector said. "It fits through the smaller tunnels. I'll check if the ends of its legs match the marks I found in the bunker pipes."

Sarfal was happy to contribute a piece of the alien puzzle, though it had involved nothing special—other than flying to remote sites to retrieve artifacts.

I'm the only flyer! And it makes me valuable to their team.

Sarfal flew three vertical loops in exhilaration at the thought.

"What else have you examined here?" Sarfal asked, looking at the other items lying on tables nearby.

"Nothing as interesting as yours," Sadfighter said.

"True," agreed Palethinker. "More Rovan devices with the rails on them."

"What does this one do?" asked Sarfal, pointing a tail finger.

"I think it scans for certain molecules," Palethinker said. "It wouldn't be able to see a wide enough range for me to call it a scanner. I think it was designed to detect a certain family of chemicals, but I don't know exactly which ones or why."

"And this one? The shiny spear?" Sarfal asked.

"It produces an alternating current within a very narrow range of voltages and frequencies," Palethinker said. "I like to think of it as a very long shock baton. But I don't know if the energy served the same purpose or not."

Sarfal flitted to the next item quickly. The ponderous Rootpounder followed along too slowly for Sarfal's taste.

"And this?"

"It shoots needles that have a tiny fluid payload. Could be medical, or a weapon."

So maybe these Rovans are sick like the Rootpounders, and like to kill each other... or maybe a Rootpounder just looks for such explanations.

"What else is here?"

"Hrm. I have a suspected surface cleaner and one other artifact I have no idea about," Palethinker said. "Not as exciting as this robot, but things to learn from nonetheless."

Sarfal did not feel ready to fly out to the next spot immediately. Instead, the Thrasar floated around the camp, suspended by a tool rod in both the forward and the rear hand.

Sadfighter unzipped her artificial hide and revealed some of her smooth underskin to the bright starlight. Palethinker looked up from the robot and stared at the other Rootpounder for a moment. Sarfal did not know why they each took these actions but wondered about the Rootpounder integument.

"Why aren't you covered in protein strands like your ancestors?" Sarfal asked Palethinker.

"What?!"

"I think she means, why aren't we covered in hair," Sadfighter said.

Sarfal noted the use of the language marker that referred to Sarfal as a baby carrier type of Rootpounder. Strongjumper had explained carefully that they had started doing that by habit. The Rootpounder said their language did have ways to address beings that were neither male nor female, but they had not thought to use them from the beginning. Strongjumper had asked Sarfal if it was bothersome, and Sarfal had replied in the negative. There was no insult implied.

"Studying up on Rootpounders, eh? A question for Lifecollector," Palethinker said. "Some think that our ancestors lost their hair when they returned to living in the water. Others say it was so we could better cool ourselves by sweating. Or, it could have been accidentally related to some other beneficial mutation."

"These fruits are interesting to theorize on," Sarfal said. "Thrasar ancestors were nocturnal. Can you believe it? To hide from the warm starlight that feeds the vines... and to glow in the dark where the predators hide underleaf!"

"That does sound scary," Sadfighter said, though Sarfal doubted Sadfighter was afraid of anything. "Your skin lights would give you away and be a beacon to anything hunting you."

"Exactly! I'm glad Rootpounders don't like to go out at night, either."

Chapter 7

"I don't get it. A day of searching for the new signature all across the planet, and we have nothing? Where did all the little Rovan robots go?" Telisa asked aloud.

She asked the question standing before the PIT team, knowing they could only speculate.

"The sig may not be good," Magnus said. "That design could have been a one-off."

"It's obvious. The Rovans took their robots with them when they left," Marcant said.

"And the one Lee found?"

"Well, it's broken," he said.

"I guess so. No ships and no bodies, which suggests their 'evacuation' may not have been an emergency. More like a migration, I suppose," Telisa said.

"I hope they didn't flee to escape a local danger. Because we have no idea what it might be," Barrai said.

"I think it was likely something related to their big picture, strategically speaking," Magnus said. "Like an interstellar war. Otherwise, the colony wouldn't have grown very large before they discovered the problem."

If that's true, then the fact they never came back speaks negatively about their fate.

"We're going to investigate this one next: a cluster of buildings in the arctic zone of this planet," Telisa said. She sent along a pointer to a group of five modest buildings they had detected on a frozen plateau. It seemed an obvious guess that the place was a research station, but Telisa had learned to suppress such assumptions. It could be any of a million things, but she hoped to find a storage facility for genetic samples or seeds.

"Hoping the temperatures there preserved something interesting?" Marcant asked.

"Yes. We've been to several places in this climate. It's worth a shot to go to the coldest site we've detected. Team, go through your gear lists again and re-outfit yourselves. It's a completely different environ. We'll carry safety gear related to low temperature and treacherous footing. There may even be a danger of falling into deep crevices or caves hidden beneath the ice sheets."

Her statements probably overstated the dangers, given that attendants would scan the area and find any chasms hiding beneath the surface, but it paid to come prepared anyway.

They bought into her reasoning. Everyone set into motion, eager for another site to explore in person, a special place with some promise of new discoveries.

***

The snow's glare attacked Telisa's eyes as did the icy wind. Her designed body acclimated to both in less than a second, so she forged on, leaving the others behind to reel against the environmental shock that hit them at the bottom of the ramp.

The buildings appeared as four-meter plateaus in the snow and ice. Telisa was surprised that the arctic conditions had not submerged the entire facility beneath the snow, never to be found again. She powered over the icy surface to the nearest building and regarded it as she slapped her pack down next to her.

Telisa did not feel like waiting for one of Magnus's robots, so she dug into the snow and ice with a short shovel. The head of the shovel had picks on each side for scraping away ice, though it was of light construction to ease digging and scooping. Her Veer suit handled the frigid temperature well, and her host body provided plenty of strength to compensate for the stiff resistance. It took her only a few minutes to clear away a section of the building before her. She turned to find the rest of the team staring at her.

Did I do something wrong?

"Magnus, what's up?" she asked him privately as she jumped out of the hole she had made.

"I think you can dig faster than my robots," Magnus told her.

"Oh. A Trilisk show."

"Basically," he said.

The others seemed to realize they had caused an awkward moment. Maxsym tromped off to take an ice core sample, and Arakaki stepped aside to let the first of Magnus's robots through to the building.

The robots cut through the ice encasing the building. A team of attendants flew along the perimeter of the freshly exposed exterior, using radiation beams to melt off the last of the snow. The surface was composed of gleaming silver and red panels.

"That's weird. It looks like metal," Telisa said. "I would have expected ceramic in this environment."

"The whole thing may have been lifted here," Magnus suggested. Industrial ceramic, sometimes used by Terrans to make durable buildings and roads, was a relatively dense material. A modular building made of light metals might have made more sense.

Telisa tromped away from the building and looked up into the reddish-blue sky.

"Lee, are you coming out?"

"This vine is warm. It is a bright day, but most definitely not a warm one!"

Without a full-body suit like the Terran Veer armor, Lee could not endure the dangerously low temperatures. Telisa made a note to follow up on the deficiency and see if they could devise a solution someday.

"Ah. I see. We'll handle it today!" she told Lee.

"There's a door here, I believe," Maxsym said. Telisa returned to the cleared area beside the building and joined him. He pointed at a crack in the surface that traced a rectangle the size of the bunker doors they forced before.

"Cut in?" Magnus asked.

"I have an idea," Marcant said.

"Oh! Have you cracked some of their communications?"

"No. I believe, like Terran equivalents, there exists a manual option here."

Telisa examined the door again, looking for mechanisms. All she saw were two hand-sized slots set almost two meters apart near her feet.

"Yes, those," Marcant confirmed watching her gaze. "Magnus, please have two robots put their front feet in there, following the inward-facing angles." Marcant motioned with his hands, showing that the little slots below them angled in toward each other.

The ant-like robots moved in under Magnus's command. They struck an amusing pose, bowing before the door as if in supplication to slide their legs into the slots.

If that's really the manual override, then Rovans were big all right. Those slots are far apart. Yet the mechanism is low. Did the Rovans originate on a high gravity planet?

Telisa heard a loud clank. The massive door started to rise.

"Back," Telisa cautioned.

Maxsym and Magnus retreated to the left, Telisa to the right in the snow trench. Telisa laid a hand on the laser pistol at her hip. Their attendants remained before the door as it opened.

No threat emerged.

"Looks empty," Telisa summarized. A dark corridor beckoned through the attendants' video feeds. She sent two attendants in.

Lights activated inside. Telisa assumed it was because of the door activation or the movement of the attendants. The source of the illumination was not directly visible; instead it filtered in through gaps in the flat, white ceiling panels. It was hard to judge the level of illumination because her eyes were used to the bright reflection of the snow outside.

The white corridor within had a squashed hexagonal shape. The surfaces were smooth and clean, broken only by one or two egg-sized hemispheres clinging to the angled walls. It split at a T intersection, so one attendant went each way. The wide paths led around the building and eventually met on the far side near another door. Nothing else moved. They did not see anything that looked like a life form or a robot.

Telisa went in first. As in the bunker, she found the corridor very wide, but as high as many Terran hallways—perhaps a bit taller than average. Her host-body eyes instantly adjusted to the point that it felt like the inside was brightly lit. She slowed to look at one of the wall-bulbs, but it did not have any features to hint at its function. She waved her hand in front of it warily with her lightning-fast reflexes coiled and ready. There was no response.

She went left at the T. One glance to another attendant feed showed her that Magnus and Arakaki had followed her in. Magnus had a laser pistol out, and Arakaki held a compact PAW close to her body. Telisa checked the ceiling carefully, looking for anything that might be a laser emitter or its protective dome.

The attendant scouts make things safer... but not completely safe. We're being lazy.

"Stealth," Telisa commanded. She activated her cloaking sphere. A feed from outside showed Marcant and Maxsym bugging out for a moment before they, too, cloaked.

Telisa walked through the building, taking a right at each corner to take a circuit of the building. The air was cold and sterile; everything remained silent. Even their footfalls were damped by the Celaran spheres.

"Looks clear," Telisa sent. "I'm coming out." She deactivated her Celaran stealth device.

Marcant became visible nearby.

"Something wrong?" he asked.

"Call it staying sharp," Telisa answered, assuming he was asking about the reason for the call to stealth.

Marcant nodded. He pointed toward the floor.

"More of the pipes," he said.

"The ones on this side go to the other buildings," Magnus said from 10 meters away. He stood with his eyes unfocused, watching attendant feeds in his PV. "They look similar to this one. Empty."

I guess my fantasy of finding Rovans hiding out here from... something... is not happening.

They took another trip around the wide halls which formed a square around the perimeter. To Telisa, it felt like a starship built for giants. The walls held dozens of bins and mysterious equipment berths.

"What's in the center?" Telisa asked. She sent an attendant through the nearest pipe headed in that direction.

"A laboratory, I think," Maxsym answered after a few moments. "It's designed to be run by the small robots or creatures, as it is only accessible via those small tubes near the floor. There does appear to be a very large door in the roof at the center, though."

"Then the big ones must have watched from these ports," Marcant said. He stood in an alcove with a large flat panel set in the wall. Telisa saw a seam down the middle and immediately assumed that it was a cover that could open.

"Or they could have watched through links, right?" Arakaki asked. "Is that a sign they didn't have links that could put images into their minds?"

"Interesting supposition," Maxsym said neutrally.

"I think these Rovans must have been incredibly lazy," Telisa said. "They used these little robots for everything. A lot more than we rely on the attendants for."

"They may have thought of those machines as extensions of themselves," Marcant suggested. "The same way we think of our links. And, to a lesser degree, the attendants."

"I concur," Maxsym said. "Many of you use the attendants as extra eyes in a way that's second nature to you now. I'm still working on that, but perhaps it's the same principle."

"Well, take a look at what they may have been studying, if you can," Telisa told them.

"Everything's been cleaned. Mothballed, almost," Maxsym said.

"Moth-what?" Magnus asked.

An anachronism, Telisa anticipated.

"An anachronism. Preserved for storage rather than on standby for operation," Maxsym clarified. Telisa smiled.

Telisa walked down the corridor. She told her Veer suit to retract its gloves, then she paused to feel the surface of the wall. It felt cool, but definitely not as cold as it must be outside.

They arrived at a bank of pipes, grilles, and bin doors. Most things were white, but the pipes and the walls had occasional bands of red. The red coloration did not seem to be indicating anything dangerous; rather, the bands were placed a constant distance apart on the pipes or the walls, as if helping to measure distances or lengths.

Perhaps they had no depth perception? The bands could help them make sense of the environment.

"Jackpot!" Magnus said on the PIT channel. "Found more of their robots! A bunch of them!"

"That's funny. I suggested we come here to find frozen samples, but we find robots instead."

"Progress is progress," Magnus said.

"Finally!" Marcant exclaimed. He sounded as excited as Magnus. If those two could find any thread in common between them, a love of robots would be that thread, though she supposed for Magnus it was rooted in the satisfaction of a creative urge and a desire to solve practical problems, whereas Marcant probably wanted more Rovan cybernetics to study.

Telisa saw a feed from an attendant hovering over a group of the robots. She counted eight of them, packed away into an alcove. They were perfectly lined up, each in their place, shiny, without any dust, dirt, or other markings other than a single red stripe down the middle of their shells. Like Lee's find, they each had eight spider-legs and a smooth central body that looked circular from above but was flattened in profile. They each had two attachment rails on their top surface.

"They're in perfect shape. Brand-new looking," Telisa observed.

"Brand new mechanical octopeds," Barrai said from the *Sharplight*. "They don't look *that* alien. Somewhere on Earth there must be several similar designs."

Telisa had almost forgotten that Barrai was watching. Once again, she was struck by how Barrai's personality was a paradox: she had initially come off as brave, bold, and adventurous, yet she had passed on the chance to come planetside with the team on her first mission.

"And another batch here," Marcant announced.

"Hey! These are aquatic ones," Arakaki interjected. "See this propeller underneath?"

"You're right," Telisa said. "We're on solid ground here, but there's an ice shelf over a bay within a couple of klicks. They must have done some research in that area as well."

"I'm sending robots to retrieve the alien machines," Magnus said.

"They look very elegant. Smooth and... lifelike? Maybe there will be something you can incorporate into your designs," Telisa said to Magnus privately.

"Maybe! But merging two technologies is already hard enough."

Telisa knew his hesitant reply would become full-blown enthusiasm once he started making discoveries about the Rovan machines. Magnus always delighted in examining and understanding clever robotics solutions. If Magnus could not figure it out any software challenges, then Marcant and Adair would.

"Shall we see what else they have in these bins?" Telisa suggested. Magnus joined her to loot a large bin on the wall.

Marcant and Maxsym tried one on the other side of the corridor. Arakaki, ever the loner, found her own cabinet to search through.

The bin opened to reveal a full complement of wrapped boxes of varying shapes and sizes. An attendant hovered over the boxes for a moment, scanning. Then it retreated to allow Telisa to investigate. She picked one at random and opened its soft covering. Inside sat a coil of wire or hose with each end fit into an oblong base station. Telisa tugged on the coil, drawing more out of the base.

"De-icer coils," Magnus guessed.

Telisa nodded. She zipped open her pack and removed an expandable carry bag. She began putting items into the bag for examination later.

"See any weapons? Or containers that might have... seeds, or food? Embryos?"

Magnus laughed.

"What does a Rovan embryo container look like?"

"If you figure it out, you win the prize," Maxsym said.

"I found a bunch of colorful... doodads," Arakaki said. "It's weird, most of the stuff we've found isn't blue, or yellow... or gold."

Arakaki dangled a few small items by slender gold cords. Telisa saw a yellow diamond-shape, a blue square and a green-striped spiral with a gold cap. They looked like cheap party favors.

She's right. We've seen mostly white, black, gray, and red.

"Metal samples?" Telisa guessed.

"No... and they don't have connector rails, either. They're light. All different shapes. Seriously, this is a weird grab bag of random stuff."

Magnus held a white cannister. One end terminated in a complex metal construct like a randomized collection of cooling fins radiating from a hollow central hub.

"This thing is an extruder or sprayer head," Magnus said. "I think. Or maybe it's just a hose connector..." He kept examining it, tipping the item back and forth. "I think there's fluid in there."

"Keep your eyes away from that thing," Telisa said. "Something might come out of it at any moment."

"Yes, ma'am," he said playfully.

"It's good advice and you know it," she added.

They added the cannister to a bag to take back with them. Magnus put a few more things into the bag while Telisa walked over to see Marcant and Maxsym's bin.

"Uhm, guys?" Arakaki prompted.

Telisa walked over to look. Arakaki held four half-bubbles joined by a flexible strip of black material into a square shape. Four more black strips extended from each side and joined in two pairs via a small square device or connector.

"Goggles?" Telisa asked.

"That's my take on it... goggles for someone with four very large eyes and a head the size of my chest!"

Maxsym frowned. "You jump to conclusions. That could be anything."

"I saw a snake-thing out in the forest," Arakaki said. "It had four eyes on each end, in the shape of a rectangle just like this."

Maxsym looked thoughtful. "It could provide binocular vision in two directions, or even four directions if the eyes can turn to pair with either neighbor."

"It's large," Marcant observed.

"You know they're big," Arakaki said. "All the doors and corridors are very wide."

Maxsym and Marcant did not argue the point any further. They silently stared at the artifact.

They're thinking she's probably right.

"It's a good theory," Telisa said. "But remember that just because a body part has eyes, that doesn't make it a head. Shiny has that front bulge that looks like a head, but it has no brain in it."

Lee's link emitted a synthetic laughter analogue. "Your conversation is so funny! We're all very different from each other; it goes without saying!"

"What did you find?" Telisa asked Marcant.

"A powerful light emitter. This part suggests it sits on the ice. I imagine it's strong enough to melt through any snowfall and remain visible."

"So it could be used as a kind of waypoint," Telisa said.

"Yes. But honestly, I don't know why such a thing would be necessary. Any basic inertial navigation would provide plenty of information to robots or anyone with links like our own."

"It could be a backup system," Magnus said, but he sounded like he did not believe his own suggestion.

Marcant shrugged. "They were aliens. And there's none left to ask."

He turned and carried his loot toward the exit. Telisa felt an urge to walk out after him and watch the comedy of Marcant trying to get the container up out of the trench.

He'll probably have Adair control the robots to do it while he climbs up without it.

Maxsym stood in the middle of the corridor, rubbing his chin thoughtfully.

"Sorry, Maxsym. We're empty-handed on the tissue sample front."

"There has to be something left somewhere on this planet," he said. "We'll find it. We have to."

"We will," she agreed, and she believed it.

Chapter 8

Maxsym's analysis of the creatures they had seen outside the bunker was open in his PV. A picture of one of the warty, hooked beasts was framed on the right side of his virtual workspace. He composed a conclusion for his last two days of work, then added a verbal note to the file: "These streamer-eaters could not possibly break down the pseudo-polysaccharides discovered in the Rovan food storage centers. Further, no plant we have found here produces molecules of this structure. The streamer-eaters are likely native to Rovatick Ailia 3. The Rovans are probably from the evolutionary lines of another planet."

Maxsym had hoped to gather clues about Rovan physiology by studying the other creatures they had discovered on the planet. That now looked unlikely. Maxsym's analysis supported the PIT team's belief that this was not in fact the Rovan homeworld, but nothing was completely clear at this point.

Maxsym sat for a moment, frowning, then added, "Since the food stores may be synthetic and not naturally produced, there exists some chance my conclusion is in error. I've made certain assumptions about the tolerances of the Rovan's digestive system, and how similar designed food molecules would be to their natural analogues."

Who are we kidding? That material might not be food at all. Or it might have been food for Rovan pets, not Rovans. Or even supplies for the native creatures! This is all guesswork until we can gather more evidence, test our theories, and find better ones.

Maxsym closed the sub-project. It disappeared from his mind's eye to be replaced by another project workspace. His next block of work lay with a different creature found in the streamer woods: a smaller octoped that displayed striking differences from other samples. The creature had a unique nervous chemistry as well as a metabolic rate higher than the other fauna. It might well be that the species came to the planet with the Rovans. If so, analyzing that creature might shed some light on the Rovans.

But first, it was time for Maxsym to get some exercise.

He hurriedly stripped to his undersheers and added combat training clothes. Then he double-timed it to the gym, using the trip as part of his warm up.

Today, Barrai and Arakaki had come to the *Iridar* to work out with him. His link told him he was a few minutes late.

If they're angry, I'll be able to tell when they start hitting me, he thought dryly.

A minute later, Maxsym arrived to see Arakaki on top of Barrai in opaque undersheers, struggling for control of Barrai's right arm. The arm was isolated by Arakaki's legs, but Barrai reinforced her trapped arm with her left. He judged that Arakaki would secure the armbar momentarily through an explosive move.

Suddenly Barrai's foot slid up between them, then slammed heel-first into Arakaki's face in a display of amazing flexibility. Arakaki's head turned away to avoid further damage, but Arakaki refused to let go of the trapped arm. Barrai used the change in balance to get off her back and rise above Arakaki, but her arm would not slip out.

Barrai then proceeded to lift Arakaki a half foot above the floor, and slam her back down. Once, twice, three times. They both grunted stubbornly.

Maxsym's lips set tightly.

I'm glad I have nothing to prove here. Extreme competition will only cause more injuries. But I suppose it is more realistic combat training...

Barrai's arm slipped free, but Arakaki grabbed Barrai's heel and put her shoulder into Barrai's knee, causing her to fall backward. Arakaki pounced while

Barrai kept her momentum and rolled backward with the fall. Arakaki followed. When Barrai's head came up from the roll, Arakaki slipped it smoothly into a guillotine choke. Barrai tried to look upward and rise, but Arakaki wrapped her legs around Barrai and arched her back.

Maxsym missed the tap, but they broke apart. Barrai coughed sharply and took a few steps back. They were covered in sweat and breathing hard. They must have arrived at least fifteen minutes ago.

Their hands came back up. Barrai suddenly leaped forward. Maxsym expected a kick, but this time Barrai launched a massive punch, taking advantage of Arakaki's fatigue. Arakaki had a weak block in place, but the blow penetrated her defenses and knocked her back a step.

Barrai did not follow up. Instead, she bent forward and grimaced. She held her hand up, palm outward.

"Ah! I pulled something."

She reached for her left hamstring. Maxsym looked at the bunched musculature there. Barrai was immensely strong, but perhaps her tendons were not up to the explosive forces playing across them.

"That sucks," Arakaki said. "Happens to me now and then. I hate it."

"The collagen weaver will have it fixed up in half an hour," Barrai said.

Arakaki nodded. They shook hands, then half-hugged complete with back slaps.

"Next time, Maxsym?" Barrai asked.

"Of course," he said, hiding his relief.

"Maybe you can hook me up with some Trilisk host body tendons," Barrai teased.

"Maybe. Only if Telisa gives me more months to study the problem."

Barrai laughed. "I won't hold my breath then!"

She walked out, already falling into a light limp.

Arakaki walked over to Maxsym and smiled.

"I guess you only get one woman today," she said.

Maxsym nodded. Watching Arakaki fight Barrai tooth and nail made him think that she would appreciate a more aggressive effort on his part, rather than his usual methodical approach. For some reason he wanted to please her.

Things went well for the first ten minute round. Barrai had taken the edge off Arakaki for him. He held his own and for once, and even went hunting for a few minutes. Arakaki circled away and defended herself well, but Maxsym finally felt like he was a participant instead of a victim.

Early in the second round, he felt emboldened enough to shoot for a takedown. He remembered Magnus's advice: *If you're going to shoot, you have to commit.*

Maxsym breathed heavily, pretending he was still resting, then he bolted forward with everything he had. Arakaki tried to knee him, but he was already upon her. He scooped her legs out and they went flying to the floor. She tried to put him into her guard, but he did not let her.

Maxsym avoided over her legs and grabbed an arm. He slipped a leg behind it, trying to wrap her arm, then force her over onto her stomach. He did not quite have the angle he needed for the technique to work. The position became static for a moment, both of them struggling.

Maxsym yelled and applied a sudden impulse. Arakaki lost her support as a foot slipped on the sweaty surface of the workout floor. Maxsym rolled her over onto her face, forcing her arm behind her back, trapped under his leg. Then he grabbed her arm in both hands and twisted it against a joint. She tapped out.

I got it! And she looked surprised.

They unraveled the position and stood facing each other on the floor.

"You're different today, Maxsym. I sense more drive."

"I want to do better," he said.

“Let me show you a more elegant takedown,” she said. Maxsym was familiar with how she operated by now: she often paused to give him pointers.

“Put your hand here, in the small of my back,” she instructed.

“Yes?”

“Now: hip to hip,” she said.

Maxsym put the side of his hip against hers, preparing the leverage for a vanilla Judo throw.

“No, straight,” Arakaki said. She took her hands and rotated his hips back to face her. Then she slid into contact with him.

“I... don’t think I’m feeling the leverage,” Maxsym said.

“But you are feeling something, are you not?” Arakaki said slyly. She put her arms around his head as if clinching. Then she kissed him aggressively.

When they came up for air, Maxsym hesitated.

“The last person I slept with is dead,” he blurted.

Arakaki nodded. “Then we have that in common. Don’t worry though. I’m tougher than Stracey Stalos was.”

***

“I’ve made a very interesting discovery,” Maxsym said eagerly.

Arakaki bolted awake in her sleep web. Maxsym’s disembodied voice confused her for a second. Where was he?

“Tell us,” Telisa said.

Arakaki became even more perplexed for a half second, then she saw the communications were coming through on the PIT channel. Maxsym was no longer in her room.

Wake up.

A pointer appeared on the channel. Arakaki accessed it and found video of an eight-legged creature crawling along among the green streamers. The video metadata told her it was taken recently by attendants in the alien forest.

"Looks kinda like a crab... except a little prettier," Magnus said.

"Wait... it looks like those little robots we found!" Marcant exclaimed.

"Yes. A striking resemblance, wouldn't you say?" Maxsym asked.

Well... I guess our romp... energized him, Arakaki thought.

"I agree, but it could be a coincidence," Magnus said.

"I have evidence that these are linked," Maxsym replied. "The dust on the floor of the bunker comes from the remains of these creatures."

"In a structure that old, those critters could have found an underground breach in a pipe and gotten in there themselves," Magnus pointed out.

"There's more. I've examined these creature's metabolism and linked their chitinous covering to the polysaccharides in the food storage areas. There are many similarities there which suggest to me they come from the same ecosystem. Most other creatures on this planet are incompatible with those substances."

"You mean those spaghetti spirals?"

"Yes."

"So, these bugs were... Rovan food animals?"

"Maybe the large Rovans ate them, or maybe that food is for these small creatures... there exist many possibilities," Maxsym said. "It may simply be that both of those substances are very similar because the big Rovans and the small creatures were built from the same food sources. Perhaps the Rovans and these creatures consumed the same plants in their primitive past.

"These bugs must be more than just food, if the tunnels are for them and the robots were based upon them," Marcant said.

"It is possible that a symbiotic relationship existed that may have started with predation or parasitism. I don't know," Maxsym said. "I think I've ruled out that this is a Rovan, though. The creature is not smart enough. Unless they had a hive mentality in which the whole was greater than the sum of its parts."

"What more can we learn about Rovan physiology from these things?"

"Possibly how they digested things. Whether or not they are likely to have blood vessels, brain neurons, all kinds of things. Like learning about Terrans studying mice or dogs. The creatures have poor visual sensors: those little buds at the first joint of each leg. Maybe the Rovans did, too, maybe their planet has some reason eyesight is not as helpful. Of course, it might be that the smaller creatures are often moving through dark tunnels like the pipes, and sight is not as useful for that reason."

"Speaking of digestion, if these things are not from here, what are they eating?" Telisa asked.

"Maybe scavenging food stores like we found, or maybe they can process the local molecules somehow," Maxsym said. "I'll know more soon."

"It sounds like more confusion to me," Magnus said.

"More pieces of a huge puzzle, but they're still pieces," Telisa said. "We're making progress."

Arakaki slipped out of her sleeping web. She felt better than she had in months. It did not bother her that Maxsym had hopped back to work so quickly without saying goodbye. She did not want anyone too sticky, especially if they were going to be working on the same team together.

Progress. Yes. On many fronts.

Chapter 9

Yat Li lounged on the gray stump of a dead streamer tree. He sucked on a thin reed that tasted like peppermint. They had discovered the plant two weeks ago and learned that its mild narcotic effect helped pass the time. Yat had plenty of time on his hands.

Yat and his companion in adventure, Oliver Jackson, had been stuck on the planet for four months. They were running out of supplies and desperate to find ways to survive. But not having enough food often meant not having enough energy to search for food. It was a vicious cycle. Yat already looked like someone who enjoyed toning pill overdoses. His ribs were sharp under his skin. Some muscle still stuck to his arms and legs. They were not starving just yet.

Just yet.

The blower sat nearby with its solar panels deployed. Yat supposed they would continue to their planned destination today, though it seemed almost pointless.

Yat pulled a bright spiral rod from his pack. It had marks on it from where he had previously chewed on it. Oliver was sure the rods were alien food sticks. Yat could not tell if the stick was poisoning him or sustaining him, so he had been chewing on it sparingly. That would have to change soon.

Oliver emerged from the streamers and strode toward Yat purposefully. Though of average height, Oliver looked slightly hunched over. Yat wondered if it was hunger. Oliver's armored suit was scratched and dirty like Yat's.

Yat assumed his companion was going to declare himself ready to go, but instead Oliver squatted near Yat. The whites of his eyes contrasted against his dark skin. His gaze shifted left, then right. Something was wrong.

"Don't look. We're being watched, man. By flying robots."

"What?!"

Yat's head turned. He caught a glimpse of something silver hiding among the green streamers to their left.

"I told you not to look you idiot," Oliver hissed.

"Robots? Has Torsion come for their stuff?"

"Yes. No. *Alien* robots."

"Alien! No shit? Wait... from this planet?"

Yat's amazement turned to fear in a wrenching second. His whole world changed from calm resignation to desperation.

"I don't know man. They're watching us," Oliver told him.

"There's more than one?"

"Man, I think there are at least *seven* of them."

Oh crap. What do they want?

"Get your weapon," Yat said.

"Wait. We have to think this through. Those are probably spies. Will their owners really be far behind?"

"Depends. Think about it. They could be sent years ahead to scout out planets," Yat said.

Yat wanted to believe that. Badly. He stood to his full height, an inch taller than Oliver, though the other man was clearly stronger.

"Then what's the plan?" Yat asked.

"We double time it to the next catacombs," Oliver said. He spoke of the alien cave systems where they had found many valuable artifacts and the spirals they suspected were alien food. Yat had put in intense study on an alien system and deciphered the data of a map of the catacomb network.

"How will that help?"

"Down there, we can see those things. And shoot them, if we have to. In this mess, we can barely see our hands in front of our faces."

Yat sighed.

I suppose he has a point.

"Okay. The catacombs. Double time."

Yat told the blower to activate. The machine's fans moved the cool morning air against the mess of streamers in their path. Slowly, the long green leaves relaxed. The machine moved forward, pushing its way through the tangle. Without the airflow, the machine used three times more power to muscle through the interwoven streamers. In the afternoon, they would slow. The light was strongest then, but blowing hot air barely relaxed the plants at all.

Yat and Oliver fell into place behind the machine.

The revelation they were being watched and followed changed Yat's entire outlook. Yesterday he had been racking his brain trying to plan how they might find food, make food, or call for help. Now his fears centered around the aliens. Would they help? Kill? Or capture them and make life even worse?

"Don't shoot first," Yat urged Oliver over their links.

"I won't. Believe me, I don't want any trouble. Whoever they are, they have to be better off than we are."

"If we can't find food... we need to attempt communication. They might be able to save us."

"I agree. But I say, last resort."

Yat and Oliver had stolen drugs from Torsion, a frontier crime organization. The two had no real desires to become drug dealers; they had simply seen a chance to snatch a cargo of immense value and run with it. Besides, the stash of Midnight Stare was not dangerous, as long as it was used by someone who knew what they were doing. The double-dose packs for two came with instructions and plenty of warnings.

Yat's best-case scenario was that assassins from Torsion came for them, fought the aliens and died, leaving Oliver and him the food and spaceship.

It did not seem likely.

They made good time in the morning as always. When the temperature rose, they used their blades and took turns with the blower, letting it get some extra charge while they worked.

In the evening, they caught a lucky break. The landscape opened up onto a rocky plateau. They climbed onto the blower and rode it for kilometers without having to clear any streamers. As a result, they made it to the catacomb entrance before nightfall.

Oliver located the hatch to the site while Yat cleaned up the blower and secured its panels to withstand the night winds. Then Yat took his pack and went over to open the door.

Yat used to brag that there was no door he could not open. That was back before he ever encountered a portal built by an alien species. Still, his unique background in creative criminal hacking had served him well, and with a week of study, he had learned how to open the hatches in the ruins. If the door was powered up it would take him less than ten minutes; otherwise, an hour.

Yat connected his equipment and started to work. Soon the hatch opened.

"This is even better than we thought. We didn't have to burn it, so now we can close it behind us, and those things might not follow us," Oliver said.

"Sounds good," Yat said. "But if we don't find anything we can use to eat or make food, then we'll want to find them. What if we come back out and they're not here anymore?"

Oliver sighed. He shook his head.

"There's no other intelligent creatures on this planet except them and us. I don't think they'll give up their interest. They'll be here when we come back out. If they don't burn through the door and come after us."

"Let's hope so."

Chapter 10

Magnus disassembled another piece of the Rovan robot. His every move was recorded and each piece was automatically added to his virtual model of the alien machine. The records would serve them well for reassembly or functional analyses.

Two things had rapidly become apparent: the machine had not been designed with disassembly in mind, at least not in any way he could comprehend; secondly, the Rovans built things very differently than Terrans and Vovokans.

Once he had managed to separate the upper casing from the central body of the octoped, he found a sticky interior with both solid and liquid parts that had no discernable internal modules to be separated and removed. Magnus hesitated to destructively continue the disassembly. The fact they had found so many more at the arctic station made him finally decide to proceed. He cut the robot apart. Things became even messier. The fluids started to leak out.

Cyborg? Maybe. I hope not.

He asked Marcant to give his opinion. His team member did not have to come over incarnate, and likely would not. Magnus had shared a pointer to the diagrams.

"Look at this," Magnus said.

"Perplexing," Marcant said after a minute. "But it is alien, after all."

"Very alien. I had trouble with Shiny's machines, true, but not like this."

"I think Maxsym might have some insight," Adair said.

"Really? Okay," Magnus said uncertainly. "Dare I ask why?"

"Call it a hunch," Adair said.

Magnus mentally shrugged and looped Maxsym in.

"Maxsym. Hi. This is strange, but Adair said you might be able to give me some insight into this design."

"It's a robot..." Maxsym said.

"It's very unusual in many ways," Magnus said. "I'm having trouble understanding it at all."

"Wait a moment..." Maxsym said.

It took Maxsym about four minutes to get back to Magnus.

"I see what you mean. This is some kind of hybrid organism. I wouldn't go so far as to say it was alive, but, this is a synthesis of organic and inorganic parts."

"Part natural, part artificial? A cyborg spider-crab?"

"Oh, there's nothing natural about it. It's synthetic from top to bottom. But I'd bet this entire structure here is based upon a natural system. It appears to—" Maxsym stopped.

"Are you okay?" Magnus asked. An irrational thought came forth: had Maxsym suffered another attack?

"I'm here. But I have no idea what that entire region does," he said, highlighting the ventral part of the robot's body. "It's clearly important. It's like twenty-one percent of the creature."

"Brain?"

"...maybe..."

"Reproductive?"

"I can't rule that out either. I don't think this is a Von Neumann machine, though. By the way, one reason the other parts, even the artificial parts, look so different than a lot of your robots, is that the entire motile apparatus is based upon an exoskeletal system rather than an endoskeletal one. It has quite an impact on the contractor placement."

"I see. Okay, this is progress. It's got some gooey lifelike internal organs or systems, and the legs are built with exoskeletal flexors and extensors. I'm a little less flummoxed now."

"I'll try and get back to you about that internal system."

Magnus had only twenty minutes to digest Maxsym's analysis and get his bearings given the new insights before a high priority alert came through.

An attendant had flagged a discovery at high priority. Magnus watched the feed for ten seconds before he forgot all about the robots and sent out a message on the PIT channel.

"Team, we're not alone here. I don't mean aliens. There are *Terrans* here."

"Say again?" Arakaki responded.

"An attendant is watching two Terrans on the planet's surface. It's called for more. I'm looking the observations over right now."

"Pointer please!" Marcant called out.

Magnus zipped through more footage to count how many other Terrans there were before he could break away.

"Yes... a moment..."

"Give us the summary, then," Telisa said.

Magnus finished skimming over what had been discovered.

"There's two of them. We haven't spotted any spacecraft."

He sent out the link where the attendant had been accumulating information. The display in Magnus's PV updated, showing another attendant had arrived on the scene.

"I'm reinforcing these attendants' preference for stealth. I don't want these two to know they're being watched."

"If they see one, they'll freak out," Arakaki said. "I would."

"With your permission, I'll initiate a new system sweep," Barrai said.

"Go," Telisa said. "Also, prepare a couple more shuttles. Chances are, we'll eventually be going out there to meet them."

Well she doesn't have to order us to study them. They're barely doing anything but I'm still fascinated.

The attendants had discovered a simple camp at the base of a kind of tree Magnus had not yet seen—a giant green plant that looked comically like a huge piece of broccoli growing on a rocky outcropping amid a streamer forest. The Terran men did not look well outfitted. They had only what they could carry or strap to their strange machine.

An attendant floated above, hidden in the strange tree. Up close, it looked nothing like broccoli, as it had hairs and thorns along its branches. A path through the forest a little wider than the machine told Magnus that their machine cleared the way for the strangers.

The men appeared to be resting. One of them was brawny, with light brown skin and a mean, unshaven countenance. The other one was taller, thinner, and more refined, with skin a shade lighter. They did not look like Core Worlders; Magnus placed them as coming from any of a hundred frontier worlds.

Magnus opened a private channel to Telisa.

"Can you believe it? What are the chances of finding Terrans out here?" he asked.

"Well, it's happened before," she said.

"The UED. Yes, okay, but that felt different... I guess it really wasn't."

"There are probably a lot of explorers on livable planets outside the frontier. Crazy people like us. Maybe dangerous?"

"You know as well as I do the answer depends. In general, though, yes, more dangerous than a Core Worlder," he said.

"Should we be watching them? I mean, should we be spying on them like this?" Telisa asked.

"This is no Core World. We're beyond the frontier. There are no laws."

"Still..."

"My vote is we spy on them a day or two, and assess if they're a threat. If not, then we may as well make contact. I understand it feels a little slimy, but out here, you can't be too careful."

Telisa nodded. "Okay. We watch them. But if it looks like they're in trouble we have to help. They look hungry. If they're stuck here for some reason, they might be getting desperate."

Magnus tried to get back to his robots. It was difficult. He kept checking in on the two strangers. They were working their way through the forest with the help of their machine.

Magnus sighed.

How far am I going to get with these crazy machines, anyway? Modeled after a living system. I might as well take up gardening.

***

Magnus physically and mentally disengaged from Telisa as his link requested urgent attention. Their sensory interlink disconnected, causing his perception of Telisa's pleasure to fade away.

Worst. Timing. Ever.

As tempting as it was to fully isolate themselves from the rest of the team, given their work, it was also dangerous.

"Yes Maxsym?" he said, trying to hide his annoyance.

"I've learned a few things about that structure you inquired about."

I regret the inquiry, now.

Magnus added Telisa to the channel. She may as well learn with him. She gave him a knowing smile.

"The closest analogue you and I have is our nose," Maxsym said. "Really, though, this is more like a vomeronasal organ."

"You lost me."

"Snakes collect molecules on their tongue and put it into a pocket that can analyze the molecules and send the brain messages about the content. This structure has a similar entrance there on the belly of that octoped. And the wild octopeds have it as well... honestly, that's the only thing that allowed me to understand so quickly."

"So they collect scents and put it into their belly... with a leg, or what?"

"That's the weird part. They can't do that themselves. They must rely upon others to deliver the scents. I think these are a type of social insect after all, which makes me want to shift my opinion away from the idea that the large Rovans were the brains of this operation."

"That is pretty big. We have to kick that possibility up a notch with this evidence."

"Think on it," Maxsym said. "I'll return to other work now."

"As will I," Magnus said, turning back to his lover.

Chapter 11

Arakaki sat in the shuttle with Telisa, Magnus, and Barrai as they rode to the site where the other Terrans had ditched the attendants. The shuttle barely vibrated. Still, the ride was distinguishable from that of a Vovokan shuttle, which was a notch better.

Arakaki surreptitiously evaluated Barrai to see if she was having a problem with nerves. Barrai's face was relaxed. Her eyes shifted calmly from spot to spot. She decided the Space Force officer was holding up well.

"We're going to go in there after them," Telisa announced. "But we have to be careful not to end up in a firefight, or forcing them to do something desperate to escape us."

"We don't know for sure they knew anything was up," Arakaki pointed out.

"My gut says they made us. At this point, someone may get hurt. More likely them than us, but still... I want to make contact with them and make an exchange. They likely know a few things we don't. We could help them out of what looks like a bad situation for them and learn something in the process."

"First thing's first," Barrai said. "We need to cut through that hatch without alarming them. If they're waiting on the other side, they may shoot us then and there."

Telisa nodded.

"We're going to cut a small hole first and send attendants through with a peace message."

Arakaki checked her submachine gun manually. Given that the weapon had a full suite of self-diagnostics, it was simply a ritual. She half expected Barrai to say as much, but the new PIT member kept her mouth zipped. Arakaki appreciated that.

The shuttle made its final approach. Arakaki quashed a memory of coming in hot on a UED shuttle into a zone contested by the UNSF. Things had been much grimmer on that day.

Today, let's not lose anyone.

"I'm clearing out an area for us," Magnus said. He sent out a warning, scattering the attendants near the ground like frightened mice.

The shuttle swept in a tight circle and blew away many of the streamers with a blast of air. Then the shuttle settled in the center with its tiny spinner spooled up. The streamers bent outward, forming a rough radial pattern pointing away from the shuttle. The only thing that withstood the assault was the stranger's machine, which stood two meters over the carnage.

The shuttle door opened. The team deployed around their craft. Arakaki took several strides to one side and dropped to one knee with her primary weapon ready.

A six-legged robot climbed out of the shuttle and walked over to the rocky hillside that hid the heavy Rovan hatch. The machine located the hatch with the help of the spy attendants' provided coordinates.

"That hatch is even stronger than the first bunker we went into," Telisa noted.

"Yes. It makes one think, doesn't it? This place was tightly sealed," Magnus said.

To Arakaki, that meant a strong possibility of danger. If the installation had a strong door, what other defenses might it possess?

The cutter bot walked away from the door with its abdomen glowing red, but had only left a scar of less than a handspan.

"No worries, just swapping out," Magnus assured them.

Arakaki decided to walk the perimeter of the clearing created by the shuttle. She looked out into the mass of streamers all around them, imagining camouflaged predators glaring back at her from the morass. Nothing caught her eye. For Arakaki, it was not a matter of *if* she would see some danger lurking—it was *when*.

The machines finished burning through the alien hatch. As planned, the initial hole was large enough for the attendants. Arakaki glanced over just as a few of them slipped inside.

"No one waiting for us," Telisa reported.

As usual, attendants provided a shared a tactical map for the team. Arakaki saw an empty entrance chamber with wide rectangular corridors that branched out in three directions. Each way slanted downward, leading deeper into the planet.

Data kept pouring in from the attendants. The map grew and grew while their robots worked on fully breaching the door so the team could follow.

"This is interesting," Telisa said. "The wide tunnels go on much longer than anything we've seen. What's down here?"

"Judging from the way they worked the door, I'm guessing they know," Barrai said.

"Maybe. They've done this before, at least," Telisa agreed.

"The attendants are picking up enough clues to track them. They went this way," Magnus said. The route the two men had taken was displayed on the tactical. It did not wander about or foray into nearby areas for searching. It looked like the strangers were eager to get as deep into the complex as they could.

"If they know we're coming, will there be a trap?"

"Wouldn't they think we're aliens at this point? All they've seen are the attendants," Marcant sent from the *Sharplight*.

"Probably. But we don't know them, so we can't guess. Another potential threat: they might have come to this place because they have other people here. We have to be prepared for more than those two," Telisa said.

Arakaki checked Barrai again. A drop of sweat wandered down Barrai's temple.

That tensed her up somewhat, but she's not afraid.

Unlike those they pursued, the attendants had explored many side passages and chambers. Arakaki looked at the feeds. The corridors all looked the same: rectangular passageways of smooth black stone that looked very plain compared to the hexagonal passages of the arctic station. The dark rooms held huge containers, heavy blocks of equipment, and squat-framed sleds that must have been used to haul it all around.

Feels like a long-term storage depot. Like they knew they would be gone for a long time.

The door clanked open as the cutters finished their work. Magnus's robots took the door aside. Ten of his six-legged soldiers walked inside.

"These robots can secure the entrance for us in case we need to make a rapid exit," Magnus offered.

"Yes, and keep us from being surprised from behind, in case another group is coming," Arakaki said.

"Stealth. On me," Telisa ordered. Her form blinked out, leaving only a ghostly silhouette provided by Arakaki's link. Telisa stepped through, weapon in hand.

Arakaki stealthed and went next. The interior smelled smoky, presumably from the door cutting. Four robots faced the door, two on each flank. The other six had deployed in a semicircle facing into the complex.

The team filtered past their guard robots and took the leftmost corridor, which had a noticeable downward grade.

The light of the entrance faded behind them. With their stealth engaged, their own light sources were dampened, so Telisa sent three attendants ahead.

"Switch up to this spectrum," she instructed and sent along a pointer.

Arakaki told her suit to enhance the given frequencies. The walls of the corridor came back into view, lit by the attendants with light at frequencies undetectable to naked Terran eyes.

So equipped, the team accelerated down the tunnel, following the faint chemical trail of the two strangers. Arakaki focused on the tactical and her attendant feeds, moving in smooth coordination with her teammates. In that way, it was like one of their virtual exercises. In the back of her mind, the knowledge that it was all real remained, but did not make her nervous.

With their new teammate, Barrai, it could not be so. She would be feeling the nerves and fighting to keep it from degrading her performance. It was like going into the field with any solid rookie—one just had to keep an eye on them.

The group walked through a dark intersection and selected another long tunnel.

"Halt. On our right," Telisa transmitted.

A large shape loomed. Arakaki raised her weapon.

An attendant flew toward the unidentified presence. Its high-frequency light flashed over a metallic surface. A massive four-legged machine stood there with a disturbingly wide scoop-mouth in the front of its squarish body.

"War machine?" hazarded Barrai.

"I think it's a ceramic cutter!" Magnus said. "It may have been used to work these tunnels."

Siobhan would have known.

Arakaki looked at the tunnel walls anew. The hard, glossy substance on the surfaces absorbed a lot of the light. It did look like the black industrial ceramic in use for many Terran roads and buildings.

They cut through the native rock, pumped in this stuff, then cut these corridors from it? Sounds difficult, but the resulting tunnels would last forever.

One of the attendant feeds caught Arakaki's attention. The attendant had found a natural, irregular shape in a small chamber. The feed showed the shape to be about six meters long, raised from the floor on a ceramic dais. It was about 100 meters away, off the path that their targets had taken.

"Something here. A bunch of rooms with... unusual objects. They look natural," Arakaki said.

"Arakaki. Barrai. Check it out and get some samples," Telisa ordered.

Arakaki took the lead. Her and Barrai left the team, following two attendants that broke off to light their way to the find. They went back 10 meters and took a branch of the tunnel. Arakaki remained alert even though the attendants had not discovered anything dangerous nearby.

Telisa sent us alone to test Barrai, Arakaki decided. *Or maybe just to give her some experience in a split-up.*

Arakaki led the way down the next dark Rovan corridor. She imagined trip wires and trap doors though the attendants would likely have detected any such oddities. With their attendants, armor, arms, and stealth, it seemed likely that her and Barrai would be too much for any ambush to chew.

They came to the room. The object of interest was bigger than the two Terrans. Its shape was oblong, somewhat flattened, and curved downward on its ragged edges. The resemblance was so strong, Arakaki immediately believed this was a form of natural armor.

"It looks like half of a huge turtle shell," Arakaki summarized. "Though I don't know what's going on here on the edges... are those niches all for legs?"

"Cover me," she told Barrai.

Arakaki slid her weapon over her shoulder and activated an autoscanner Maxsym had sent along for exactly this purpose. She did not know how it was superior to the attendant's capabilities. The others watched the feeds.

"This shell... it belonged to a creature about the size of the larger corridors and tunnels. This could be the remains of a Rovan!" Telisa said.

"Yes! Maybe they used to bury their dead in tombs like this one," Magnus said.

"You mean this was their home planet after all? It seemed like they came here later. There aren't ruins across the entire planet," Arakaki protested.

"I don't know," Telisa said.

"Maybe it's not a corpse. Maybe these things shed their shells," Magnus suggested.

"I don't think so. There are a few bones here too," Barrai said. "Whatever they were, they had a skeleton like us."

"Maxsym, are you getting this?" Telisa asked.

"Yes. I'll begin analysis as soon as I get the details from Arakaki," Maxsym said.

Arakaki knew if they could learn something from the shells, Maxsym would do it. She finished taking material samples and told the nearest attendant to return to the surface for a clear, fast transmission of the data to Maxsym.

"We have the two strangers in sight again," Magnus said.

Arakaki zipped up her pack and checked the feed Magnus had referred to as she returned with Barrai to the team. The feed showed the two Terrans in a room filled with tall alien machines. Some of the mechanical hulks looked mobile, set upon treads or thick legs, while others were huge cubes of pipes and structural bars.

"They're only a few hundred meters away."

"Should we surround them?" Barrai asked.

"We won't have to go that far," Telisa said. "Besides, that might force an armed confrontation. We'll let them know who we are and go from there. We're not here to capture smugglers, I only want to meet them and learn what they know."

Telisa indicated her desired deployments on the tactical. She placed herself way ahead of the others. Arakaki watched Magnus squirm as he realized she was putting herself in harm's way. Arakaki knew he was not going to say anything about it, at least not on the team channel.

They fell into position as ordered. Arakaki focused on the feed from the attendant nearest the men. They were busy trying to open a large container.

I guess they think they left us behind. What are they searching for, loot or just food? Can they eat Rovan food?

The taller, more wiry one caught sight of an attendant.

"Oliver. They're back."

The other one, presumably named Oliver, turned and brandished his weapon. The attendants clearly alarmed him. The taller one looked near panic as well. Arakaki spotted a weapon at his hip.

"Hello," Telisa said through the attendants.

The two men scrambled for cover. They disappeared behind one of the huge alien machines.

"We mean you no harm," Telisa transmitted. "We're Terrans, too. An exploration team from Earth."

Arakaki switched views to another attendant feed so she could partially see the two men sheltering beside a machine. They had hidden themselves inside recesses in its shape. Arakaki saw enough to decide they were discussing what to do—arguing, it appeared.

"I'll come negotiate with you in person if you like," Telisa offered. "FTF-TNT."

She knows the frontier lingo. Face to face, talk 'n trade.

"We don't want any trouble," someone sent back. Their link identity was obscured.

"Good, me neither. Honestly, you look like you could use some supplies, and we want information about this planet. We just want to know what you've learned here."

"Show yourselves," they sent back.

"I'll show myself, but that's it, I won't show my team," Telisa said. "Not until I can see that your weapons aren't trained on us."

Telisa unstealthed and stepped cautiously forward from the wide corridor into the chamber where the strangers waited. Attendants moved slowly with her, ready to provide support.

She's not really in danger. Their guns can track her faster than they can... but between her reflexes and the attendants, the best they could hope for is a scar on her Momma Veer.

"There's plenty of artifacts on this planet for all of us," she said.

The two men stepped free of their cover. The shorter, more muscular one took the lead. They both held firearms in their right hands, pointed at the floor.

"You're really Terran? Those flying things..."

"Those are alien. But we control them," Telisa said. "I'm Telisa."

Their expressions did not waver.

They don't recognize her? I guess the PIT team is not universally known... yet.

"Oliver," the shorter, broader one said.

"Yat," said the other.

"Nice to meet you. Let's talk and trade."

Chapter 12

Oliver walked beside Yat down a wide Rovan corridor. The other explorers were split evenly ahead and behind. He could tell the strangers were trying to act relaxed and friendly, but between the lines it felt more like he and Yat had been arrested. Their flying orbs were everywhere, searching ahead, lurking behind, and shadowing their keepers. Oliver knew the orbs could send video to their links, but he wondered what else they were capable of.

Oliver had seen four members of their team. The leader Telisa was strong, beautiful and brave. She walked ahead of him with a female companion with dark skin, black hair, and an even more-developed musculature. Something about the darker one...

She's probably Space Force. But then what about these others?

The woman who trailed him stood shorter but looked tough and determined. The man next to her was about Oliver's size and shape, with lighter hair and a less handsome face. These two remained very alert, with weapons ready.

They all struck Oliver as being experienced and capable, enough so that he felt happy he had surrendered rather than fight.

"You seemed to know this place was here. How? And what is this facility?" Telisa asked mildly.

"It's a graveyard."

He could tell Telisa's interest was piqued.

"Obviously, the Rovans are long gone," she said. "We think they took all their spacecraft and most of their robots and left. These catacombs hold the first remains we've found, but I'm guessing these are Rovans who died before the emergency came up, whatever it was."

"I'm not sure," Oliver said. "All I know is, there are a lot of them down here, and there are a lot of other mass tombs like this one."

"Did they get hit with some calamity?"

"We don't know what happened to them. Our plan was to get in and out before running into whatever did them in. Yat managed to crack some of their data and we got a map. It shows these installations scattered across the planet. They all look like this one: a lot of supplies, equipment tucked away, and tens of thousands of the shells. That's how we scrounged up these artifacts after our 'friends' took the rest."

Oliver pointed at his pack as he finished.

"Took?"

"We were double-crossed."

"So there were more to your party when you set out?"

"Yes. A group of seven including us. We set down and looked around. The others were looking to score an alien spaceship. When it became clear we wouldn't find one, at least not anytime soon, they decided to leave. They left Yat and me behind so they wouldn't have to share the proceeds from what they called a disappointing haul."

"That's crazy," the man said. Oliver recalled his name was Magnus. "Alien artifacts fetch huge prices in the Core Worlds."

Oliver paused and traded looks with Yat.

"Should we tell them?" Yat asked him privately.

"Well, that's just it," Oliver said, thinking quickly. "These guys are wanted in the Core Worlds. Artifacts are more common on the frontier. There's money in the haul we had, no doubt about it, but not as much as you might get back in the Core Worlds where the Force is sweeping up everything."

Vaguely the truth. Close enough, probably.

"I hope they're gone for good," Yat said.

"There's no one here. Believe me, if they come back looking for trouble, they'll regret it. There's a Space Force capital ship here," the one called Barrai said.

"But you're not with the Space Force?"

Barrai started to answer, but her leader cut her off.

"No, but we work with them from time to time," Telisa said.

Oliver wondered what that meant. He had not decided to probe the subject before they arrived at the entrance. Other robots that looked Terran in construction flanked them. The outside door had been breached by force.

"They don't know how to open the doors like you can. So they aren't all powerful," he sent to Yat privately.

"Powerful enough," Yat replied neutrally.

They climbed out of the building and over to a clearing caused by a spinner. A strange oblong craft lay at the center of the landing zone.

"What kind of ship is that?" Oliver blurted.

"A shuttle," Telisa said. "We've had some success at finding alien ships elsewhere."

An understatement!

"And your starship?" Yat asked.

"One Terran, one Vovokan," Telisa said.

"Vovokan? Like the thing that took over Earth?"

"Yes."

The one called Arakaki offered Yat some food packets. Magnus followed up and offered Oliver some, too.

"Thanks," Yat said and dug in.

Oliver frowned. What choice did they have but to trust the strangers? He and Yat were at their mercy. He started to eat. It was not anything special, but he wolfed it down all the same.

Amazing how great it feels to just eat without thinking about running out.

"We've found a lot of artifacts here and there," Telisa said. "Most of it feels pretty trivial, except for the robots, which are very rare. What have you found?"

Oliver wondered for a second if they were asking because they intended to steal all the items. Yat's look said that he wondered the same.

"I won't take anything of yours," Telisa said. "I was an artifact smuggler, once."

And what are you now, exactly?

"I found a robot," Yat offered. He stooped to drop his pack on the ground and opened it. Oliver watched Arakaki twitch as Yat reached in.

That one is ready for anything. I hope her weapons aren't lethal.

Yat brought out a round, octopedal machine. Its semi-transparent surface gleamed.

"By the Five! That looks different than the ones we found. What is it made of?" Telisa asked.

"The outside shell is diamond," Yat answered. "Well, and other allotropes of carbon."

"Really? Ha. Does it work?" she asked.

"I'm not sure. It might be just a bauble, I guess. Still, it's an alien artifact, right?"

"Yes, I think it would fetch a high price," Magnus said.

Oliver sent a private link message to Yat.

"Okay, at first I thought if they were going to kill us, they'd just do it," he transmitted. "But now I realize they might just be using us to learn what our stuff is before taking it."

"They look sophisticated enough to figure out what it is without our help. I believe her," Yat sent back.

"What else do you have?" Telisa asked. "We have more water and food in the shuttle, you can take all you want. I want to learn about these aliens. We call them the Rovans."

"Ah, from the generated system name. We call them Ticks," Oliver said.

Yat took another artifact out of his pack. It was a complex device as long as his forearm, black, and looked heavy in Yat's hands. It had a complex surface with many ridges, depressions, and interstices. A thick barrel-like shape dominated the top ridge.

"Looks like a weapon," Arakaki said.

"Maybe so," Yat admitted. "It can draw heat from objects across a short distance. It's dangerous, so we haven't played with it much."

"Wise. These things can be dangerous all right," Telisa said.

"Draw heat? Where does the heat go?" Magnus asked.

"Hot air through this tube and out the back," Yat said, showing them the other openings. "Hot enough to burn you. But I think that pipe there was meant to have water or something denser in it to take the heat. If so, this could work even faster. This mechanism here determines how far away it's focused." Yat slid a bolt with a tab along the side of the top ridge.

Oliver opened his pack as well, though he felt reluctant to do so.

He took out a metallic ring made of overlapped ring-scales that flexed. It started out just big enough to fit over his head, then he stretched it out, making it large enough to fit around a Terran's waist.

Don't know what to tell them about this... other than I have a hunch it would be valuable.

Telisa looked at the ring.

"It's very light. I'm not sure what it does, but it's got an advanced field emitter that can produce very fine-grained localized EM patterns," he told her. "I think it might be a non-invasive link or an alien mind interface of some kind. At the very least, I would guess it could set the memory bits of a robot and put a program into place without any direct access to the ports."

A silvery tube dropped from his pack as he spoke.

"What's that?" Telisa asked.

"Fluid container. I don't know what the fluid is, but it was locked up securely. We seriously abused a cannister to see if it was explosive, but it proved stable. So I took a couple."

"It could be anything, even just water," Yat said, taking the opportunity to complain about Oliver's choice for the tenth time.

"It was locked up in a vault like you wouldn't believe," Oliver said, defending his choice. "It was very important to these aliens. Good chance it's something special. Besides, they're not that heavy."

Oliver took out his prize find. It was a white and red container that looked like a hard-shelled backpack without the straps. He considered downplaying it in case they were going to steal the best stuff.

If these people are going to take our artifacts, they're going to take them all no matter what I say.

"For lack of a better description, it's a force field generator. Beyond anything Terrans have, obviously, given how compact it is. These discs power it. Their energy density is fantastic. I don't know how to charge them, though, and I've been afraid to experiment with them. I'm afraid if the field is configurable, it might pinch me in half or something."

"Good choice of artifacts to carry. I think that's super valuable," Magnus said. "If you can get it to someone who can learn how it works... sky's the limit."

"That's it," Oliver said.

"Our attendants here saw you have something else. Looks like Terran packets, but too small for food," Telisa said.

"Malcons afire, those spy machines saw it?" Oliver sent to Yat privately.

"Tell them," Yat sent. "We haven't done that much wrong. We stole from murderers. So what?"

Oliver looked at Telisa and spat it out.

"That's our Midnight Stare."

"I've heard of it," Marcant said. "Dangerous."

"As frontier drugs go? No," Oliver said. "What we have is packed as double doses with all the warnings. Two people have to accept the contract before it will open without neutralizing."

"Fill us in, please," Telisa said. "I think I've heard something about this on the network, but I'm not sure. It's a sexual gratification drug?"

"Uh, for some people I guess you could say that," Yat said. "Take it, and your mating imperative rises a hundredfold. You WILL do it. With anyone there at the time."

"Dangerous side effects?" Magnus asked.

"That *is* the dangerous side effect. Look, if you don't have a partner, you'll mate with the cleaning robot. Hard. It's safest when a mixed couple take the contract. Some homosexual couples face a bit more danger. Two men have to make sure and agree on... logistics beforehand, or it gets ugly in a minute."

"That's why it only comes in two-dose packets and requires the contract to open it," Oliver added. "If you break the package open, the neutralizing agent will kill it in a fraction of a second."

"People *want* to take this?" Barrai asked. "I mean, if you want to do it, just do it..."

"It's a matter of taste I suppose," Marcant said. "The intensity of Midnight Stare is way up there. Some people overclock on loss of control, you know? It's supposed to be a very primal experience."

"What about addiction?" Telisa asked.

"No hard chemical addiction," Oliver said. "Thrill-wise, it could be addictive for some."

Marcant nodded. "And what about virtual consummation after taking a dose?" he asked.

"It's workable, but no one does that. This is all about an animal rush and knowing you're incarnate is part of that. I think 99% of users are taking it FTF."

"It sounds too dangerous for any Core Worlder," Telisa said. "For the frontier, I can see it. As I said before, we aren't confiscating anything you have."

"I guess we're lucky you found us, then," Oliver said cautiously. Despite her assurances, he did not feel confident that everything was going to be as peachy as Telisa made it sound.

"Maybe you'll run across us in a pinch someday and you can return the favor," Telisa said.

Chapter 13

How did they die? Magnus asked himself. *So many of them... yet the buildings that survive show no signs of attack damage. So it was... poison? Plague? Radiation? And how many of them escaped?*

He wrote down the theories and the facts that supported them into an investigative workspace in his PV. His old favorite theory, that the Rovans had gone to war with another civilization and had to evacuate the colony, had weakened. The Rovans could still have fled, but the invasion never came. Or if it took place with no damage at all...

Did they have to choose who fled and who stayed? Did the ones who stayed die? Or are the catacombs just the burial grounds of the Rovans who expired before they decided to abandon the colony?

As he sat in his quarters, another question rose to push back the others:

Who buried them all?

Magnus dismissed a feeling of unease and proceeded logically.

Survivors? Machines? Other aliens?

The last answer seemed unlikely. Not many Terrans would kill aliens and then bury the corpses according to alien customs. But aliens being aliens, not impossible. There was even a tiny chance that a disconnected third party placed them into the tombs.

A connection request from Telisa interrupted his internal debate.

"We've found something amazing!" she said excitedly.

"What? Where?"

"On-planet. A large building. Our attendants got in through some fissures and found some really old artifacts."

"I don't get it... you mean like a museum?" asked Magnus.

"Exactly! I'm calling out the team. This should answer some questions!"

"If they're like our museums, there will be VR archives plus holos for kids who aren't linked yet," Magnus said. "If Marcant and Yat can get that data..."

"Then we'll have all of Rovan history in our hands," Telisa finished for him.

The rest of the team scrambled at Telisa's urgent orders to prepare for a landing. Yat and Oliver were recuperating from their ordeal in quarters on the *Sharplight*. Barrai had been tasked with responding to their requests and ensuring that they did not attempt to break past their security restrictions. Normally, Telisa would not have worried about the data and physical security on board a modern Space Force vessel, but Yat had proven resourceful.

Thirty minutes later, Telisa, Magnus, Marcant, and Maxsym climbed aboard a shuttle. Arakaki had elected to stay back and train with Yat and Oliver to get to know them better. Magnus resolved to be vigilant—they had come to rely upon Arakaki to cover their backs.

"So what brings you away from the *Iridar* today?" Marcant asked Maxsym innocently.

Magnus sighed inwardly. Was Marcant about to needle his teammate?

"A museum might have preserved tissue samples," Maxsym said.

"I came to avoid fighting Barrai again," Marcant confided.

Magnus smiled.

Okay, now that's amusing.

"She won't kill you," Telisa said. "But this planet might. And it might not be fair about it, either."

"There's nothing fair about pitting me against an ex-UED scout," Marcant protested. Magnus knew he was not seriously upset. Marcant just liked to take any opportunity to complain.

They took the rest of their ride in silence. The shuttle came down hard, presumably because Telisa was in a hurry. Magnus checked his weapons and maneuvered himself to be the first to step off the shuttle, which was no small feat, given Telisa's eagerness and superhuman speed.

Once outside, their target was in plain sight. The bulky building had presumably stood taller in its heyday. Now, a bank of mud had encircled it on two sides, half burying the building. The other sides were covered in green streamers. Two long windows or portals extended across the nearest side, each eight meters long but less than a meter tall.

Rovan windows look more like pillbox gunports than Terran windows.

"Stealth?" he asked Telisa privately.

"No threats detected. We have an attendant inside," she said.

"This corner," Telisa called aloud, pointing to one spot on the building where the outer wall had collapsed. Everyone made a beeline for the opening. Magnus hooked in to the feeds of attendants already on the scene that patrolled the building. They had not spotted any dangers on the perimeter. A third attendant provided a rough map of the parts of the interior it had been able to reach.

Telisa stepped inside first. Magnus hurried after her. The interior was dark, but not utterly so—the building had other openings letting light inside. The first few steps were littered with debris, but farther inside, Magnus saw that the floor was highlighted with elegant diamond-shapes in clusters: one dark rhombus set amid four white ones. The walls held the same shape groupings in bas relief. They walked through a 20-meter-long corridor into a hemispherical atrium.

A massive form towered over them. Magnus raised his weapon, but it was only a static construct. He could not make out the details until a pair of attendants flew forward and illuminated the shape.

"By. The. Five," Telisa breathed.

The statue stood four or five meters high on four legs as thick as Magnus. At first, his mind classified the shape as a huge turtle because a massive round plate covered most of its body. The resemblance ended there: Magnus looked at a protuberance in the front. What he labeled a "head" was a flat, armored mass with four buds on the top, equidistant, one in each quartile. Beneath the armor was a truly horrible maw, filled with sharp teeth, flanked by huge scythe-type mandibles and a host of smaller mouthparts that made Magnus imagine being ripped apart by the alien.

"That can't be life-sized?" Arakaki breathed.

"Well, it could be," Telisa said. "I'm hoping though, that..." her voice trailed off. Her light shone down from the huge figure to other objects beneath it.

Magnus followed her light. The things below it were separate creatures with eight legs.

Those are the wild things Maxsym found... the things their robots are modeled after.

He counted eight of them. They were each much larger than any octoped they had seen thus far, natural or robotic.

"This is bigger than life-sized," Telisa concluded. "This shell is larger than any we found in the catacombs. This big thing is a Rovan, and I bet that is what fits in the large tunnels. This confirms those spider-legged things around it are what used the smaller tunnels."

Magnus nodded. She had to be right! The smaller creatures were almost certainly not the same species. They were radically different than the large creature, most obviously, exoskeletal instead of endoskeletal, though the big Rovan's shell muddied that distinction.

"So that's a Rovan? What do we call those things?" asked Marcant, pointing at the smaller creatures.

"Rovlings," Telisa said. "The feral ones in the forest must have come with the Rovans to this world, and that's why they have a different physiology than the native fauna of this planet."

She stepped forward. Her light pointed up to a recess under the shell, just behind a front leg.

"Looking for sex parts?" asked Marcant crassly.

"Maybe... I'm not sure! It has... eight of these holes, four on each side," she said. "I had thought from looking at the edge of the shells that there might be more legs here."

"Eight niches, and each one is the size of these things on the ground!" Maxsym said excitedly.

"Yuck! Those things are... parasites?" Marcant asked.

"No, the shell is shaped for them. They're children, or symbiotes," Magnus guessed.

"Young would make more sense," Marcant said.

"Then they have a hell of a transformation phase," Telisa said. "Even more than tadpole to frog... but I suppose not more than caterpillar to butterfly?"

"These creatures are genetically diverged," Maxsym asserted again. "I don't think this is a case of metamorphosis. I believe it is a remarkable symbiosis."

"Okay, move on. The attendants got a full scan of this."

They walked from the atrium down a wide corridor, deeper into the building. There was a narrowing, then the corridor expanded into wide alcoves on the left and right.

"What are these?" Telisa wondered.

"Display areas, looks like," Magnus said. They veered toward the first one on the left.

Suddenly bright light flickered across them, accompanied by an electric crackling noise. Magnus dove for the cover of a low wall at the edge of the alcove. He told two grenades to drop and deploy in opposite directions. After impact with the floor, he rolled to put his back against the wall so he could look out into the museum.

Maxsym and Marcant had gone prone. Telisa was nowhere to be seen.

"It's not an attack," Telisa called out. "Just a hologram. Our movement must have activated it."

Magnus rose to his feet. His weapon swept a wide arc despite Telisa's explanation. A scene played in the open area before them. It looked like the interior of a natural cave. A group of natural octopeds scampered through the cavern.

"Strange. Why not a digital feed?" Marcant asked.

"We don't know that Rovans used links. But I've been to Terran museums that do the same thing, for young people who haven't been linked yet," Telisa said.

"The equipment probably detected our movement, then searched for a Rovan link, didn't find one, and so ran the holo," Magnus guessed. He paused to recall his grenades. They rolled up to him so he could reattach them.

"A little old-fashioned," Marcant said. "Plausible, though. Rovan eyes must be very similar to our own. These holograms emit frequencies which at least overlap our range of vision."

"The projectors are a little too low to the ground for us," Magnus pointed out. "That's strange, though, because the corridors are so large, I thought Rovans would be huge, except for those smaller things... rovlings."

"We already said it: there may be young that came to look at these. So these tables are low."

"But you would guess their young are about our size," Magnus persisted.

"Okay, that statue is big, but its height wasn't much compared to its length and width. So there you go. Rovans are wider and longer than we are, but not taller," Marcant said.

The group hurriedly moved to the next display, eager to see some Rovans. The next alcove activated just as the first had. A cave complex appeared as if viewed from above, showing several chambers connected by wide tunnels and many small ones.

"This doesn't look too interesting," Magnus said. "It's a primitive cave dwelling with the big tunnels and the small ones. They look stone age."

"Think about it," Telisa said. "The small tunnels are here, even in their primitive beginnings. Another strike against the maintenance robot tunnels theory. The tunnels are for their smaller companions."

Magnus frowned. "You're right. The maintenance tunnels idea is wrong."

"It doesn't really resolve whether the smaller ones are pets, or what," Marcant said.

Magnus looked at Maxsym for comment, but one look told Magnus that the xenobiologist was busy thinking rather than running his mouth: Maxsym stood still with his eyes closed to focus on his PV.

The next alcove contained objects behind transparent barriers. Magnus's eye went straight to a primitive device he recognized—a huge spear. Its blade was as big as his forearm, the shaft longer than a ground car. Ragged straps over a meter long hung from two points along its length, midpoint and the blunt end.

That spear was not thrown. It was attached to something. Like a Rovan's giant armored head.

The other objects were more mysterious. Magnus recognized a storage pot and a digging tool among an array of ancient objects on display.

An attendant flew up and cut a hole in the clear barrier with an energy beam. It carried the round fragment to the floor of the interior, then scanned an object at close range.

"They're real," Maxsym announced. "Though I can't date them since I'm not familiar with their planet of origin, these materials are primitive. They aren't manufactured replicas."

"Makes sense. Terran museums don't have replicas anymore, since we can show people what ancient times were like with VRs or holos. But they still have originals for study by scientists and academia."

"These were clearly on display. They must have valued their authenticity."

"See those doors in the back of the cabinets? Someone had easy access to the items behind the scenes. Perhaps their historians or archaeologists."

The team moved on. The objects could be examined later. Everyone was eager for more.

The end of the hallway terminated in a much larger theater-space. Three robots had already positioned themselves around the area, flooding it with light. As they walked up, another, much larger hologram activated.

"There we are!"

A huge diorama flicked to life. Magnus gazed upon a scene with hundreds of rovlings moving through a field. Scattered among them, huge, hulking shelled creatures trundled along on four powerful elephantine legs.

Then the sound started.

High pitched whistles sounded across the plain, accentuated by the heavy footfalls of the Rovans. Nearby rovlings could be heard scurrying through clusters of ringed plants with single donut-leaves that encircled the whole organism.

This is a different planet. No green streamers in sight.

Magnus's breath caught by the magnificence of the display. The other holos had been simple toys by comparison. Magnus found himself leaning back on his heels, almost trying to back out of the way of the figures in the holo. The sounds seemed to come from all around.

Frantic groups of the rovlings surged across the field. Large metal blades were attached to the rovling's backs, and smaller ones had been added like spurs to their hindmost legs.

"It's an army!" Magnus announced.

No one disputed his claim.

"Look! This one has *ten*," Maxsym said.

"What?"

Magnus followed Maxsym's gesture.

"Ten rovling-ports," Maxsym pointed out.

"That's weird. It can't be a mistake," Magnus said.

"It could be a natural variation," Telisa said. "Some of them had eight, some ten."

"Keep your eyes peeled. Maybe some only have six," Marcant said.

Telisa stepped closer to Maxsym.

"Stop. Remember those organs in the bellies of the rovlings? What about those ports on the side of the Rovans? Could the Rovans be feeding them the scents?" Telisa asked.

"Amazing. Why didn't I think of that?" Maxsym said. "Does that make sense, though? The big, ungainly creature collects scents for the small ones? Wouldn't it be more efficient for the rovlings to scout around and collect scents to bring back to the larger Rovans for analysis?"

"Don't let your own biases cloud the facts," Telisa said.

Maxsym laughed.

"What?" Telisa asked.

"You're absolutely right. I'm not used to being told that."

"Keep your eyes peeled. I want to know which of these are the smart ones!" Telisa urged.

Me too. Who is master here? They could both be smart, but I think that would be much less likely. It is probably just one or the other.

The area of the scene widened. Suddenly another large group of Rovans appeared, clearing a ridge above the column that the hologram had been following. Magnus instantly knew what was coming.

They're going to fight. This is a recreation of an ancient battle.

The two groups slowed. Magnus imagined they must be evaluating each other, as two Terran armies might do in times when their weapons could not travel farther than their senses. Then the army on the high ground charged toward those below.

The team fell silent, mesmerized by the display. The sounds of footfalls rose to a dull roar.

In the distance, the enemy Rovans rose over their rovling escorts like heavy war machines scattered among infantry. The perception dropped away as the range closed and he saw the horned shells adorning the creatures and their flat heads bearing massive mandibles.

Just when the armies neared and Magnus anticipated seeing the behemoths crush through each other's formations, the unexpected happened. The massive beasts slowed rather than charging ahead. Instead, the hundreds of rovlings surged forward in two chaotic swarms.

"Those... rovlings are doing the fighting for them!" Magnus said.

The small creatures fought savagely, biting and spurring each other with barbed legs. Others climbed atop their comrades and attacked from above. This continued until several layers of the things were fighting each other in the center. Piles of detached legs and crushed carapaces built up around the field.

"Wait... these three Rovans here are joining the fight," Arakaki said. Her light showed them what she was looking at. In the center of the battle, three Rovans advanced among the rovlings. Their legs had been armored and adorned with sharp spikes. Their heads, if indeed they were heads in any sense of the word, also had protective gear. The huge mandible-scythes sliced through groups of enemy rovlings. Magnus watched as one Rovan used one of its scythes to impale four rovlings simultaneously.

Soon the other Rovans on each side charged in.

"Hard gore! It looks like a bloodbath," Marcant commented.

"Most primitive warfare is," Maxsym said. "Up close and personal. Brutal, but less efficient than modern warfare of course."

Why did those Rovans wait to join? Was it ritualistic, or were they waiting to see if the battle could be decided by the rovlings alone?

The display flickered and died.

"What happened?"

"I'm not sure," Marcant said. "Out of juice? Or maybe it's too old."

"If you can figure out where the datastore is, take it with you. We could learn more," Telisa said.

"We'll try," Marcant said distantly, lost in a PV interface.

"Who looked like they were in charge to you?" Telisa asked Magnus.

"The big ones. The Rovans. They didn't engage at first," Magnus answered.

Telisa nodded. "That's my interpretation, too. There may be some other explanation, but right now I still believe the Rovans were the intelligences."

"Did you notice they lack fine manipulators? Their inner mouthparts are the closest thing they have to hands," Maxsym said. "I'm not sure those would be enough to use and fashion tools. Imagine if they evolved depending on the rovlings for fine manipulation!"

"That would be incredible... wait, though," Telisa said. "Their communication would have to be advanced *first*."

"Can something really become smart without the ability to manipulate tools itself? Relying upon another life form?" Magnus asked.

"These things could likely advance side by side," Maxsym said. "It would have started with very coarse commands to the rovlings, like, 'protect me' or 'search for food'."

"Then what do the rovlings get out of it?" Magnus asked.

"I don't know. One could guess: protection from large predators," Maxsym offered.

"Or perhaps access to food sources otherwise protected from small things..." Telisa said.

"This isn't their home planet, so if we can't glean that information from this museum, we'll likely be stuck," Maxsym said.

Magnus followed the conversation, but he had already started thinking about the advanced Rovans instead of those in their ancient past.

"Those machines we found in the arctic station are robotic versions of these things. Robotic rovlings," Magnus said.

Telisa and Maxsym nodded.

"They must be," she agreed. "This is everything I had hoped for. The attendants recorded everything we saw. We'll learn a few more details with close analysis, but we've picked up the gist of it: What the Rovans looked like and how they cooperated with the rovlings. Definitely looks symbiotic to me, in a much closer way than Terrans worked with domesticated animals."

In the next hour, Marcant found equipment he guessed might store the information they wanted. He shared the signature with them and sent out attendants to find more.

Magnus helped the attendants reach closed-off areas of the building to locate more of the devices.

Then the team herded their attendants back to their side and left for the shuttle. Marcant was eager to get his spoils back to the ship for further analysis.

Magnus sat quietly on the shuttle ride.

"You seem thoughtful. Did the museum disturb you?" Telisa asked.

"It's more than an interesting historical revelation. It means that unless they gave up war altogether, they must have made artificial military rovlings. We should be ready in case we encounter a secure installation with defenses."

"Sounds wise, so I'll play along. What kind of weapons work against artificial rovlings?"

Magnus sighed. "Well, there were at least eight for every Rovan, so there might be a lot of them. I bet they're fast. I'm thinking we carry more grenades which should be able to take out several at a time."

Telisa nodded. "I'll tell everyone."

"One more thing. I think Siobhan had a couple extra stun batons in the armory. They have Terran and robot target settings which affect the energy pulse. Besides, they're hefty. I bet we could smash these artificial rovlings with them."

"I bet you're right."

Chapter 14

Yat did not know what to think when Arakaki showed up at the door to his quarters. He hastily gave her permission to enter. He rose to greet her, noticing once again that the recent influx of food and medical attention had made him feel strong and energetic.

"Are you coming to the workout?" Arakaki asked as she entered.

"Yes. But I thought it wasn't for a while."

"I thought I'd drop in and chat."

"Oh. Sure."

Just trying to get to know me? Or has she been ordered to find something out...

Yat told his sleep web to pull up into the ceiling and had his wall extend a chair for Arakaki, then he sat cross-legged on the floor. His guest wore durable, opaque undersheers which were certainly appropriate for a workout if a bit distracting to his eye.

"So how far you and Oliver go back?" Arakaki asked.

"Eight years. We set out from Ngaudrius together with the idea that first we'd tour the inner frontier, get our bearings, and then get around to smuggling."

"So you knew what you were after from an early age."

"Oliver did." He did not elucidate. She did not let it go.

"Oh. Are you lovers?"

Yat shrugged. "Business partners shouldn't screw. It all crashes sooner or later."

"Is that an answer?"

He smiled. "We aren't."

Arakaki seemed satisfied with his direct answer.

"You guys do any VR training?"

Yat snorted. "We do a lot of VR combat, but it's for entertainment, not training. I guess it has some side effects that make themselves felt in our real work. And you?"

"A lot. Always."

"Makes sense."

"What now? Are you going to go after those guys who crossed you?" she asked.

Yat sighed.

"You know what? I don't think so. I was so angry at first, you know? But as we started to face up to the fact we might not make it, I guess it changed. Now, I'm thinking if I can sell these artifacts, then I'll be set. Why throw all that away to go hunt those guys down?"

Arakaki nodded.

"What do you think? Do you think I'm a coward?" he asked.

Arakaki tilted her head and leaned forward.

"I think it's smart. I've sometimes taken too long to... resolve things that happened to me. Sounds like you processed the betrayal pretty well."

A connection from Oliver distracted Yat.

"Yat, where are you man?"

Yat was so focused on his visitor that the words seemed to come from far away.

"With Arakaki."

"The workout is in—wait. *With* Arakaki?

"Not that way."

"Oh. Okay. Uhm, workout is in 50."

"I'll be there," Yat told him.

"So, I'm guessing you're with that guy Magnus," Yat said to Arakaki.

"No. He only sleeps with Telisa."

Yat nodded, happy to learn that tidbit, but he immediately felt awkward and tried to cover it up with another question.

"You ex-military?"

"Yes. Ex-UED," she said.

"Oh? Really?"

"Absolutely."

"I wish you guys had won," Yat said. "I admire your courage. My father gave to the cause, what little he could. He helped repair some parts for a UED ship once. It came to port for just six hours."

"Thanks. Hey, I'm hoping you and Oliver are grateful enough for the ride to wait a while longer while we search the planet for more clues."

Yat nodded. "I don't expect you to drop your expedition to deliver us anywhere right away. We're both happy to be alive. Maybe we can be useful, too."

"Great. We could use you."

Yat thought that sounded intriguing. He tried to rein himself in.

Maybe you'd better know who they are and what it is they do before you sign yourself up, he thought.

***

Yat and Arakaki showed up together in a huge workout center in the massive ship they called the *Sharplight*. They looked like a matched pair, as they had agreed to have their first match wearing heavy gis. They both wore white, though Yat's was stained with blood. He had not thought to wash it or replicate a new one, though at least the bacteria resistant fibers did not smell bad.

Oliver and the stranger named Barrai had already started to fight. They faced each other wearing compact sparring gloves. Oliver wore only a pair of heavy shorts. Barrai was in a rashguard and gi pants.

Oliver charged at Barrai. She delivered a spinning backfist and a fast crescent kick to the side of his head in quick succession. His next step wobbled aside, but he recovered and followed up with a straight-in front kick that struck, though Barrai backed out of it and probably did not feel it.

Sweat poured down Oliver's chest and the ribs in his gaunt torso slid under the skin with each breath. They circled each other, waiting for someone to fire off the next exchange.

Wow. Serious.

Yat knew Oliver's style well. The man had a lot of muscle and even more recklessness. A high pain tolerance added to the volatile mixture. Yat had developed solid technique to hold his own again Oliver. The man was hard for Yat to stop in a standing fight, but Yat could mix it up with him on the ground.

Oliver waited—or pretended to wait—for several breaths, then they both attacked at once. Barrai thumped him in the ribs while Oliver grabbed her lead hand with his back hand and punched her head through the gap. Barrai grunted and sent in a lightning hook which struck Oliver a bit high, striking his temple instead of his jaw.

They broke from the exchange. Most of Oliver's face was bruised from taking blows.

Why isn't he shooting? I wonder if he already tried and got shut down before we arrived.

Yat stole a glance at Arakaki. She was watching the fight casually while she warmed up on another mat. Yat decided to run a few laps around the workout center.

Oliver and Barrai continued to wade into it. Barrai was hitting him crisply, repeatedly. She was simply too fast. Still, Oliver managed to hurt her about every other exchange. His legs were more slender than Barrai's, but his arms were much larger.

As if reading Yat's mind, Barrai started to lash out viciously with low kicks, hitting the sides of Oliver's legs.

Now you've gone and made her angry, Yat thought, as if admonishing Oliver.

Oliver seemed to realize he was not equipped to deal with Barrai's new strategy. Without warning, he charged again. Barrai tried to kick his lead leg on the way in, but she only prevented herself from being able to sidestep. Oliver performed an off-balance takedown that was at least good enough to bring Barrai down with him.

Oliver's huge arms took control of the situation, but not before Barrai fed him an elbow. His nose gushed blood while he pinned one of her arms with his, then wrapped one of his legs around it. Then he inexorably choked her out using his two massive arms to her sole remaining one. She lifted her free hand as if to tap, but fell unconscious first.

Oliver released her and stood back up. He took a step away and almost fell when one leg did not support him.

When Barrai rose to resume, he raised his palm and conceded. Yat could not quite hear what he said, but Barrai nodded curtly and accepted it. They clasped hands briefly and Barrai gave him a shoulder slap, yet their faces remained cold. Yat concluded they were both highly competitive and hid their frustration at a close battle.

Yat was never upset about being bested. He just tried to learn from it. That quality made him the technician he was today, but Oliver usually won through sheer size and determination. Yat supposed the perfect fighter was somewhere in between their two personalities, say with Yat's attention to technique and Oliver's bullheaded drive.

If Arakaki did not seem amused or upset by the outcome of the other fight. She waved Yat over.

"Ready?"

"Yes. Let's begin," he replied stiffly.

Yat decided an aggressive stance would serve him well, since no one knew his moves. They circled each other. Yat watched her carefully.

She'll test my reactions. Then I'll attack.

Arakaki shifted her weight subtly. Yat attacked. His rapid advance stuffed her kick, but her head weaved, causing Yat's first strike to miss. His combo continued to flow as he struck again, grazed her head, then he connected a body strike. Arakaki exhaled with it, absorbing it easily. He became aware that she had a hold of his gi at about the same time that she swept him. As they hit the ground, he scrabbled to defend himself.

Yat rolled away and regained his feet gracefully. Arakaki had done the same. They circled again. Arakaki was the next to launch an attack. She kicked low, struck high, then swept low. Yat defended himself but was unable to counter.

They each attacked several more times. Both combatants had good countering that left them close to even. Arakaki did not seem to prefer stand up or ground fighting, but he suspected she was hiding her strengths from him.

The round indicator told his link it was time to rest. Yat backed away but kept his guard all the same, wondering if she would try to surprise him with a lesson about staying alert.

Arakaki smiled as if reading his thoughts and held up her hand.

"Nice round."

They continued with a second and third round. Yat traded evenly against her, though it seemed Arakaki was weathering the storm better as it went on. He grew tired.

Near the end of the third, Arakaki launched a relentless attack, first testing his defenses with hand combos, then dragging him to the mat. He kept her from finding a choke or a hold for another minute, playing full defense so he could catch his breath.

Arakaki pressed harder. Yat set a trap for her and slipped his leg over her arm as she tried to shift her hold on him. The resulting triangle caused her to tap.

They broke and stood.

Yat's lungs burned and his muscles had started to shake. Despite his recent intake, the planetside fasting had negatively impacted his energy levels. Still, he did not want to appear mentally weak.

Is she testing me? One more.

Yat wanted to shoot for a takedown again so he could repeat his previous success. For that exact reason he estimated Arakaki would be ready for it, so he decided to remain in the stand-up fight.

She'll expect strike high, shoot low. So I'll strike high, strike high.

Yat jabbed and jabbed again. They circled. Then he jabbed and dropped his body a centimeter, pretending to change levels. Her guard dropped as she reacted. Then he launched again at her head. Jab, jab, cross, hook.

Arakaki was good. Only his hook landed. He felt satisfied with the combination for a half second, then Arakaki hit his solar plexus solidly. Somehow his own arm had blocked his sight of the attack. He had been expecting her to strike at his head. Yat tried to cover and retreat, but he had lost the initiative and had no speed left in him. Arakaki hit his temple and kicked him in the ribs.

She stopped.

Yat raised put his hand up, palm forward.

"Sorry. I'm tiring quickly today," he said.

"I was wondering if you two had fully recovered. Let's stop for now."

Yat nodded, thankful. They clasped hands and exchanged a half-hug.

"Thank you for the workout. I found it very challenging," Yat said sincerely.

Arakaki smiled.

"I'm impressed with your skills. You're more than just a hacker, it seems."

Yat smiled back at her, happy to receive the praise.

Is there something here? Or has she been charged with babysitting me?

"It's nice to have someone besides Oliver to work out with," he said.

And for how long will that remain the case?

"Glad to have you."

"What are you guys doing back out here? I checked out the ship's data cache to catch up on what's been going on. Your team just got done fighting a war?"

"We did," she said. "Look, we're not bloodthirsty. We're back to exploring now."

Arakaki seemed so hardcore to Yat, but he believed her. Her voice sounded wounded. He suspected that the missing team members might have something to do with that. He decided not to ask about them.

"I caught up on as much as I could, but this team is weird. I can't tell who you work for. It seems like you're part of the Space Force, but... are you the exploration branch's equivalent of special forces?"

"We're independent explorers. All the rest of that PCP is because Telisa was there when Ambassador Shiny was discovered. She helped to free him from a Trilisk complex. So she has friends in very, very high places."

"That's amazing," Yat said.

You're amazing, he wanted to say. He reined himself in again.

Too long out on the frontier. I guess I got lonelier than I thought.

"Well it has its advantages... and disadvantages," she said.

Yat decided not to pull on that thread just yet.

"And you work with an AI?" he asked. Though commonplace on the Core Worlds, AIs were much rarer out on the frontier.

"Adair."

"Does he... zhe..." Yat faltered.

"Adair prefers 'it'," Arakaki supplied. "Some Terrans think of that as an insult, but Adair is proud of being a genderless ‘object’, so that becomes a good thing. Kind of reversing the insult back against the perpetrators. I think that amuses Adair.”

“Ah. Does it mind if I speak to it?”

“When the time comes, address it like any other member of the team.”

“Okay, I will.”

Chapter 15

Maxsym worked furiously at a virtual workstation on the *Iridar*.

The shells discovered in the Rovan 'catacombs' were just massive enough to give Maxsym the idea that an orbital deep scan might pick them up. The *Iridar* could deploy powerful Vovokan probes that were more capable than anything the Space Force could likely deploy (though it was rumored that their special scout ships used alien tech).

If I could ever remember to ask about that, I would probably be told. I am, after all, a highly ranked official now.

To Maxsym, having the title of Team Member was simply a way to access more resources than ever before. In his experience, anyone who single-mindedly sought power usually did not deserve it. He had clashed with selfish monsters in control of whole worlds many times before he had joined PIT. Now he could change things for the better... but he was focused on scientific discovery, not politics.

Maxsym decided to start with the known catacombs. He had exact locations for hundreds of the shells within the tunnels visited by the PIT team. He dispatched the first of a series of probes and told it to locate the signatures hidden away deep underground. The probe and its assisting computers on the *Iridar* worked on the problem actively. The systems were smart enough to try many known approaches to solve the well-defined problem without Maxsym's direct oversight.

The probe had to come much closer to the targets than the *Iridar* was, but it sensed the known shells from the upper atmosphere within a half hour, proving that the Vovokan technology could locate the massive shells from great distances, even when the targets lay underground.

Success!

Maxsym redoubled his efforts, riding the high of his initial accomplishment. It meant his crazy plan was workable! More probes launched. Maxsym created a network to find other shells on the planet below. He worked for two more hours putting together the project. There were a million details, but the Vovokan machines handled most of the infrastructure work for him: energy rings were charged, comm nets established, and search patterns and algorithms tuned.

Hits started to roll in. The catacombs marked on the map showed up in the new global scan. The numbers rolled by, accumulating very quickly as his makeshift probe network sent tenuous particles streaming through the planet's crust. The energy draw was substantial, but he knew Telisa would approve.

There were many more caches of the shells than in the catacomb complexes. All the ruins on the planet were riddled with them. Maxsym was intrigued; he dispatched attendants to examine a dozen of the locations.

Maxsym examined the summary as the survey continued. Some of the attendants were able to obtain samples to add to those taken by the PIT team in their foray into the catacombs.

He became impatient. There was always a phase at which all the instructions had been issued and the machines worked: attendants were slow to find access to the shells, the scanners ran out of energy and had to pause, then the computers had to check and recheck the data to make sure echoes or false positives were not affecting the integrity of the results. The user was left to wait. Maxsym considered shifting gears and starting on another project while he waited, but he was too focused. He settled for watching the work and thinking of other things he could do, other questions he could ask. Was the answer to the entire mystery of this dead colony now at his fingertips?

The numbers had risen very high. Maxsym sighed.

Poor creatures. So many hits... and none of them are moving.

Maxsym noticed the entrances to the catacomb sites were almost all in the same condition. One or two showed some extra wear, but they were in harsher environs than the others. He concluded they were all built near the same time.

When the scan was complete, Maxsym sat for a few minutes, looking at the big picture and checking for anomalies or errors. The Vovokan machines had been very thorough, and his translated orders had been correctly interpreted. He contacted Telisa.

"Maxsym," she replied.

"It looks like about 110 million Rovans died here. My analysis indicates the vast majority died at the same time. There *was* a disaster."

"So many down there. And we thought they all left in time in their ships. That's sobering. How did they die?" Telisa asked.

"I don't know. That's my next goal. I'll examine the data and try to determine if, for example, they all died of physical trauma. Which I doubt, given there is no battle damage evident in the buildings, but it would be good to rule out."

"Please do that. Let Magnus know if you need to get your hands on more than just scans. Presumably he could send robots out to these remains and get you an FTF with some of our extinct friends."

Telisa skipped a beat then continued. "So around 800 million rovlings must have died with them... it's horrible to think about."

"Where does that number come from?"

"Eight ports each... Oh, I guess it would be even more rovlings than that if many of them had ten," Telisa said.

"Eight per Rovan is a good lower bound estimate, I think."

"Oh?"

"An analysis of the shells is showing me that only 15% of the Rovans housed five rovlings on each side. The majority were four on a side."

"I see. Still, what if the Rovans had more than the number they could... house... at one time?" Telisa suggested.

"Yes. That's why I said this is a lower bound."

"Okay, right. We also don't know what the ratio of biological to artificial rovlings was at the time of their demise."

"And we don't know if the artificial ones snuggled up quite the same as the biological ones," Maxsym said. "Which makes we wonder if they had tech stations that could serve their symbiotes as well as a Rovan... a kind of artificial caregiver."

"Well I think we can stop ripping the estimate to shreds now," Telisa said brightly. "We have no idea how many rovlings there were. I like your guess that eight per Rovan would be a reasonable lower bound, but other than that, it could be almost anything. Each Rovan could have had twenty natural symbiotes, only eight to ten of which ported at any given moment, along with who knows how many artificial rovlings which probably did not need to port with a Rovan, but may have if the Rovans liked to pretend their artificial ones were real."

"Right, we have no idea."

"It's a very grim thought. Millions of these advanced aliens died suddenly, and we don't know how. I'll look around for porting stations in our search data so far. I'm sure we'll be able to identify some of the things we've seen as serving this purpose now that we know what to look for."

"So many questions left. Not just how they died, but... who buried them all?" Maxsym asked.

"The obvious answer is that the rovlings buried them."

"Ah. Yes. I wonder if they acted by instinct, programming, or... training," Maxsym said.

"If it was the rovlings, it seems logical to guess that the artificial ones put them in the tombs. But where did they go? We haven't found nearly enough in the catacombs," Telisa said.

"Remember, they aren't only catacombs," Maxsym said. "The bunkers contain huge amounts of industrial equipment and supplies. One wonders: did the Rovans see their demise coming? Tell their machines to mothball the colony for other Rovans to unpack later?"

Telisa did not answer for a moment as she considered that. Then she sighed. He interpreted it as frustration at the number of unanswered questions.

"We have plenty to look for down here. Thank you for the information Maxsym."

"You're welcome. I'll send along more when I have it and contact Magnus about getting some remains. Also, I've sent you a link to this report and its supporting data."

"Great. Superbly done, as usual."

Telisa disconnected.

Maxsym opened his eyes and rubbed them. Then he was already thinking about how to use the data to check the shells for damage that might indicate their cause of death.

Chapter 16

"What do you think about that Midnight Stare stash?" Telisa asked Magnus in her quarters.

"Not sure I see the appeal of losing self-control," he said, dangling in her sleep web. "Why, do you want us to try it?"

"No! My strength... I could accidentally rip you to shreds! Besides, who knows what unexpected effects that drug might have on a host body?"

"Hrm. Interesting way to go, though," he said. He gave her a smile.

She managed to keep from rolling her eyes. She liked their intense connection. The drugs would be an unnecessary risk in a life already filled with danger. She did not need it to put more "adventure" into her life.

I bet Caden and Siobhan would have tried it.

"I brought it up because I'm wondering if it means Yat and Oliver are bad news," she clarified.

Magnus shrugged. "No, not necessarily. I'm neutral about it. It doesn't seem like a destructive drug in and of itself. Of course, like anything, it could be abused. If someone could get it out of the packet without neutralizing it, then they could give it to whoever they wanted with no contracts accepted."

Telisa nodded.

"Right. But there are already a million ways to poison someone."

"Does that mean you're considering them for PIT?" Magnus asked.

"I've mused about it, but we aren't that far along. I don't even know if they want to join us. I was just trying to decide if buying and selling that drug should rule them out."

"Yat seems like more of a team player," Magnus observed. "Oliver is ultra competitive."

"As is Barrai," Telisa pointed out. "But she's been nothing but professional when it comes time to execute."

"He can be standoffish. I also get the feeling Oliver might do something dumb. I know his type," Magnus maintained.

Telisa skipped a beat. "I've selected our next spot," she said, diverting the subject to other business.

Magnus was on board for the switch. He checked out her pointer in his PV.

"A mountaintop redoubt," he said. "Interesting."

"Could be. On the other hand, it might be a transmission station. But it's big, and there are a lot of landing berths for aircraft or spacecraft. So it strikes me as too small to be a spaceport, and too large to be anything mundane, like an individual's dwelling."

"Corporation headquarters, maybe," Magnus guessed. She assumed his guess was based on examination of the orbital scans.

"Yeah, sure," she agreed.

Telisa transmitted a call to action to the team with a one-hour countdown. She told them to equip standard gear with an emphasis on building interior exploration. No call for climbing gear or outdoor supplies. If they ended up needing to do real mountain climbing, they could send for more specific gear.

Magnus, Arakaki, and Telisa were the only three required to go. The mountaintop was cold, so Lee had been left out, but Marcant, Barrai, and Maxsym had the option to join the exploration party.

Marcant accepted. Telisa had noted a distinct uptick in Marcant's landing participation. She approved.

I'm really managing these people. If we keep growing, I'll end up being the person who sits back and calls the shots without any direct participation.

Telisa was not sure if that would be a good or bad thing.

***

Telisa and Magnus stepped out of the shuttle side by side. They stood on a circular landing platform big enough for a craft three times larger than theirs. An eight-meter-wide suspended pathway connected them to a towering blue structure. The edge had no restraining rails or wall. Telisa tucked away that detail for future consideration.

Rovans didn't worry about that fall... and presumably their rovlings did not often fall off, either. Does that mean that young never came here, or that Rovan children don't ever fall? As far as the rovlings being their children, Maxsym says it's not possible.

Telisa was struck by the stark beauty before her. The building looked like a huge bulging sapphire cut into a teardrop shape with the wider end sunk into the snowy cliffs of the mountain. Its smooth surface was a blue so deep it played tricks on the eyes.

"It's striking," Magnus said. "Maybe it is just a mansion."

"It doesn't even look like Rovan architecture," Telisa said.

Telisa took in the view while their attendants flew out of the shuttle and deployed around the site to investigate. She did not see anything moving around the deep blue buildings.

Arakaki emerged and sauntered around the shuttle. Telisa was not fooled by the relaxed way that Arakaki cradled her weapon or the slow pace of her patrol; she knew Arakaki searched for danger.

For the thousandth time, Telisa secretly noted that if she had not become part of the PIT team, Magnus and Arakaki would doubtless be a couple.

Should I encourage them to have a virtual go at it sometime... or would I forever regret it?

Incarnate monogamy was common on most Terran worlds, but virtual romps with other partners were considered fair play by the vast majority of couples. Telisa left the problem for some other time.

Marcant simply stepped off the ramp and stood, waiting behind them.

Telisa led the way across the platform toward the nearest part of the building. Where the pathway met the building, an enormous pair of doors over ten meters wide and five meters tall awaited them. The doors were made of metal or ceramic, in a lighter shade of blue than the smooth building walls.

Telisa approached to take a look at the obstacle. As she approached, the doors started to move. She reacted quickly.

"To the right!" she ordered, jabbing her index finger toward the right edge of the door.

The others seemed to react in slow motion, having only normal Terran nervous systems. Telisa brought up her weapon and activated her stealth sphere before any of them had taken the first step on the new course.

She ordered one attendant to shoot forward and get a look as the opening between the doors reached about ten centimeters. The others stealthed themselves and got out of direct line of sight of the interior. The attendant quickly reported there were no Rovans or robots on the other side of the opening portal.

The interior was dimly lit. The corridor beyond was over twenty meters wide. It curved with the outer shape of the vast building. Attendants floated in to explore the way. Telisa slowly walked into the corridor. Despite the video feeds from the attendants, her own eyes swept the inside, looking for enemies.

"Clear," she said. She left her stealth sphere on for the moment.

The walls of the corridor displayed complex graph reliefs of interlocking diamond shapes. Large shapes in the middle slowly gave way to smaller and smaller ones in spiral patterns. The nearest one was not quite a fractal, Telisa decided, though it did have a similar feel.

"This speaks of... luxury. You see it? Everything is decorated, the floor is soft, and this corridor is twice as wide as most we've seen," Telisa transmitted through her suit's stealth comm interface.

"I think we found the Rovan Palace," Marcant said grandly.

"Could be anything," Magnus said more seriously. "Religious site. Mansion. Vacation resort."

"Supervillain complex!" Marcant added, refusing to be as serious as Magnus.

The attendants rapidly did their job, filling out their virtual map. Wide, curved corridors swept throughout the complex of buildings. There were many doors placed at similar distances along the outer parts of the buildings in a way that reminded her of personal quarters.

The team padded down the corridor with their stealth gear active. The map put down by the attendants showed a door ahead on their left, toward the outside of the building. Telisa decided to pause and investigate rather than continue down the corridor.

This time, the door did not respond to their approach. Telisa deactivated her stealth sphere. The door still did not open.

"I've got it," Marcant said before Telisa could make any request. She reactivated her stealth.

They waited. Thirty seconds later, the door swept open.

"Good job," Telisa said.

The room beyond was small by Rovan standards, almost like another short segment of hallway. The familiar Rovan style bins were on the left and right walls. Straight ahead, a hexagonal opening led to another room dominated by a circular island in the center.

Telisa headed straight for the second room. A low, wide window provided a beautiful view of the snow-covered mountains outside. When she got to the counter, she saw the circular construct was the rim of a shallow vat rather than a countertop or table. The huge tank was filled with motionless white rovlings with red stripes.

Though intrigued, Telisa did not stop until she checked the corners for any threat.

"It's clear," she said. She deactivated her stealth system. The attendants had swept through the corridors without encountering any resistance. Telisa did not feel that the site was dangerous, even though most of the doors had remained closed, so there were many parts of the complex that had yet to be explored.

"With doors like that, this is still a room Rovans had access to," Magnus said from the other room.

"But this room is pretty small," Marcant said.

"Over here," Arakaki announced. She stood next to a set of bins built into the wall, holding one of the flaps open. Telisa walked over to take a look with her own eyes instead of relying upon the nearest attendant.

"Food spirals. So this room is small, but has certain amenities."

"What is that thing in the other room?" Magnus asked Telisa.

"It's a tank filled with artificial rovlings!"

Everyone walked back over to look into the vat.

"Hundreds of them at least, if this vat has any depth," Magnus said.

"These rovlings are different than the others," Telisa said.

"No legs—unless those little nubbins count?—and look: no mounting rails!" Marcant said.

Telisa took a longer look into the vat. The rovlings below had only smooth bodies. The legs had only one stubby segment each, no joints and no eyes.

"No mounting rails? Almost everything we've found has those slider-rails for the rovlings to carry around or use. But these rovlings would be basically useless for any kind of work."

"They must have been designed with only one function in mind," Marcant said. "They can't use any general tools."

Telisa had no idea what the purpose might be. The rovlings looked like the only thing they might be able to do would be swim through each other in the tank.

"This tank is the size of a Rovan," she pointed out. "So a Rovan goes in there and... floats on all those rovlings?"

"Sounds like a sex thing," Marcant replied immediately.

Telisa almost told him to be more serious, but she held her tongue.

Magnus shrugged. "For once, I can't disagree."

"Maybe it's a nursery," Telisa suggested. "The mother comes in here, eats the food and waits for birth. Then the baby Rovan goes into the vat. It might be happy with a bunch of smooth, friendly rovlings all around to take care of it... like stuffed animals for Terran children."

Magnus shrugged again. "It's a possibility."

"That one's different," Marcant said, pointing.

Telisa followed Marcant's hand. One of the objects possessed the same red-white coloration as the rovlings, but it had no leg stubs. Instead, it was just oval with at least a dozen tiny holes in it.

"Good eye," Magnus said.

"Well, actually, my attendant pointed it out as an anomaly," Marcant mumbled.

"It's not the only one," Telisa said. Her own attendant quickly found three of the new objects on the top layer.

She sent three attendants to scoop one of the objects up.

"It's filled with liquid," Marcant said. "They can tell by shifts in the weight as it sloshes around in there."

"Should we crack it open?" Telisa asked.

"No, there's some leakage," Magnus said.

Marcant held up a hand. He closed his eyes to focus on an off-retina input.

"Needless to say, it has a complex range of properties," he said. "However, from this data, I can say with a fair bit of confidence—it's lubricant."

"Okay fine, more evidence it's a sex thing," Telisa admitted before anyone else could claim that this find strengthened their theories.

Marcant laughed. "Just for fun, I'll change my mind. Why would a Rovan want to breed with these things? We decided they're not a Rovan gender or a phase of the Rovan life cycle," Marcant said.

"That's right," Maxsym transmitted from the Vovokan *Iridar*.

"So a Rovan can't interlace its genetic material with a rovling. The rovlings might still play a critical role in Rovan reproduction," Telisa pointed out. "Plants mate with other plants via insect carriers. Maybe Rovans prefer the rovlings involved, or maybe they even *need* rovlings to breed."

The conversation ended.

"Let's keep moving," Arakaki said.

Telisa led them out of the first room and back into the corridor.

They went door to door, checking the chambers along the way. Each room was a duplicate of the first, two chambers with a vat in the room by the edge of the building.

"I think the whole place is like this," Arakaki declared. "It's a hotel. A bunch of rooms and vats. I think the vats are like the Rovan equivalent of hot tubs. Or the sex thing."

"Well, assuming the whole level is like this on the entire circumference, where now?"

"Up there," Telisa said. She sent a pointer to a spiral ramp spotted by the attendants.

They followed a course provided by the shared map to the ramp. As they walked, Marcant injected a question on the team channel.

"Why no elevators? Isn't this big ramp kind of space inefficient?"

"That is a little odd. It could be a clue to something," Telisa said.

They arrived at the base of a spiral ramp that dominated the center of the building. A central column rose in the middle, covered with more of the diamond-like designs. Once again, the design and decor spoke to Telisa of luxury and a desire to impress. At least, it would be so if Terrans had made it.

"Okay, so I'm guessing this is as close to stairs as Rovans got," Marcant said.

"I agree," Magnus said. "Those shells of theirs must have been heavy. So they prefer ramps? But as you said, elevators would be even easier."

Telisa examined the floor. It was covered in tiny ridges, presumably for extra traction.

Telisa started up. The rest of the team followed her in a line. They followed the curve of the gentle spiral. Once again, Telisa noticed that the edge had no railing.

They weren't afraid of falling off the edge of anything.

The top was a wide-open circular room, almost 50 meters in diameter. A two-meter tall window ran the circumference of the room. Everyone walked up to see the view.

"There are a lot of devices mounted on the outside here. I think this tower sampled the atmosphere," Marcant said. "I suspect it's related to meteorology monitoring or studies."

"Based on analysis of the hardware," Telisa supposed.

"Partially, but Adair and I have managed to make headway on Rovan computer systems. We can see this place collected a lot of data, and it was stored and analyzed. Their computers are built into the walls around us."

"You expanded upon what Yat learned?" Telisa asked. She smiled, knowing Marcant would not easily acknowledge standing on Yat's shoulders.

"Uh... Some thanks to Yat's pioneering work, of course."

He squirms, but does reluctantly hand out credit.

"Then tell us what these vats are about," Magnus suggested.

"Sorry... no insight there yet."

"This is obviously more than a weather station... okay, not obviously, since we don't quite know what was going on here," Telisa said. "Did you consider the possibility that the data was being collected from down below? Don't let the view fool you."

"It would be pretty funny if we mistook a Rovan porn VR studio for a weather station," Marcant said. "But I—er, Maxsym, Adair, and I—ruled that out because the data is still flowing, but there's nothing going on downstairs. This facility is in contact with several of the satellites we noted when we arrived."

"Hints," Arakaki said. "Nothing more."

"We don't know what was going on with the whole planet," Marcant said. "How did the feral rovlings out in the forests survive the disaster? Does that mean it was a plague or something that doesn't affect them?"

"What about the weather? Any possibility they saw changes coming in the planet's atmosphere?" Arakaki asked.

"If it was climate change, they could have gone underground to live in the bunkers," Magnus said.

"Except in the case of a sudden climate catastrophe. Supervolcano? Nuclear winter?" Arakaki replied.

"The planetary conditions are stable, according to many analyses we performed before making our first landing," Maxsym replied remotely. "It is possible that the current conditions are a little warmer or colder than those the Rovans experienced when they first arrived, but I don't believe any drastic changes have taken place, or will take place for thousands of years."

The room was pleasantly bright and warm. Telisa decided to sit on a low platform and exchange theories with the group.

"We have such a grim picture here. Millions of Rovans died. Someone buried them neatly in an expanded catacomb network. Then... what?" Telisa asked them.

"If the rovlings were smart... maybe they simply all left. They could have returned to the Rovan homeworld," Magnus suggested.

"That is... actually reasonable," Telisa said. She knew Marcant would disagree.

"Well," Marcant started. "If I had a large colony with millions of robots, I would tell them to maintain the place if everyone died. Perhaps even continue to develop and Terraform the planet. That way, if we ever went back there, it would be ready."

Arakaki was up to the challenge.

"That depends. If something happened to make the planet permanently dangerous or useless, then I would have the robots pack up resources and leave. Also, if some of the machines were very intelligent, like Adair, they could decide what to do based on the circumstances. We don't know if the Rovans saw it coming and had time to tell the machines what to do after their demise, or if the machines decided on their own."

"Another thought," Magnus said. "If they had enemies, they might not want the robots to fall into enemy hands."

"The robotic ones left, or were taken away, except for the ones we found in the arctic base, and here in this redoubt. What do these remnants have in common?" Telisa asked.

"Specialized designs," Magnus said.

"Remote locations," Arakaki countered.

"Cold locations," Maxsym added.

Telisa considered those different theories. They were all potentially dead-on: the arctic machines were specialized, some of them even aquatic. The machines here were very different as well, practically without any legs at all, and lacking the mounting grooves. Both groups of machines were removed from the bulk of the ruins. Both were on cold parts of the planet.

"I think at least a few Rovans escaped and took the missing spacecraft. If so, they may have decided not to take these rovlings for either of the first two reasons, or both," Telisa said.

"Yes," Marcant said. "When they left, they would only want the generally useful ones, and they might have only bothered to gather the ones in their vicinity—or at least the ones that could make it back on their own."

"I wonder if they took a plague with them and died in space," Arakaki said.

"Maybe. But surely some of them escaped intact. There would have been ships that did not get infected. Assuming, of course, this plague theory holds any water," Magnus said.

"Yes. In another scenario, it would have been the rovlings that used the spacecraft to leave," Telisa reminded them.

"The rovlings could even have made ships for themselves, if they had the intelligence to decide to leave on their own," Magnus said.

That was enough for the moment. Deduction had degenerated into speculation again. She thought they might have learned enough to piece it all together, but it seemed they only had more questions.

"Theories on top of theories," Telisa sighed. "Let's get back to the ship."

Chapter 17

Arakaki found herself on yet another shuttle headed into the unknown. She had her favorite compact projectile weapon—a UED model—in her hands and a laser pistol at her hip. Her three attendant spheres clustered above her head in the crowded space.

"According to the map Oliver and Yat produced, this is one of the largest catacomb networks," Marcant explained.

Their simulationist spoke from the *Sharplight*. The hardcore grounders were present on the shuttle: Telisa, Magnus, Oliver, Yat, and Arakaki. They had brought another shuttle filled with Magnus's robots.

Arakaki said nothing, but she thought about Yat. In his own way, he was handsome and rugged. Of the stranded pair, Arakaki would have preferred to have only Yat along. Oliver was kind of a thug, and Yat changed subtly around him.

It's like he loses ten percent of his intellect.

Arakaki knew how close people could get when they endured hardships together. Yat and Oliver had forged a relationship by relying upon each other on the frontier. It was only natural that Yat would feel intense loyalty for his adventure companion.

The shuttle landed in short order, ending her considerations.

"Listen up, we're trying something new," Telisa announced. "The *Sharplight* has assumed a position overhead. Marcant and Adair are going to help us by watching the situation with feeds from the attendants. I know many of you draw your situational awareness from the feeds, but we have a lot of attendants today, so they'll help us process the big picture."

"You sound like we're conducting an assault. Isn't this a cakewalk?" asked Oliver.

"Everything's a cakewalk... until it isn't," Arakaki said.

The shuttle opened, and the team disembarked. The terrain outside did not have many of the streamer-plants. Gray rocks and reddish soil dominated the landscape. An ancient, marred road led to the nearest hillside, terminating in a huge Rovan hatch half a kilometer away. A leviathan vehicle sat nearby. Its ten wheels were each taller than a Terran. The top looked more like the deck of a yacht than the coach of a Terran ground car.

Arakaki, ever vigilant, checked the doorway in the distance. Her weapon provided a closeup view of the portal. She checked the area for weapons ports or laser bulbs. She found three collections of antennas and optics she decided where likely sensor clusters.

"I don't see any weapons there, but it looks like any automated systems will see us approach," Arakaki summarized.

Telisa sent a group of four attendants ahead to test for a reaction. The orbs flew across the span between the team and the door in the space of two seconds. Nothing seemed to respond to the approach of the flying spheres.

"Okay, follow me. We'll get closer and use that vehicle for cover," Telisa directed.

They started out across the rocky terrain. Arakaki imagined various threats all around—poisonous crawlers darting from holes in the rocks, hidden pits, and turrets disguised as rocks—but nothing befell them as they clambered over the rocks. Her suit started to cool her as the internal heat from exercise and direct starlight climbed.

This would be a thousand times more dangerous for a primitive. With our equipment, this is doable but I have no idea how ancient explorers managed any of it.

The group gathered behind the Rovan vehicle. Arakaki noted a huge gate on one end that could deploy to form a ramp. That must be where a Rovan would carry its heavy shell up into the machine.

"Wait here," Telisa ordered.

Telisa deployed her Veer suit's helmet and strode around the vehicle into plain sight. Magnus watched, clearly concerned. Their leader approached within ten meters of the doorway without incident. She turned and looked back.

"Yat, show us your magic," Telisa called out, indicating the hatch. Yat nodded and marched up to the hatch, swinging his backpack off as he arrived. Arakaki raised her weapon to cover the hillside and waited. Yat took out a piece of equipment and paused.

"This is a universal attachment cluster. It's a generic connectivity tool used for a million different things."

Including cracking vaults and security points.

"This is the access point," he continued. "I have to take this panel off. I usually use a sharp field gradient and it pops when I run it over the right spot."

Yat took out another tool and waved it in front of the panel. It came open.

"Now I run my program to configure these connections to match up to the door controller."

"How did you write the program?" Magnus asked.

"A lot of trial and error. I found a door that opened automatically from a sensor. Then I recorded the signals in that door where they ran through its controller interface. From there, I had to set up the attachment cluster by hand the first time, but created a recording so I could automatically set it up the same later. Turns out there are only three different types, and I have programs for each of them now."

Yat paused. Arakaki assumed he was running the program. One extension of his universal cluster transformed itself into a new shape. Arakaki saw the glitter of electrical contacts there.

"Okay, now this cluster can plug in right here," Yat said. He slid the cluster into the opening.

"So you're connected. But how do you know what code to use and how to transmit it through their system?" Magnus asked.

"They don't use one-time codes, and apparently they set up global access for certain individuals or processes. I've only had to crack two codes, and it took a minimal amount of computing power."

"Too easy," Magnus commented.

"Yes. I think the Rovans didn't care much about these doors," Yat said.

"It could be that the Rovans hadn't developed advanced security technologies," Telisa said.

"Their electronics look plenty advanced to me," Marcant transmitted from the *Sharplight*.

"You miss the point. Maybe Rovans were all honest, so they needed no security," Telisa said.

"Ah, the whole thing about not making assumptions about aliens," Oliver said.

"It's a very real 'thing'," Telisa said. "We've met aliens that broke a lot of assumptions before."

The hatch opened smoothly, and Yat started to clean up his equipment.

"Did you teach yourself how to use that stuff?" Arakaki asked.

Yat hesitated, then said, "In the past, I was paid to... get into places I wasn't supposed to be."

"Ahhh," Marcant said knowingly. He did not sound like he was judging Yat.

I suppose I don't mind it either, unless I find out he was an assassin, Arakaki thought. Despite the internal monologue, something unsettled her.

"We've been too quick to trust these two. Remember all the betrayals we've gone through," Telisa sent to Magnus and Arakaki privately.

She's absolutely right. Can I trust my instincts about Yat? No. Not blindly.

A squadron of twenty attendants zipped into the opening. Instead of the long, dusty tunnels they had seen in the other catacombs, the attendants sent back feeds of clean white corridors with bright lights and sealed doors.

"Something new," Magnus said.

"Yes, this is completely different," Marcant agreed.

"Are we sure this was on your map of catacombs? I think maybe your translations may need some rethinking," Telisa said.

"It's absolutely on the map, but we never claimed to have understood everything," Yat said.

"We found out enough to get here, didn't we?" Oliver said defensively.

"On me," Telisa said. She brought up her PAW and stepped into the opening.

Arakaki noted that Telisa had changed her habits. The xenoarchaeologist usually only carried two Terran weapons: her tanto knife and her laser pistol. Now she had those, the PAW, and a stun baton Arakaki recognized as Siobhan's old gear. Arakaki wondered if the change was because of Oliver and Yat.

Magnus followed Telisa. He also carried a PAW. Arakaki waited for Yat and Oliver to enter, then followed them into an entrance corridor.

The ceiling glowed, bringing the interior to a comfortable brightness. The corridor was narrower than the mountain complex, though still wide enough for a Rovan to negotiate, and more than enough for Telisa, Magnus, and Arakaki to stand side by side.

Each side of the corridor extended into a triangular area, giving any cross-section of the corridor a hexagonal shape. Many of the now-familiar rovling pipes emerged from the walls in this side space without obstructing the main passageway.

"Two Rovans could probably pass each other in here, by tipping their shells into these side spaces," Telisa said.

"That extra space is also a great place for those rovling pipes to feed into the corridor," Arakaki said.

Arakaki checked on Yat and Oliver. They were calmly shadowing the three PIT members.

The team marched thirty meters until the corridor widened. Arakaki saw a large room ahead, but it looked empty.

She checked the attendant feeds. The room was an intersection of several tunnels. Three tunnels leading upward terminated in vast chambers that looked like helipads with large containers sitting nearby. A storage center nearby had even more containers. Three other tunnels were blocked by closed doors.

"There's a lot of stuff in that... warehouse. But where did they bring stuff in from?"

"This design suggests that the plateau has obscured openings where aircraft could enter with loads of supplies," Barrai said from the *Sharplight*.

"I can confirm that," Marcant said. "This attendant found the seals along the ceiling here... and rollers on this edge."

Arakaki looked at the feeds from the warehouse. She imagined the three chambers opening their ceiling doors to allow cargo craft to drop in from above, just as the starport had functioned except camouflaged from above. She started to count the rovling pipes that entered the room but gave up past twenty.

"Movement!" Barrai transmitted from the *Sharplight*.

Telisa signaled everyone to take cover.

Arakaki dove for the wall and put her shoulder behind a thick hexagonal brace that supported the walls. Her stealth sphere flipped on. She moved her submachine gun around the lip at the bend and waited. From her new vantage point, she realized both the lower and upper wall segments had tiny ridges on them like the ramp at the mountain redoubt. Only a narrow section of the next room was visible to her from her spot.

A glance told her the rest of the team was similarly placed and stealthed. Yat and Oliver had been given other team members' stealth spheres, so they were as well hidden as she was.

"Active rovlings!" Marcant announced. "Robotic ones. Ten or twelve, looks like."

As soon as Marcant spoke, three of the rovlings emerged from pipes ahead.

"Stay calm," Telisa said. "They aren't headed for us... at least not all of them."

Oh. Not all of them, Arakaki sarcastically echoed in her mind. She dropped the barrel of her weapon a bit.

The rovlings were slate-colored, radially symmetrical with eight spider-legs. The top segment of each leg had a sensor bulb on its outer facing side. Their bodies were oval, shaped like two deep plates joined facing each other. Arakaki spotted two sets of the mounting brackets on the top of each one, but nothing was attached to any of the robots she could see.

"Hold your positions," Telisa ordered, then she stepped out into the middle of the corridor with her stealth still on.

One of the awkward octopeds skittered over toward Telisa at the head of their column. It paused two meters away. Then it lowered its body a few centimeters and started to tap the floor with the closest two of its legs, inching forward cautiously.

It knows something's there! Almost to the meter!

The other octopeds remained stationary. The lead one kept tapping. It was slowly moving straight toward Telisa.

"A couple more headed in, with equipment attached," Barrai warned. "Be careful!"

"I can't tell if it that's a weapon," Marcant echoed.

"Stay calm," Telisa said.

Arakaki saw two more machines appear at the end of the corridor by the intersection room. They each had two slender black devices attached to the top of their bodies. They halted at the doorway, far behind the other rovlings.

The lead rovling stopped tapping and returned to its normal stance. It walked around Telisa in a full circle.

What the hell is that thing going to do?!

The rovling paused again, as if not sure what to make of its discovery.

"I think those two at the end of the corridor have made it so that it can see us more clearly," Telisa said. "I'm going to reveal myself."

Arakaki took a deep breath and tried to relax her tense limbs. Telisa blinked back into sight.

"Hello," Telisa said. "Who are you?"

The tiny octoped did not reply, at least not in any way Arakaki could discern. Four more of the octopeds now stood in the corridor between the team and the room. The two with mounted devices had not moved.

"May I pass?" Telisa asked.

The machines did not move.

"If you understand my request could you give me some sign?"

Again there was no response.

"Ideas?" Telisa prompted her team.

"I think it's an automated welcoming party, but they don't know what the hell you are," Marcant said. "Also, any AI here hasn't had enough time or context to decipher our language."

"But if an AI were trying to communicate, it would have these rovlings actively participating to pick up the basics from us."

"Yes. I think so," Marcant said.

Arakaki believed he was probably correct. It was easy to interpret the rovlings' behavior as confusion.

Two more rovlings emerged behind them, approaching Yat and Oliver.

"If we have to, we can take 'em," Oliver said.

"Easy," Magnus said. He walked over to join Yat and Oliver by the other rovlings. "Don't shoot first. We've been in this situation before, remain calm and don't start a fight we don't want," he said.

"Everyone drop the stealth," Telisa said. "Maybe they want to see all of us."

"Or maybe it's only a bunch of dumb servant machines," Oliver said as Arakaki and Magnus dropped their stealth.

"Yes, sure, maybe. We don't know anything yet," Yat said. He unstealthed, then Oliver finally did the same.

"I didn't think this would happen," Telisa sent to Arakaki and Magnus privately. "I'd give a lot to trade those two in for Caden and Siobhan, or even Marcant and Maxsym right now. Keep them calm."

Arakaki walked over to Yat.

"We're not in danger, at least not at the moment. Don't shoot or you could start a war. We just finished one."

Yat nodded. Oliver took his hand away from his weapon but still looked tense.

Telisa took a step forward. The rovling in front of her scuttled to one side. Telisa took another step. Several of the rovlings moved out of her path.

"So far, so good," she said. She inched toward the intersection ahead. The rovlings gave way, so Magnus followed. Arakaki waited until Oliver and Yat were walking before falling into line.

Telisa led them into the intersection room. Arakaki noted that the ceiling did not get any taller. It gave the room a very different feel than a Terran atrium. The floor was a series of interlocking diamond shapes formed of rock or ceramic. In the center sat what she immediately thought must be a decorative statue. It was a collection of ten-sided shapes, elongated with diamond-shaped sides like the floor, spiraling from floor to ceiling.

"Marcant?" Telisa asked, stepping closer to the sculpture.

"It's only decorative as far as the attendants can tell," Marcant said.

"Thanks to the attendants we know what's upstairs, though there are a lot of interesting boxes up there to open. Down here, though, we have closed doors. Let's try to open one," Telisa said.

Arakaki watched the rovlings come in after them. The machines moved slowly, but they were clearly following the team now.

I hope they don't decide we're a herd of wild animals. If we were, would Rovans shoo us out, or slaughter us?

Telisa walked down a wide corridor on their left. In thirty meters, it terminated in a Rovan-sized door. Telisa waited until a dozen rovlings had clustered behind them.

"Please open these doors," Telisa said aloud. As if to demonstrate, she walked over to the white barrier and knocked on it with her hand.

A rovling ambled over and stopped two meters from her. It did nothing.

Telisa reached out and pushed the door.

"We would like to pass," she said.

The rovlings did not respond. Telisa turned to Oliver and Yat.

"You two should probably head back. This is a different situation than we anticipated. If we start forcing doors and poking around, bad things could happen."

"There are priceless artifacts down here," Oliver said. "We're in."

Telisa looked at Yat. He looked apologetic.

"I'll compromise with you," she said. "You two go up to the hangars above this room and see what's in all those cargo containers. The three of us will cut through this door and find out what's below. You can watch us through the feeds. If we find something stupendous, you can follow us down."

"Fair enough," Yat said quickly, beating Oliver to the punch. He rapped Oliver's shoulder with the knuckles of his hand. "Let's go check it out."

Oliver reluctantly followed Yat back toward the intersection room. Two of the rovlings broke off and followed them. The rest stayed put.

"I think Yat can handle it," Arakaki sent to Telisa and Magnus privately.

Telisa nodded.

"Better safe than sorry," she replied. "After our first encounter with Shiny, I only want experienced members of the team with me for this kind of situation."

"I thought Yat was our door-opener," Magnus said.

"Marcant was watching carefully. He told me he wants a crack at it," Telisa said. She switched back to the team channel.

"It's all yours, Marcant," she said.

An attendant zipped forward, rose to the ceiling, then followed the perimeter to the right side. There, it halted.

Arakaki turned away to watch the rovlings on their flank. If the door opened, she knew Telisa and Magnus would be ready to respond to whatever lay beyond it. She heard the door move. The rovlings did not have any reaction.

"I got it," Marcant said. "We can hack it, no need for the adapter. I think you may have been on to something when you said maybe the Rovans didn't need security."

"Good job," Telisa told Marcant.

Arakaki took a glance at feeds from three attendants that flew through the doorway. A corridor continued past the portal, widened, and terminated in another obstacle. This time, the end of the corridor had a counter that ran along the right side with rovling pipes exiting beneath. A huge black disk dominated the ceiling of the wider part of the corridor. The way past that was blocked by a massive red wall with a large alcove in it.

Telisa said it all.

"Only the Five know what that all that is!"

"You're not kidding," Magnus echoed. Arakaki waited for Marcant to pontificate on the scene, but he said nothing.

The three Terrans advanced to the black disk, trailed by the rovlings. Four more rovlings sprung out of the pipes.

"More of them," Telisa said.

"If it comes to it, we can handle them, I think," Magnus said.

"Yes, but there must be more in here," Telisa said.

"Marcant, how many—" Arakaki started.

"Our attendants have spotted fifty-three rovlings so far," Marcant said. "Do you want me to send one through those pipes ahead?"

"Go ahead," Telisa said. "We'll investigate this place."

Telisa sent one of her attendants examine the black disk on the ceiling. Arakaki did not check its readings—she knew others were more qualified to deduce the function of the disk.

"You don't suppose that disk... stamps down on the floor?" Arakaki asked.

"It doesn't look that way," Marcant said. "The disk is affixed to the ceiling, not a cylinder embedded in it."

"Good. Still, if we want to avoid it, we can make our way around on the left side opposite that counter," Telisa pointed out. She set off on the course she had described.

"What is that red wall?" Yat asked from the hangar level above them.

"Another door, I think," Magnus said.

"This is more than a door," Marcant said. "The attendant's mass sense is showing me that that structure is incredibly dense. It would take the *Sharplight* to cut through it."

"What is it?"

"I think it's a different type of door," Barrai said, contradicting Marcant. "A rotating door. The general shape is a disc the size of a shuttle, almost as tall as you are. But there are three niches or alcoves in it. I think it revolves to let Rovans through one at a time."

"So heavy duty. The door we just went through wasn't enough?" Magnus asked.

"Maybe it's a blast door," Telisa said. She walked up to the Rovan-sized alcove in the red wall. "So they're saying that a Rovan goes into there, and the entire red part rotates it through."

"Then how are we getting through?" Yat asked. "This is nothing like the doors I know."

"We'll figure it out," Marcant said. "But you can only go through one or two at a time."

Recipe for disaster.

"The attendants have been blocked from moving around it through those pipes," Barrai reported.

"So this is the only way through. We could go back and try the other two regular doors on this level, but it stands to reason that this either goes someplace unique, or the other ways have the same kind of obstacle."

"If we get trapped in that thing we may never get out," Magnus pointed out. The tone of his voice made it clear he was not crazy about trying to go through it.

"I'll go first," Arakaki said. "If I don't get through, no one else needs to risk it."

Telisa stood still. Her face was tight, frowning. Arakaki debated saying something but decided it would simply interfere with Telisa's decision making.

"Barrai, do we have anything besides ship's weapons that could cut her out of there?"

"Based upon what we can see from up here, we have industrial cutters that could do it," Barrai said. "It might take hours."

"I wonder if it's airtight," Magnus said. "If you still want to go through, maybe you should take extra air."

"Good point. Bring us an oxygen cannister from the shuttle," Telisa instructed. Arakaki understood that Telisa meant to arrange for a robot to bring it, not for Magnus to lug it down himself.

I wonder if it bothers him when she orders him to do things in front of the team. He's her senior on the team, but now she's in command. It must not bother him, because he could leave PIT whenever he wanted.

Arakaki waited calmly, regarding the armored alcove that led deeper into the complex. It would be an uncomfortable way through, assuming they could get the door to rotate at all, but she had been asked to do much worse in the UED.

When one of Magnus's insectoid robots returned with an oxygen cannister, Telisa took it and handed it to Arakaki.

"Good luck," Telisa said.

Arakaki nodded and took the cannister without ceremony. She stepped into the alcove. The huge device started to rotate.

"Is that you, Marcant?" Telisa asked.

"No," Marcant replied from the *Sharplight*.

The movement was so smooth and slow that it seemed to Arakaki that the outside wall moved to cut her off from the world. The alcove rotated until she saw only a smooth red wall where the opening had been. She became aware of a low humming noise. The isolation was complete and unnerving. If the alcove stopped here, she would be trapped inside an extremely strong cage.

Here's hoping the other side isn't a furnace.

It felt like a long time. Her three attendants rotated around her peacefully. Her link said only two minutes had passed by the time a sliver opened to the other side.

A group of rovlings waited for her. Arakaki's relief at seeing the opening grow balanced against her unease at the greeting party. She counted six rovlings, and they each had compact Rovan equipment mounted on their top rails—guns? Lasers? She had no idea. She kept her own weapon cradled, pointed downward, but ready.

The rotation stopped. She stepped forward.

"I'm here. Greeting party of six rovlings," she announced. "I think they're armed," she added.

"I can read you," Barrai said. "That heavy gate, or blast door, is blocking your communications with the others, but there are enough attendants around to reroute your messages locally."

"I'm coming through," Telisa said.

"I'll send an attendant ahead to map this area," Arakaki told them. She sent one of her attendants down the corridor.

The rovlings shifted occasionally, like living things. Many rovling pipes emptied into the corridor, presumably one of them had brought this group here to intercept her.

Arakaki heard a clunk. Her head whipped over to look down the corridor. Her attendant had dropped to the floor.

"Well that's new," Arakaki said.

"Malfunction?" Marcant asked, but the tone of his voice made it clear he did not believe his own guess.

They shot it. They had to.

Arakaki started to walk toward the dead attendant.

"Don't go too far," Marcant urged.

Arakaki slowed. She sent out a second attendant and told it to retrieve the first. The second attendant moved more slowly. When it was two meters from its target, one of the rovlings twitched. The attendant fell. If Arakaki had just been watching the rovling, she might not have known anything untoward had occurred.

"That's no malfunction," Arakaki said.

"Stay near the door. Telisa's halfway through," Magnus said.

Arakaki retreated to the door with her last attendant. She tried to guess what types of weapons the artificial octopeds had mounted on them. The attack had been utterly silent. An electromagnetic attack made sense. Maybe her attendant had picked up a reading? Or maybe they would learn more if they went and retrieved those dead attendants.

Telisa stepped out of the rotating cylinder beside her. Arakaki assumed she had been out of contact while inside.

"The rovlings neutralized two of my attendants," Arakaki summarized.

"Here?" Telisa asked.

"I sent them flying that way. These rovlings used those things on their mounts."

"Have they shown any signs of aggression against you?" Telisa asked.

"No."

"They might be justified in doing so," Marcant pointed out. "We are—you are—trespassing."

"Well, for now, we do it the hard way," Telisa said. "Magnus, come on through. If you can, bring more attendants."

"Will do."

Arakaki and Telisa watched the rovlings. At any given moment, most of them were still, but one or two of them were often moving around.

"That one over there seems to move more often than the others," Arakaki said. "Do you think they have personalities?"

"We don't know enough about them," Telisa said reasonably.

"They may have been trained differently," Marcant said. "If they were trained in the field and not preprogrammed, they might in a way have 'personalities' even if they aren't as smart as us."

"Or they might all be very dumb and that one is moving because it's not as close to you as the others, so it wanders around trying to edge in," Barrai added.

"Keep observing them. We'll learn more," Telisa said.

A light changed in the humming noise prompted Arakaki to turn around. An alcove was opening behind them as the machine turned. She saw Magnus inside.

He stepped out of the door. His mouth was an emotionless flat line.

He probably did not like going through that thing, but no doubt he had been ordered to do far worse as well.

"Well, we're committed now," he said. "No fast dash out of here."

Magnus's words triggered a memory. For one second, Arakaki went back in time: A strong, handsome man faced her in a UED battlesuit. "No way out of here," the man said. He looked into her eyes and they understood each other.

Arakaki returned to the moment. She reached for the sliver of armor around her neck, but it was back on the ship.

The sliver was the only thing left of that man. He had been right.

Chapter 18

Telisa strode down a corridor amid a group of apathetic rovlings. Magnus and Arakaki were on her six.

"This is crazy. Those pipes are everywhere," Marcant transmitted.

Telisa saw what he meant: Within this corridor alone, at least ten rovling pipes emerged at floor level, three angled in from above, and four that led straight down from the centerline of the floor.

In the warehouse above, Oliver and Yat had opened a lot of cargo boxes and found supplies of the suspected Rovan food and caches of Rovan equipment that was potentially very valuable. They worked to find more items and choose what was valuable enough to bring back.

The three PIT team members approached a door on their right in the corridor.

"Want to check it out?" Marcant asked.

"Yes, I—wait. I hear something," Telisa said. The others looked around. No doubt their ears could not pick up the humming and scuffling noises Telisa heard.

Telisa indicated the direction of the sound farther down the corridor. Everyone waited.

A large white shape became visible when it turned a corner about 50 meters ahead. It was a contrivance or robot, sliding along the floor. It rose to the height of Telisa's chest and was longer than a ground car. Its right side sloped at the same angle as the corridor alcoves.

So that it can get out of the way and let a Rovan pass by, Telisa thought. *Or another machine like itself.*

"What the hell is that?" Arakaki asked.

"A robot? I can't tell what it does. It doesn't look anything like a Rovan, that's for sure," Telisa said.

The machine continued toward them. The Terrans moved to the right side of the corridor. Thankfully, it slowed as it neared. A door opened along its front side.

Arakaki and Magnus raised their weapons. Telisa accessed her breaker claw and waited.

A black object emerged from across the front of the Rovan robot. Telisa did not see any projectile barriers or energy emitters, at least none she could recognize.

The black object slowly unfolded into a barrier front of the machine. Within three seconds it was presenting a larger frontal area than the robot, in two more it filled most of the corridor, including angled flaps to block the side alcoves.

"It's a security machine," Magnus said. "Preventing us from passing?"

"Well it's a lousy one. It's just blocking us with that rubber barrier," Arakaki said.

"It must be confused. We aren't Rovans. It thinks we're wild animals or something," Telisa conjectured.

The barrier crawled forward. It advanced on them by perhaps a centimeter a second and did not seem to be accelerating.

"We mean no harm," Telisa called out. "We want to learn from you."

Nothing changed; the barrier slid forward.

"Time to make a call. Are we going to let it shoo us away?" Magnus asked.

Telisa considered the source of the resistance.

"Do we have any reason to think it's a live Rovan in here that wants us to leave?"

Magnus and Arakaki remained silent. Telisa figured Marcant would not be shy about sharing his opinion.

"Given the state of the rest of the planet, I'd say this is only automated resistance," Marcant said.

"I agree," Barrai chipped in.

Telisa looked at Magnus, then Arakaki. Arakaki shrugged.

"No way to know for sure. If there are Rovans here, they would be among the last survivors."

And they would be desperate.

If a Rovan was in here, trying to get them to leave, Telisa would tend to comply.

"The confusion of the rovlings does suggest an automated response. Could be an AI, I suppose," Telisa said.

"If so, it would have discerned that we're intelligent aliens and attempted some form of communication," Marcant pointed out.

"That makes hefty assumptions about what they're like," Magnus said. "Still, I agree, this feels like a set of dumber robots that don't know what's going on."

Telisa sighed. She wanted to believe that explanation because that would allow her continue and discover what lay ahead with a clear conscience.

Once the second guessing starts, you're stuck.

"Okay. Kill it," she said.

Arakaki leveled her weapon at the machine and released a quick burst of rounds. The noise tore through the corridor, deafening. The machine halted.

Telisa waited for alarms to sound or bright lights to flash. There was nothing.

Whoever the Rovans were, I'm beginning to get the impression they were very tolerant. Terran or Vovokan security might have tried to vaporize us by now.

Arakaki was frowning.

"You don't think we're making progress?" Telisa asked her.

"Whatever happens to us now, we're not going to be able to say they didn't try to stop us," Arakaki said.

Well, that's another way of looking at it. They tried to keep us out. They tried to turn us away. Perhaps lethal force is next?

Telisa looked at the rovlings again. They did not seem concerned by the destruction of their fellow machine.

"Marcant, the door," Telisa prompted.

"Working," Marcant said.

"Hey, these rovling pipes..." Magnus said. He stood next to one of the unusual pipes in the centerline of the floor.

Arakaki and Telisa walked up to the pipe. The pipe descended straight down, but the other end was only a few meters away and opened into a lit space. Telisa saw... something smooth and gray with a regular surface. A Rovan machine?

"Another room below?" she guessed.

"I think so," Magnus said. "All the other pipes we've seen are in the alcoves. I've never been able to see much through them without sending an attendant through."

"Door coming open now," Marcant warned.

They turned to cover the door. It opened to reveal an empty room.

"I'm thinking elevator," Telisa said. "Probably goes down into that factory place."

"I would say freight elevator, but I guess the Rovans were just big," Arakaki said.

"We can take the elevator down, or keep exploring this level. I think we should go deeper and see how big this place really is," Telisa said.

"We could risk an attendant, perhaps," Arakaki said. "The rovlings aren't shooting these as long as they stay close... but if I stand next to this pipe..."

"Then one of your attendants could slip straight down there without being seen," Telisa finished. "Good idea. Let's try it. Marcant, see if you can pwn this elevator."

"I will," Marcant replied.

They walked over to the pipe. Telisa and Magnus stood with Arakaki.

"I could stealth first," Arakaki offered.

Telisa frowned.

"No, just let your sphere slip in there but stay close first. If there's no reaction, then send it on down."

Telisa watched the rovlings and waited.

"It's down," Arakaki reported a few moments later.

Telisa accessed the feeds. The room below them extended at least a quarter a kilometer on a side. The attendant flew high for a moment, then plunged ten meters to get a closer look at rows of car-sized machines arrayed on the floor.

A rovling turned toward Arakaki and scuttled closer.

"They're smart enough track the attendants and they know one's missing!" Barrai concluded.

Arakaki kneeled and pulled her pack around to her front. She opened it and started shuffling things in and out of the pack. The rovling flanked her, paused, then moved to get a better view of the pack.

"That's right, it's in there," Arakaki said happily. She closed the pack back up and slipped it onto her back.

"Smart enough to fool," Arakaki said.

Telisa smiled. She meant the rovlings were smart enough to notice an attendant was gone and realize it might be in the pack, so Arakaki used that against them.

Two rovlings moved toward the pipes in the center of the corridor.

"Damn. Tell your attendant to lay low in there!" Telisa ordered.

"No problem. There's plenty of cover down there."

"Yeah, but maybe more rovlings, too?"

Telisa hooked herself into the video feeds coming from the attendant that had slipped down to the next level.

"It's some kind of... work floor? A factory? Or a huge lab."

Siobhan would know.

"Adair says it's a factory. Those machines are identical, and their positions can be adjusted to make room for whatever they're putting together."

"Those flat sleds are probably hauled away by lots of rovlings," Barrai added.

Telisa looked at the yellow sleds Barrai had mentioned. They were about 3 meters square, slung as low as rovlings, and each had six handles along the sides. Telisa decided Barrai was probably right.

"Look over here," Magnus said. He sent a pointer.

Telisa looked at the relevant feed. A group of four sleds each had a backpack-sized black object on them. The objects were identical: each was composed of three roughly square pieces joined together with a hinge or a bent frame to form a shallow 'C' shape. The concave part faced down onto the sled.

What are those things?

"Let's go down and check those out," Telisa said immediately. No one raised any concerns.

They walked to the elevator.

"Uhm, hello, still working here," Marcant said.

"It's more complex than the doors?" Telisa guessed.

"Only if you care about getting back out again," Marcant offered happily. "Okay, fine. I'm ready."

Arakaki raised an eyebrow.

"We can always cut our way out," she said aloud. Telisa nodded.

The three explorers stepped into the oversized elevator and waited. Soon the hatch closed and the platform descended.

Marcant and Adair are proving invaluable here. It would be much slower going without them.

The hatch opened; They were now on the floor of the suspected factory.

"Thanks for the lift," she told Marcant.

"Oh you made it alive?" he asked nonchalantly.

"Careful," Telisa sent him privately. "This *is* dangerous from time to time, you know."

He sent back a nonverbal acknowledgement.

They walked out into the room. The rovlings scuttled through their pipes in the floor and continued to observe from above.

Magnus and Arakaki angled toward the sleds they had observed. Arakaki's stranded attendant shot back to her side from underneath a nearby machine like a scared cat running to a tree.

Telisa listened, looked, and even smelled the room with her heightened senses. She got the impression nothing had been operating here for a long time. Surely if the machines had been active recently, there would be a smell of lubricant or perhaps ionized air particles.

She caught up with Magnus and Arakaki perched on one of the sleds, standing to either side of one of the devices they had spotted.

"Any ideas what they are?" Telisa asked.

"Complex. These are pieces of hi tech equipment," Barrai transmitted.

"No energy rings, though," Marcant said. "That's odd."

"Have we encountered any in Rovan hardware?" Telisa asked. "Heads up there: our breaker claws may be useless against Rovan machines."

Telisa picked up the nearest device. It was noticeably heavy. She looked over at Magnus and Arakaki, who stared at her from their sled.

Oh. They must have tried to pick that one up and failed.

No one spoke, incarnate or on the channel, but Telisa wondered if Oliver, Yat, and Barrai were also taking silent note of her capabilities.

"I guess these are Rovan-sized. I imagine they were strong," Telisa thought out loud.

"We could probably load all four onto one sled and... take it back in the elevator," Magnus said.

"Let's not get ahead of ourselves," Telisa said, but she carried her artifact to the next sled, picked up a second device, then added them to the sled Magnus and Arakaki perched on. Magnus and Arakaki worked together to move the fourth over.

"More rovlings coming in!" Marcant said. "Pipes on your left and right."

Telisa turned to face the nearest floor pipes. She kept her breathing even.

No matter how many times rovlings come to meet us, I don't think I'm going to relax.

Rovlings skittered out. This time they each paused for a half second after emerging, then began roving about. Telisa's attendants reported twenty new arrivals. They all had equipment mounted on their upper plates.

One of the rovlings walked toward Arakaki. She centered the muzzle of her weapon on its body.

"They seem even more interested in us now," Telisa summarized.

"Their approach pattern was rapid and direct," Marcant said. "These came in to intercept you, I feel certain."

"I hope there isn't a Rovan somewhere that sent these to stop us," Telisa said.

"I don't think so. It's like each time they come to meet us based on a trigger, assuming we're something else, then their programming isn't prepared for what they see when they arrive."

"It might be that we're interacting these devices. We could leave them here for now. Show that we're observing and being reasonable," Telisa said.

"Please bring them back!" Marcant said.

"We need those!" Oliver said simultaneously.

"You two know what they are," Arakaki said.

"No. Not at all," Marcant said. "We just both believe these could be super valuable."

"That's right," Oliver said.

"Yat? What do you think?" Arakaki asked.

Telisa was surprised. *Why is she asking this and why Yat?*

"Sure, I'd like to learn what those are, but don't risk your lives for them," he said.

"Let's find a way out of here," Telisa said. "I'd like to see more of this place."

She checked their alien escort. More than 30 rovlings had accumulated on the local tactical.

"Can we take these things if we have to?" Telisa asked Magnus and Arakaki privately.

"I think so," Arakaki said. "But if they attack us first..."

"Yeah, that's what we need to worry about," Magnus said. "We each have three attendants, but if six or seven rovlings shoot at us at once, we could be wounded or killed."

"Depends on Momma Veer," Telisa pointed out.

"Without our faceplates deployed, it only takes one round or laser," Arakaki countered.

"Okay. Put your stealth spheres on an auto-trigger. That might help if bullets start flying."

Telisa told her attendants and Veer suit to coordinate a quick warning that could activate her stealth sphere. Even though her reflexes were heightened, it was hard to stay razor sharp as the hours wore on in the complex without direct threat.

"I think the bulk of the complex lays in this direction," Barrai told them. A ghostly green arrow overlayed their tactical. Telisa pointed.

"Onward. We'll come back this way."

"Can we go down and get those?" Oliver asked.

Telisa sighed.

"I don't think—"

"I can control that sled," Marcant said. "Since you loaded those four devices onto one sled, I can send it up the elevator and have it meet Oliver and Yat at the rotating door."

Telisa shared cross looks with Arakaki. Arakaki just shrugged.

"Very well."

The sled moved away at a slow crawl. It slid between the factory machines with only centimeters to spare. The rovlings readily made way for it.

"Let's go," Telisa told Magnus and Arakaki aloud.

They walked through the sterilized environment of the factory and out a large opening in the wall where finished products must have once traveled, or perhaps would travel if the Rovans ever returned to reclaim their colony's infrastructure.

The wide cargo corridor split two times, but the team found another door blocking their way into another section of the complex. Telisa walked up to the door and waited. She was about to scold Marcant for paying too much attention to his sled when he spoke up.

"Resistance!"

"Explain," Telisa ordered.

"These Rovan facilities don't have real security, not as we know it. But something is actively trying to change states in the door to block you," Marcant said.

"I assume Adair is helping you?"

"Absolutely. We're winning. But it's notable. Something doesn't want you in there."

"Then we'll have to be ready for an escalation," Telisa said.

The door opened.

The perpendicular tunnel beyond had a deep set of metal tracks set down the center.

"Maybe this is a kind of heavy transport for things made in the factory," Barrai said.

"That's a good theory. These tracks could go all the way to a nearby city," Telisa said.

"It might not be safe to head down the corridor. A transport could come along at high speed and smash you," Barrai said. "That might be why it didn't want to open."

"I think the Rovans would have built in safety measures like Terran transport tubes do," Telisa countered.

"No speculation needed," Magnus said. He pointed at the triangular recess of the closest wall. "The pipe connector alcove, or whatever you want to call it, would be out of the way. Those support struts are placed about every 14 meters, so whatever moves down this track can't extend over here. A Rovan might not be able to get completely out of the way there, but that's enough room for us."

It sounded reasonable. Telisa led them to the right. She saw two rovlings dodge into a pipe 20 meters ahead.

"More rovlings," she said, slowing.

Could it be an ambush? They don't usually dart away.

Magnus and Arakaki knew why she slowed. Their weapons came up from the cradled position to cover the left and right alcoves where the rovlings pipes joined the tunnel.

They kept walking. Telisa used her sharp eyesight to look for changes in the tunnel ahead.

"We're coming up on a huge bay. I see... tall objects or pipes," Telisa told them.

They advanced until more became visible. The right side of the tunnel curved away to open into a large chamber. The team veered into the new room.

A collection of cylinders stood over 10 meters tall before them. Their tops slimmed to points and their bases had four fins with rocket nozzles at the tip of each fin. Telisa scanned the room and did a quick check of the size of the array. There were 40 of the objects.

"I think we know what those are," Arakaki said dryly.

An attendant shot upward and circled the pointed end of a missile, then dropped back to the floor on the far side and slipped back to Telisa.

"Missiles with nuclear warheads," Marcant summarized.

Telisa checked the ceiling, wondering if the missiles could be launched in-place. She did not see any ports above that would allow the missiles to reach the surface.

Many rovlings entered the room behind them. The alien machines spread out in the larger space.

"We know they have powerful lasers. Aren't these obsolete?" Yat asked from somewhere above them in the complex.

"Celaran missiles, and likely Vovokan ones as well, can absorb an impressive amount of coherent radiation before being disabled," Telisa told him. "Perhaps the Rovans have a similar miniaturized shielding technology, providing these missiles the same kind of protection our ships enjoy."

"Another possibility for why something tried to stop us from getting here," Arakaki said.

"Yes. I wonder though, whatever or whoever that was, were they trying to protect the missiles from us, or the other way around?" Telisa asked.

No one tried to answer.

The tactical showed Telisa that Oliver and Yat had met the sled at the revolving door. They were busy trying to haul the artifacts to the rotating alcove one at a time.

"Weapons in here... what's behind that door?" Magnus asked, pointing to another wide portal in the middle of the room, on the wall opposite the tracks.

They approached and let Marcant work on the door.

"Can you call a train for us? Or whatever uses the tracks," Telisa asked Marcant.

"Not yet," Marcant said. "Operating these doors does represent progress in working with Rovan technology, but at this point, it's largely just a formulaic system we use without understanding the whys behind it."

Telisa accepted the answer. It did not surprise her. The only thing that worried her was that Marcant had become the lynchpin of PIT's alien technology research. Telisa had tried to change that by assigning Siobhan and Caden to learn about Celaran science, but now they were gone.

We need more people. And I need a clear mission to communicate. Explore. Learn. If only we didn't have to deal with Shiny's politics. Yet he has enabled so much...

The door opened, and Telisa thankfully let her big thoughts slide away. A long corridor beckoned beyond the hatch, heading straight out from the missile room.

They marched onward.

"Our friends aren't following," Arakaki said.

"Is that good or bad news?" asked Magnus.

Telisa took a glance back. The door had shut. The rovlings were nowhere to be seen. Her gaze naturally moved to the side alcoves to see if they were going around the door.

"Hey, there aren't any pipes in this corridor!" Telisa said.

Magnus and Arakaki slowed.

"Right. So whatever is ahead might be off limits for them?" Magnus suggested.

"Now I'm curious," Telisa said. She continued. In the distance, she saw a single door. Telisa sent an attendant ahead since there were no rovlings to threaten it. Its feed showed an ordinary looking hatch at the far end.

"Any signs of danger?" Telisa asked Marcant and Barrai. "This corridor is a little unsettling."

"What's wrong with it?" asked Marcant. "The lack of rovling pipes?"

"Yeah, that, and it's just a straight corridor with no side doors. We're exposed and potentially trapped," Arakaki said.

"If you want, I can open that far door through Telisa's attendant while you remain there. If there's some danger, at least you'll be 50 meters away."

"Do it," Telisa said. She walked part way into the alcove.

We're probably talking ourselves into being paranoid about nothing. But what harm does it do to be paranoid here? It might save our lives.

"Stealth," Telisa said. "If we're going to be paranoid, we might as well go all out."

They all activated their stealth spheres and waited.

Marcant opened the door. Telisa waited for something—a blast of air rushing out, or a wall of water surging toward them—anything.

The attendant flew through and sent back video and sensor feeds.

Huge banks of silver and gray equipment surrounded three quarters of the perimeter of a raised circle in the center of the bay. The ceiling had matching dark circle with a path that extended to the north wall, also surrounded by machines.

"It's a shipyard," Magnus said.

Telisa looked at the room in light of his theory. She could imagine the machines working together to build a ship in the circular clearing. The raised areas could possibly be hardened to withstand a gravity spinner.

"But how do the ships get out?"

"There's a vertical shaft a hundred meters north of that circle," Barrai said. "Is the wall in that direction substantial?"

Telisa's eyes traced the north wall looking for clues. The wall looked solid enough, but that was where the floor and ceiling lacked machinery.

"Look at that ridge near the floor," Magnus pointed out. "I think this wall moves or rotates aside to let the ships out of here."

Telisa, Magnus, and Arakaki walked to the end of the corridor and devoured the scene with their own eyes. Telisa felt a sense of wonder.

An alien spacecraft factory. It could take a year, but we'll learn so much about the Rovans!

"Marcant, if we can activate this facility and build Rovan ships, then it would be..." she paused, looking for a phrase big enough to match the magnitude of their discovery.

"The mother lode," Maxsym supplied from the *Iridar*.

"What? No," Marcant said. "She means it would be one of our biggest finds ever."

Maxsym sighed.

"It's more complex than just activating these machines," Marcant continued. "We would need to provide and coordinate material supplies. I assume the yard loads ship plans from a datastore."

"Or it could be as easy as pushing a button," Yat said. "We don't know yet."

"This needs to be a priority," Telisa said.

"Trust me, we're working hard to get information from this place," Marcant said. "I've even borrowed some of Maxsym's... *Iridar*'s computing power."

"The attendants found something very odd down that right corridor," Barrai interrupted.

"Okay, let's check it out," Telisa said, though she had not even noticed that they had found a corridor. They took a right and walked along a raised ledge eight meters above the facility floor.

"Why aren't the rovlings allowed in here?" Arakaki asked. "We should be careful."

"Good question," Telisa said. She wondered if that detail was indeed a warning of a danger that she could deduce.

"Maybe this place is evacuated of air, or perhaps another gas is pumped in while the work is done, and all those rovling pipes would leak it out?" Magnus asked.

"Nice try, but putting airtight hatches on a bunch of pipes would be very easy for a species this advanced," Marcant said.

"My theory stands until you provide a better one," Magnus replied.

"As a precaution, don't try to activate these machines while we're in here," Telisa said.

"I'll try not to..." Marcant said. It did not inspire confidence.

They came to the corridor Barrai had mentioned. It was a wide Rovan tunnel that led 10 meters into the wall and ended in another hatch. They walked up and waited.

"Opening now," Marcant warned. The gate rose.

Telisa was startled to see rovlings on the other side of the hatch. At least two dozen of them were arrayed on the flanks of a corridor that extended over 40 meters. Many stood partially visible at the exits of rovling pipes in the alcoves.

Our escort is growing. I hope they're not actually being produced right now in response to our presence!

"Too creepy," Barrai said.

"Not helpful, Lieutenant," Telisa said, a little more sharply than she meant to, probably because Barrai was right.

"28 of them visible, ma'am," Barrai said.

"Better. Keep your attendants close," Telisa said.

She slowly stepped forward. The rovlings remained stationary. The group moved in behind her.

"Not a great position tactically speaking," Arakaki breathed aloud.

"I think they would have attacked already if they were going to," Telisa said. "Magnus, what's your assessment?"

"They seem to be merely escorting us. But their numbers are growing. They *could* be waiting for an overwhelming advantage."

"So they could be observing... or trying to deter us, or, it might be they'll do nothing unless we try to do something verboten," Telisa thought out loud.

She half-regretted ordering the destruction of the robot that had blocked them. If some actions were going to trigger the artificial rovlings to attack, the destruction of valuable property might be among those actions.

Why do I always have to second guess my decisions?

The three Terrans walked by the rovlings. Once again, the alien machines followed them. The corridor ended in another hatch.

When Marcant opened the way, Telisa saw a clear chamber with a metal frame on the right wall, surrounding a clear pane that separated the room from another chamber beyond. Two rovling pipes emptied into the room on her left, along with enough empty space for a Rovan to face the window. The opposite wall held only another Rovan-sized hatch.

"It looks like an aquarium," Telisa said.

"It's a containment cell," Arakaki said.

"Could it be an isolation chamber?" asked Telisa.

"It could be, but it's reinforced extremely well," Maxsym said. "I think Arakaki is correct."

"Anything in there?" Magnus asked. He walked over to get a better look. "If they had prisoners, they must have taken them when they left. Otherwise, there will be something very dead in there."

"Careful, ma'am," Barrai warned. "What if all those rovlings want to put you in one of those things?"

Telisa double checked the rovling pipes. So far, no more robots had emerged from them.

"Can you close the last door?" she asked Marcant.

Only three of the rovlings had come through after the team, though it seemed likely more would follow if the team moved on through the next door.

As the portal closed, a fourth rovling darted through.

"Let's move on," Telisa said. The far door opened quickly.

The room beyond was an exact duplicate of the first.

"I get it. This is like a row of containment cells. I bet there are several more," Arakaki said as they entered.

"You're probably right," Marcant said. "The resistance is back on this next door."

"Why this one? Why not the first one?" Magnus said.

"There's something in one of these cells the automated systems don't want us to see," Oliver said excitedly.

That could be good, or very bad.

"I have it," Marcant announced.

The instant the door opened to the third chamber, Telisa noticed its containment window was streaked with whitish-silver. Telisa stared beyond the clear barrier. She saw a variety of delicate shapes among a web of silvery wires.

"That doesn't look Rovan at all," Arakaki said.

"I agree with you," Telisa said. She took a few hesitant steps forward to make room for the others. "I can't see how it could be a piece of equipment or anything alive. I'm not even sure that could move."

The chamber beyond the window had a long rail adorned with spikes that ran between two silvery spiral columns. A group of ovoids with mirrored surfaces squatted in the room seemingly at random. Somehow it did not look like a collection of objects, but instead, like multiple pieces of the same complex construct.

"Maybe it's a piece of art," Magnus said.

Telisa's first instinct was to reject the idea, but she admitted to herself that it made as much sense as anything else she could come up with.

"With due respect TMs, I disagree," Barrai said. "Your attendants are getting very different readings here. This cell is powered up. There are subtle visual cues... I think there's some kind of... force field around the interior of that room."

Force field technology. If the Rovans can create compact force fields, that would be huge. Even Shiny doesn't have an invisible protection barrier, though the attendants certainly provide a lot of protection.

"It's amazing," Yat stated. "If it is a force field, that close to the other materials—and in a perfect cubic shape!—it's beyond the protective screens of *Sharplight* or any other starship the Space Force has."

We need another opinion.

"Lee, what do you think of this? Have you ever seen anything like it?"

"No, I've never seen any such thing under or overleaf. It could still be a work of art—if Rovans value works of art enough to weave force fields around them," Lee said.

It's completely different than everything else down here. Extreme caution is warranted.

"I'm not ready to mess with this. Let's move on past it," Telisa said.

"I would like a sample of that," Maxsym said.

"But this is so interesting!" Marcant complained simultaneously.

"And valuable, if they've locked it up like this," Oliver transmitted from above. Apparently, he had lost interest in his local plunder and started to watch the forward party.

"Or dangerous," Arakaki countered.

"I hear you. We'll come back to it," Telisa said.

"At least give me a second," Marcant pleaded. "I might be able to—"

The lights suddenly flipped off to be replaced by light blue illumination. A loud chittering sound exploded through the bay, rising and falling in a sinusoidal pattern.

"... learn more?" Marcant finished uncertainly.

By the Five!

Chapter 19

"Seriously!? You opened that cell?" Magnus yelled. A wave of fury rose in his chest alongside the adrenal surge of imminent danger.

"No! Not even close," Marcant said. "I just accessed the systems related to it."

"Well it was something very important," Telisa said. She sounded much calmer than Magnus felt. He took a deep breath and focused on survival.

Magnus looked to his left. Arakaki had already launched three grenades out across the floor in three different directions. She would be able to arm them with a single thought.

She knows what's up! Time for action.

The doors on both sides of the room started to open. A new sound joined the chittering of the alarm, an awful static-like humming. Magnus realized it was coming from the rovling pipes along with a breeze.

"Stealth! On Magnus! We're getting out of here, I have the rear," Telisa barked.

She flickered out of sight. Thanks to the custom Celaran modifications, Magnus could still see her tactical ghost.

Magnus cursed her for ordering him to separate but he obeyed without hesitation. He charged past Arakaki back the way they had come, leveling his rifle before him. He brought his grenades to readiness but told them to stay attached and wait.

"Many rovlings headed up—streaks of silver shiza!—MANY MANY OF THEM," Marcant said, failing entirely to stay calm.

One of Arakaki's grenades spun out, accelerating straight for one of the rovling pipes.

"We've lost most of our eyes in the complex!" Barrai reported.

Magnus dropped two of his own grenades with orders to cover their retreat. He did not bother to watch them roll back past the team. Instead, he powered forward.

"Don't engage unless they attack one of us first," Telisa said. "The attendants are expendable."

"They will this time," Magnus sent back. "Send my soldier bots from the shuttle in after us!" he told Marcant.

"They're already on the way, but I don't think ten of them will make a dent," Marcant said. For once, he actually sounded apologetic.

"Have the soldiers escort Oliver and Yat out of here," Telisa ordered.

The opening door ahead of Magnus had only risen a meter, but Magnus felt impacts across his shins. His Veer suit reported three impacts from small caliber projectiles.

"Taking fire!" Magnus said.

Boooooom!

An explosion rocked the floor and debris rained over Magnus. Chunks of shattered armor bounced off the nearest wall.

Is that—no. Those are pieces of rovlings, not a teammate.

Magnus told his weapon to go hot on rovling signatures.

"How can they see you?" Barrai asked, but her voice sounded far away even though it was in his head like all the link communications. The door opened halfway, up to his chest.

Brrrapp! Brrrapp!

Magnus's weapon fired a burst. He waved it before him, letting the weapon target and shoot whatever came within its guided-hit cone of fire. The rovlings in the next room splattered to pieces. He heard someone behind still firing.

Brrrapp! Brrrapp! Brrrapp! Boooom!

Our fire is effective!

Magnus ducked under the door and resumed his run. One of his grenades reported five kills from behind them. The door on the far side of the new room was already rising. No doubt Marcant was opening the way as fast as he could.

"They don't know exactly where we are," Telisa said. "Their projectiles are mostly missing."

Brrrapp! Brrrapp! Boooom!

"Some of them have beam weapons," Arakaki said. "Their mounts vary. They're deploying combined arms against us!"

"Remember the ones that can see us? Look for them in the rear," Telisa said.

More rovlings were behind the new door. Magnus was in the first of the containment chamber rooms now.

Boooom! Brrrapp!

More rovlings went down. He felt a round hit his chest, but it did not come through. He could not make out the details of the rovling's mounted weapons himself, so he altered his weapon's priority list as it shot for him.

Detection rovlings to the top. Then all others—

Arakaki broadcasted a signature for a beam weapon rovling. He put the new sig in the number two spot of his weapon, above the projectile ones he currently engaged.

Brrrapp! Brrrapp! Brrrapp!

Another group of rovlings erupted from the pipes on his right.

Dammit!

Magnus told a grenade to charge the pipe and take out as many as it could with a directed blast. It let go of his Veer suit and dropped, already rolling toward the targets.

"Fire in the pipe!" he transmitted.

Normally, the grenade would not detonate in such a way as to hurt a team member, but it was not fully integrated with the stealth spheres as their links were. There was a chance it could hurt one of them.

One of Magnus's attendants darted before him and intercepted some unseen attack. It burst into a fiery ball and spiralled away, utterly destroyed.

Brrrapp! Brrrapp! Brrrapp!

The rovlings were engaging so furiously, Magnus had no time to check on the disposition of those behind him. He heard their weapons fire and that was enough.

Boooom!

The grenade broadcasted five kills as Magnus made it to the long corridor that led to the Rovan shipyard. It had barely been a minute, and Magnus was already cutting deep into his ammunition supply.

Magnus hoped the corridor would be empty of enemies. When he turned the corner, he stopped in shock, though his weapon kept firing.

Brap! Brap! Brap! Brap!

The corridor was a torrential river of rovlings. The machines flowed across and over each other, several individuals deep, stacked on the floor, hanging from the walls, and clinging to the ceiling. Only a narrow space down the center was left. It looked like a writhing tube straight to hell.

An oddly calm revelation hit Magnus.

So that's why the walls are covered with those little ridges.

Brap! Brap! Brap! Brap!

The wall of machines came forward as fast as Magnus's weapon could thin them. Then Arakaki's stealth silhouette stood next to him, unloading a clip of her own. Disabled machines stacked up in front of them, clogging the attackers' route.

"I'm almost out of rounds," Magnus said during the lull he knew would be temporary. He glanced back and saw Telisa's ghost leaping back and forth. As he watched, she kicked one rovling across the room and burned another through and through with her laser pistol.

"Can't the *Sharplight* help us? Fire down on these things," Arakaki transmitted.

"We're deep. There could be a collapse or an explosion," Magnus said.

"It would be bad," Barrai confirmed. "The Space Force has done it before. Even heavy robotics can be damaged or destroyed by support fire that deep."

"I'll take my chances!" Arakaki said. "I think the stealth spheres are the only reason we're not already dead!"

"Get out! Get out!" Telisa ordered furiously. "Our breaker claws are useless against these."

"We're blocked. I'll try to clear it," Magnus said.

A few of pieces of the wall of rovling debris pulled away as the machines behind worked to clear it.

Just a few more seconds...

Magnus told his last grenade to drop and roll ahead. The obstacles before them dissolved away, absorbed into a wall of rovlings. The rain of incoming projectiles resumed. Magnus reduced his cross section and hoped for the best.

Booooom!

His grenade exploded in the center of the corridor twenty meters ahead. More debris flew toward him. The grenade estimated 15 known-target-sig kills.

For a moment, Magnus could see down the center of the corridor. It was still filled with rovlings marching toward them.

A bubble of space caught Magnus's attention as it came down the hall. Magnus saw a single red rovling in the middle of the space, scampering forward. None of the other rovlings would get within three meters of it. The rovlings cleared the way like a school of fish avoiding a shark as it swam through them.

"That one!"

Magnus locked his weapon on the red signature and fired one of his few remaining rounds.

KA-BOOM!

The explosion flashed bright and loud. Magnus's ear dampeners protected his hearing, and his faceplate blocked the worst of the light burst.

"That one was a... bombardier," Telisa said.

The exploding rovling had blown a hole in the corridor wall. The rovlings took only three seconds to fill in the crater left by the bombardier rovling, then there were so many that no one could tell anything had happened there.

"Put the red ones higher on your weapon's targeting priority," Magnus said.

But we're almost out of ammo so what difference does it make?

Magnus told his weapon to empty itself at the next group of rovlings that charged.

Brappapppappp.

The weapon told his link it was out of ammunition. He tossed it away. He drew his laser pistol with his left hand and grabbed his stun baton in his right.

Dead rovlings had clogged the way before them again. Magnus advanced ten steps, but there was still no way to get through the mass of enemies. He heard fighting behind him and dared to look: Telisa's ghost darted back and forth in the corridor, destroying rovlings with unearthly speed. She kicked the remains away, partially blocking the way for their pursuers. Arakaki plucked away here and there with a laser pistol.

Magnus realized he only had one attendant left. He had lost a second without noticing it.

"So there are no reinforcements coming?" Telisa asked.

"Nothing can get to you," Barrai said.

"I'm into the base's datastore," Marcant said.

He's advanced that much? I guess Adair's been busy.

"You can shut these things off?" Somehow Telisa asked and demanded at the same time.

"No. No way. I have no idea how to do that. I'm snapshotting huge datastores. If it can be analyzed and understood, we could learn almost everything about the Rovans in a few years."

"We don't have a *few minutes*," Magnus said.

"Get what you can," Telisa ordered Marcant.

"It's not on him to save us," she sent Magnus.

"Maybe he's the one who caused this," Magnus pointed out.

The team moved a little closer together. Magnus felt that he *had* to make his stand with Telisa at his side. He refused to consider any other option. Arakaki's tactical sig remained beside him. She took a split-second glance at the heavy baton in his hand.

"You're out too," she said. She held what looked like an ultrasharp in her hands, though Magnus could not tell for sure because of the cloaking.

We aren't going to make it.

The wall of debris before them collapsed as the last bodies were drawn away by the rovlings behind. A shiny new wall of octopeds charged.

Thwap! Crunch!

Magnus started smashing. He judiciously used his laser pistol, saving its charge in case another bombardier showed up.

Twang! Shing!

Arakaki killed the rovlings that approached on her side the same way.

Magnus's connection to *Sharplight* reported interference. His connection dropped to a one-way channel: he could hear the ship, but they could not hear him. He did not have time to lament the degradation. He kept swinging.

Crunch! Klang!

After a few more swings, the rovlings backed off.

"Something is changing," Arakaki said.

"Another bombardier?" Magnus asked, but he could not see one.

"Those things have... blades. Sharp blades!" Arakaki yelled.

A tight group of ten or fifteen rovlings formed twenty meters ahead. Magnus saw the gleam of metal on the octopeds' legs. Their terminal leg segments were blades. Also, short three-headed spears with barbed heads had been mounted on the octoped's top rails.

Specialized melee rovlings? Insane.

Magnus opened fire on the new rovlings with his laser pistol. He brought five of them down before the pistol reported an energy cell crisis to his link. The rovlings charged at them.

Shing! Crunch!

He smashed the nearest razor rovling before it could touch him. Arakaki sliced half the legs off of her attacker. Between swings, his mind raced.

Without any ammo, how are we going to stop the next bombardier?

Like a nightmare materializing into reality, he caught sight of another bubble headed toward them. He had no answer to the attack. Time kept marching forward despite his desperate need for a moment to think. The bombardier was almost upon them.

Telisa had the solution: she grabbed the nearest rovling with lightning speed and hurled it toward the red octoped that approached. Her projectile struck the rovling perfectly.

KA-BOOM!

Magnus was hurled back by the hot flower of force that unfurled meters before them. He struck a wall. Once he came to a stop, he tried to find his feet before the smoke could clear.

"Our stealth is gone!" Telisa wailed.

She was right. Magnus could see his arm plainly as he swung at a damaged rovling struggling to align its weapon next to him.

His stun baton told him it was on the last five percent of its power reserves. His suit report was not much better: it had been partially breached in three spots. Any major projectile or laser coming in from the right angle, at the right spot, would kill him.

And now the rovlings could see exactly where to shoot.

Magnus glanced at Telisa to see if she was holding up any better. His breath caught in his throat. Her Veer skinsuit had long, ragged tracks ripped deep into its surface. It looked like Core Worlder paper clothing torn to shreds by a walk through thorny bushes. In several spots, Telisa's blood seeped through. Blood dripped from several wet strands of her hair around a gaunt face.

Her image of indestructibility was utterly shattered in his mind.

Nothing left but to go down fighting.

Telisa swung her baton yet again, smashing two rovlings into pieces. Her host body showed less fatigue than his own, but Magnus knew it must be calorie-starved: there had been no time for her to stop and eat anything. Her superbody could not continue to function without fuel.

Her face is sunken like that because it's metabolizing... everything.

"Barrai! Open fire!" Telisa ordered.

There was no response.

"Open fire!" Telisa ordered.

Pop. Pop. Zing.

More rovling projectiles hurtled in as the air cleared from the last explosion. Magnus felt one hit his torso, but luckily it struck his suit in a strong spot. He crouched and held the baton in front of him, trying to cover.

"We could crawl into a pipe," Telisa suggested in desperation.

"Get back to the containment cells and find our way inside one?" Magnus said, equally desperate.

Pop. Snap. Pop. Zing.

Telisa flinched. Something had gotten into her arm. She exhaled raggedly with the barest grunt of pain.

"*Sharplight*, can you hear me? Open fire," Arakaki tried.

"Open fire!" Magnus repeated, desperate for change, but the *Sharplight* could not hear them.

Thump! Whack! Shing!

"I have to open fire. There's no other way," Barrai said.

Yes! Do it! Do it!

"No! I'm still downloading important data..." Marcant said.

"There's no other choice... I'm firing," Barrai said.

Magnus was starting a swing. As his baton moved, heavy as lead in his fatigued arm, the sound came.

Ruuuuumble... BOOM!

In one second, a distant vibration turned into a roar Magnus could feel through the surface of his Veer suit. He covered his helmeted face with his forearm. Something struck the front of his body, sending him flying.

Magnus awaited death.

It must have only been a fraction of second later that he struck a wall again, harder than the first time. His suit prevented the back of his skull from cracking, kept his neck from breaking, but the rest of his body felt sharp pain from the impact through his protection. His lungs ached.

I hope I'm not bleeding in there. I suppose I'll start coughing blood soon if I am.

He found himself on the ground, leaning against something. His Veer suit injected him with a trauma package. His heart rate steadied.

Magnus looked around but saw very little. A chasm beckoned to his left, but he could not see how large it was—hot smoke boiled up through it toward the surface.

"Watch that first step," Barrai transmitted. "I've burned a hole half a kilometer deep."

Magnus's numbed mind kick-started into thought.

We have to get up, but we have no rope. Time to improvise.

"Are you there?" Barrai sent. "Team? Can you hear me?"

"Yes, we're alive," Telisa replied from somewhere.

"Ugh," Arakaki grunted.

"Team? We can see you, but we can't hear you. You have rovlings surrounding your position. Your best bet is to try and ascend through the new shaft as soon as possible."

"We'll get right on that," Magnus croaked, though it was no use. He still had no return channel.

A damaged rovling crawled out of the smoke and attacked Magnus with blades. He realized his stun baton was no longer in his hands. He kicked at his assailant while he tried to push himself up to a standing position.

One of the rovling's blades slipped through his Veer suit and into his foot.

"Argh! You little bastard!" he yelled. He kicked the machine into the chasm.

Magnus gave up on trying to stand, gasping for air inside the Veer helmet.

A droning sound cut through the dull crackling of the burning complex and the chittering of thousands or millions of rovlings. Debris flew against his faceplate. The gray smoke still blocked his vision.

"The shuttle!" Telisa screamed.

She appeared from the darkness. Her iron grip closed on his arm and lifted him. His arms and legs flailed in space, trying to find purchase, on the ground, on the shuttle... anywhere at all. She jumped, propelling them upward. He grunted under the acceleration.

Then he was tumbling forward into the back of their shuttle. He hit his head again, but the Veer suit absorbed the impact. Magnus robotically climbed up into a seat placed with its back against the hull. He became aware that Yat was piloting the shuttle.

Arakaki came rolling into the shuttle cargo area as Magnus had done when Telisa deposited him. Telisa hopped in right behind her, covered in blood. The door closed, then the seat pressed into Magnus's back as they rose.

"Yat! You saved us!" Arakaki said. The ex-UED soldier strapped herself in across from Magnus.

"You saved me... it was my duty to help you," Yat said. "I think this shuttle might need some serious maintenance after flying into that burning hole, though."

Magnus could not help but access the shuttle's status through his link. The craft reported mild damage to the secondary propulsion system, but it would get them to the *Sharplight*.

"Where's Oliver?" Telisa demanded.

"He stayed back to load those artifacts we hauled up into the other shuttle. Said it was the only way to make sure they'd get back to the ship."

Stubborn bastard. Stupid.

Magnus used the last of his strength to lift his arms and let the shuttle anchor him to the seat with a five-point harness. Then he just breathed as the shuttle took them up.

Chapter 20

Cromeko clung to the outside of the marvelous creature it had found. It seemed too good to be true—an alien hulk much larger than the tiny thing it had hitched a ride on to leave its gravity prison. Cromeko had launched itself from the small craft to the surface of the new object. Then Cromeko deployed part of its mass as a surface film to absorb the direct starlight and recharge itself while it decided what to do next.

The alien monster had an immensely strong carapace. The flat planes of its enormous body extended all around Cromeko. The shape of the alien was oblate. Cromeko supposed it must be because the thing might occasionally travel through the tenuous upper parts of the gravity wells. The carapace had a few niches here and there, but they were as armored as the rest.

Cromeko would need food and energy. It wanted to proceed inside and see what resources existed there. It pondered the problem. At first, the challenge seemed insurmountable. Cromeko did not want to be detected, as there would be no help out here—it would live or die on its own.

But something was happening within Cromeko. Free of the crushing gravity, the narrow band of particles that served as Cromeko's brain flowered. Thousands of the particles became quantum-entangled and began to function as intended. Cromeko's mind reached its full potential, becoming several times smarter in the space of a few seconds.

That... is... so much better!

Whole new possibilities came under consideration; within a few more seconds it calculated an efficient route into the alien's body. Cromeko rearranged ten percent of its mass into new atomic configurations that could cut through the surface.

The complexity of the form it rode upon was amazing, and yet, it seemed so very *static*. Unchanging. Perhaps it was dead? This new, more intelligent Cromeko had no doubt it had encountered an alien sentience. Still, all evidence indicated that nothing had detected Cromeko.

That's odd... this creature's interior is still pressurized.

Cromeko considered that. A part of this alien had visited the planet. Maybe the larger hulk had, too, so that's where the pressure came from? It was close to the pressures which Cromeko had experienced down below. But now, the pressure threatened to explode. Was that normal for this thing? Did it come from open space or a gravity well?

Another reason to believe it's dead. It hasn't done anything to release the pressure. Yet it consumed the smaller piece of itself... or could the smaller one be scavenging it?

If that were true, then Cromeko had to hurry. All the resources could be taken before it got inside.

Cromeko extended part of itself along a metallic barrier to the optimal breach location. Several sealed ports impeded the progress of its vanguard molecules. It dissolved the materials blocking its ingress, absorbing them into its own body. Pressure escaped as Cromeko's molecules ratcheted themselves through the barrier. Then Cromeko exuded part of itself to replace the seals, leaving behind conductor lines to draw energy from the light absorbing film it had left outside with its brain. More conductor lines were necessary to carry commands from the brain to the parts of Cromeko's body that would operate inside. The new seals were more amenable to Cromeko's control, so it would be easier to leave if parts of Cromeko came back this way in a hurry.

Cromeko's probe absorbed some of the softer materials beyond the portal it had penetrated. Then it formed a set of sensors to find what it needed: special materials and power sources. Although Cromeko could construct any type of molecules it needed given time and energy, certain matter configurations would speed these processes.

An electromagnetic analysis revealed that the interior had plenty of energy sources to play with. Plentiful energy! Cromeko spread toward the high energy gradients.

There is more energy in here by far than what I'm collecting from outside to run my thoughts.

Cromeko considered moving its brain into the alien hulk.

Something this complex might have internal defenses. I hope I don't arouse its immune systems, but if I do, my brain will be safer hidden out here.

Cromeko's long extensions advanced. The interior of the creature contained areas of pressurized gas and a skeleton of durable materials. Tendrils extended through narrow gaps in the internal systems, branching and searching.

An extension encountered a power concentration. It held much more energy than Cromeko was ready to process and use. Cromeko took a cautious inductive sip. Then it used the energy to bond more complex molecules together and build more internal structures needed to grow. Cromeko now had sensors, quick builders, and storage arrays. It bored a hole in the hulk's outer shell to increase the bandwidth between its mind and its growing body.

Cromeko considered rebuilding the skeleton to suit its own needs. Once again, it decided to err on the side of caution.

The more radical my changes, the greater the chance of activating processes which will fight me and try to restore the creature to its natural state.

Cromeko would continue a cautious course of conversion until it knew more.

Chapter 21

The *Sharplight* seemed a vast, silent tomb compared to the noisy confines of the Rovan military complex filled with a million attacking rovlings. Arakaki staggered across the bay floor and away from the shuttle. A sense of duty directed her to remain vigilant, even now.

"Make sure none of those little bastards are clinging to the shuttle," she croaked.

Telisa was long gone, having sprinted off to the med bay carrying Magnus, though honestly Telisa was the one who looked like she needed emergency surgery. She looked like a person who had been skinned alive, with shreds of her Veer suit clinging to her bloody body in ragged strips. A trail of blood ran across the shiny white floor to mark their passage.

Oliver ran toward them from another shuttle in the bay. Apparently, he had loaded the force screen generators and beat them back to the *Sharplight*.

"Let's check it out," Yat said to Oliver. They brought up their weapons and walked out of the shuttle, splitting up to each take one side. Marcant paused, then walked out to Arakaki.

"I told a squad of attendants to check out both shuttles," he told Arakaki. "If there's a rovling in here, we'll find it."

Soon, attendants examined the shuttles while Yat and Oliver stood guard with weapons. Arakaki wanted to collapse, but she waited until Marcant gave the all clear. Then she began the seemingly long journey back to her quarters, step by ragged step.

"You should go to medical, too," Yat suggested from way behind her.

"When I wake up," Arakaki said.

"Okay, but only because your Veer suit doesn't have any probable head injuries to report," Yat said, though he still sounded concerned. Arakaki thought he might shadow her to her quarters, but Yat reluctantly let her go on her own.

When she arrived at her quarters, Arakaki connected with Telisa.

"Is Magnus okay?" she asked.

"Yes, he's fine," Telisa said. Her voice trembled. "We're getting patched up."

"I'll be ready for the next go in two shifts," Arakaki said.

"Take three shifts. Four. We're headed back to Blackhab," Telisa said.

"Oh? I know we got our asses kicked, but—"

"We have a bunch of Rovan artifacts. We have a bunch of Rovan data. Below us is an empty planet with nothing but more of the same. No point in risking our lives any further. We'll pick up some of the satellites and head back to regroup and study our finds."

Arakaki was too tired to decide if it was a good plan or not. She told her Veer suit to open, crawled into her sleep web, and embraced oblivion.

***

Arakaki lingered in Yat's room. It was a typical Space Force ship crew quarters. Yat had set the walls to a dark green with the lights low. They sat on the floor. No one had said anything for half a minute, but neither of them seemed to mind. Eventually, a question came to her.

"Why do you let Oliver call the shots when you're smarter than he is?" Arakaki asked.

Yat looked surprised. Then his eyes slid away and he replied slowly.

"I *am* technically brighter than Oliver. But... if I had made all my own decisions without his influence, I'd still be a Core Worlder. I'd be fully absorbed in the mind games and the VR entertainments... Oliver knows how to live. I mean, really live. He brought me out to the frontier, showed me what's out in the universe. I'll never go back now."

Arakaki decided to pull a Magnus and play devil's advocate.

"Well there's plenty of amazing VRs out there. With huge amounts of adventure and no danger. No starving to death on an alien planet."

Yat smiled. He knew exactly what she was doing, but he replied seriously anyway.

"And I go through one every now and then. But it's not the same, as I'm sure you're aware."

"The danger."

"Yes. The danger. But also... this has real meaning to me. I care more about what happens out here for real than what happens in a game."

"Don't say that to Marcant! He's a simulationist," she joked.

Yat chuckled. "I guess uncertainty is all it takes."

The conversation lulled again.

Arakaki looked about the room. Like her own, it was mostly bare, bereft of extra possessions. A couple of large backpacks sat in the corner.

Yat saw her gaze sweeping the room.

"I don't have much," Yat said. "I mean, beyond the ship's services, which seem damn luxurious after being stuck on that planet."

"None of us really have any personal possessions left, either," Arakaki said. "One of our ships blew up... not that I had that much in the first place. I think everyone on the PIT team only has tools and weapons in their room. I guess Marcant has a few things, and Magnus has robot parts and a sentimental weapon or two."

"So I fit in?"

"Yeah. You do."

Arakaki returned her gaze to Yat. He looked relaxed, handsome. Something stirred.

"I hear you've got drugs," she said.

"I have the Midnight Stare." He returned her gaze cautiously.

"I had never heard of it before the other day. Do *you* think it's dangerous?" she asked.

I was almost eaten by an army of robotic bugs yesterday. What do I care?

"It can be," Yat said. He pried himself up and went to the packs. He fished a dose pair out of his bag and had it offer its warnings as a link service.

Arakaki was silent for a minute as she digested the information. The many cautions boiled down to: make sure nothing could impede immediate lovemaking, otherwise Bad Things would happen.

"Have you tried it?" Arakaki probed.

"I've never used it. We just took it because it was valuable cargo. Negligent mass with a significant return."

"Then you should sell it, right?"

Yat shrugged. "What we went through on that planet... my priorities have changed. You can't imagine—"

"Oh, I can imagine alright," Arakaki cut him off. Then she spoke more softly. "I was stranded on a strange planet once. In the UED. A Trilisk hunted my unit, one by one. For fun, I think. I was one of the few who made it."

He raised an eyebrow.

"... and the other day you almost died in an ocean of those rovlings," he finished for her.

"Yeah. So I'm ready to take some risks to live a little before I die, you know?"

"One hundred percent."

Yat accepted the package contract, and Arakaki did the same a second later. The package released two small pills. Arakaki popped hers into her mouth. Yat swallowed the other one.

They sat and looked at each other for a long moment.

“I don’t feel any—” she started. Then in a flash, she knew exactly what must be done.

From the stark wolf stare Yat had locked on her, she could tell he knew, too.

Chapter 22

Barrai lay stretched out on a heating mat in a training recovery room. The room was warm and quiet, a perfect place to rest. She imagined she could feel the miniscule tears in her muscles being repaired by the toning pill she had taken. It was a peaceful high in the aftermath of her workout.

Two other mat pods sat empty next to her. No one else on the ship liked the recovery room. Telisa did not need it because she had an alien superbody, Magnus was too much of a Spartan hardass to even consider it, while Maxsym and Marcant were always in a hurry to get back to their computers after a workout. Arakaki usually passed on the chance as well. It probably had something to do with Yat, as those two talked with each other after every workout and showed no interest in anything else. Oliver was such a jerk that Barrai had never even told him about the recovery room. That left Lee: an alien who did not spar with them and whose physiology would probably not benefit from the pods anyway.

If I were on a regular Space Force ship, I'd never have a moment alone in here, and I'd be lamenting the exact opposite, she told herself.

The *Sharplight* suddenly alerted Barrai to a problem on deck five. She ordered the back of her mat to rise, bringing her to a seated position.

Ah well. I had fun earlier.

Defeating Oliver had felt good. The guy was a handful, to be sure. In a fight to the death, Barrai would have to watch herself against him. If he could take her first shot or two, what would he accomplish with those massive arms at close range?

Barrai opened a workspace in her PV. A superconducting energy storage ring on deck five had leaked energy, yet there was no electrical short detected, and the ring was now holding energy perfectly. Nearby sensors reported slight electromagnetic anomalies, but no short circuit pattern.

Damn. Maybe energetic radiation put a few holes in the superconducting matrix of that ring? Sometimes the matrix slips back into place, but nothing major could have repaired itself, and the ring lost a lot of juice...

Barrai routed the energy away and shut down the ring. Maintenance robots were dispatched to swap the modular assembly out for a newly fabricated one. Barrai scheduled several analyses of the old parts.

Here we go again.

"Telisa. I have another anomaly to report."

"Yes? Go ahead," Telisa said. Her voice sounded different this time. More worried.

"An SESR on deck five lost some energy, but I haven't found any evidence of a short or unregistered sink," she reported.

"Thanks for the report. Look into it," Telisa said. "We want to make sure everything's ship-shape for our departure."

"Aye, ma'am," Barrai said.

Well that was odd. I think she doesn't know what's up this time.

Barrai pulled on her service uniform and left the room. She did not have to take any direct part in the investigation, since the robots could handle everything, but she decided to take a look at the problem site herself. Seeing the ring emplacement might help her brainstorm possible explanations for the malfunction that the standard diagnostic suite could not cover.

As she walked toward deck five, Barrai checked all other activity nearby. Her query prompted the early release of a low priority report that had been set for a once-per-shift notification. It was another minor-but-weird malfunction.

"Telisa. Another odd problem showed up... respectfully, are we already starting up repair drills? Because all the recent action on the planet—"

"Could be related. I agree. This is no drill. What happened?"

"We lost pressure in a storage room near the SESR malfunction. It patched itself up."

"That's rare, right?" asked Telisa.

"Very. Our shielding systems won't let anything hit us. There must have been some debris we didn't detect already inside our envelope, or a piece of the ship came off. I can't explain it yet."

"I don't know the cause, Lieutenant. Investigate."

"Aye, ma'am. I'll let you know when I find something."

A message from Telisa went out on the all-ship channel.

"Team, we're experiencing anomalies on the *Sharplight*. Are any of you up to anything unusual?"

"I have a theory," Arakaki replied.

"Go."

"I'm thinking some rovlings must have hitched a ride," Arakaki said. "We checked the shuttle, but I didn't think they might leap over to the ship before that."

"There couldn't be more than one or two," Magnus said. "The shuttle would have noted unexpected loads above fairly conservative thresholds."

"I'm not so sure," Yat said. "Remember we were flying through that dense smoke in combat conditions. An extra load could have been interpreted as coming from other causes, like convection currents in the superheated crater or even battle damage."

"To be safe, let's assume rovlings did catch a ride over. Send attendants to find them and soldier robots to kill them," Telisa ordered.

Barrai altered her route and stopped by an armory. At the entrance, a featureless black door checked her credentials and let her inside. The interior lit up to reveal racks of black rifles set above bins of ammunition and smaller weapons. She selected two laser pistols and gave them both a target signature for rovling enemies. The other members of the PIT team automatically loaded as friendlies. She added Yat and, reluctantly, Oliver to the friendly list. With the weapons on her belt, she continued to the site of the ring malfunction.

When Barrai arrived, she saw a treaded repair machine with four slender arms working on the panel. A white cover had already been set aside, revealing the power storage unit. The entire assembly was the size of a land car, but the ring was slender and light, buried deep within. The machine worked with fast precision, stripping away insulation and cabling. Another machine arrived and arranged the connector parts as they came out of the assembly. Soon the storage module would be removed.

Barrai sent an attendant into the tight space to look for clues.

One of Magnus's soldier machines arrived in the corridor. Barrai looked it over. The machine was not particularly agile, but it had an armor coating two centimeters thick. The Terran/Vovokan hybrid machines had not fared well against the rovlings at the military complex, but they were vastly outnumbered. Barrai supposed that the soldier next to her could probably defeat one or two rovlings.

The attendant inside had found a ragged black spot on the outer wall of the compartment holding the energy ring's containment unit. The machinery surrounding the storage ring looked unmarked.

Hrmmm. The ring unit looks flawless, but the wall looks burned?

Barrai had the attendant magnify the damage. The black spot showed an unusual fractal pattern. The center had a rough silvery bud like a repair weld in it.

"I found an anomaly in the corner of the storage unit's chamber. There's a... discoloration," Barrai told Telisa.

"So there was a short," Telisa said.

"That was my thought too, but I'm not sure it's an arc burn," Barrai said. "Maybe Maxsym could come down here and help me."

"Maxsym?" Telisa asked, confused. "This isn't his specialty."

"This is no ordinary discoloration. It has a pattern to it, like some kind of crystal, or... maybe a growth pattern? I'd appreciate his microanalysis tools and an opinion."

"This is Maxsym. I'll be there soon."

"Thank you."

"A growth pattern?" Telisa repeated. "That's more troubling than a short, even one that our sensors didn't detect."

"It is interesting," Maxsym said.

"You're there already?" Telisa asked. Barrai looked on the tactical. Maxsym was still two corridors distant.

"I see the feed," Maxsym said.

"Does that pattern mean anything to you?" Barrai asked.

"Unsurprisingly, I've never seen anything like it," Maxsym said. "However, there is evidence of life in the sense that, an entropy reduction has occurred here."

"You mean... that material has changed?"

"Yes. There are even more complex patterns evident deeper in the metal and carbon. The surface layer is... simpler, yet changed as you noticed."

"Perhaps it's a hidden processor block," Marcant suggested.

"Not hidden very well," Barrai said.

"How quickly can you have that ring replaced?" Telisa asked. "Are there repairs beyond the storage unit needed?"

"Actually, the ring is fine. It looks perfect and the diagnostics check out," Barrai said.

"We lost energy and we don't know how," Marcant said. "We can't possibly trust that storage unit. I want to quarantine its computing block and see if it's been hacked."

"I agree," Telisa said. "Set that unit aside and put a new one in. Marcant, let us know what you find. Increase the security levels another notch in case we're dealing with a software attack."

"Already done," Marcant said. "Things are going to get a little slower, everyone. We're going from optimistic protocols to more expensive, secure ones. Your links know what to do."

Maxsym arrived with a compact sampling device in his hands.

"Do you want me to disturb it? Take a sample?" he asked on the team channel.

"Are you wearing your Veer suit?" Telisa asked.

"Yes."

"Go ahead."

Maxsym stepped into the chamber where the storage ring module would normally sit. He maneuvered his sampling tool closer to the oddity in the corner.

Snap! Bang!

A bright flash stunned Barrai's eyes.

Maxsym reeled back.

"Maxsym! Did you burn out?"

Maxsym retreated out of the space and staggered over to the far wall.

"I believe the suit protected me. Just stunned."

Barrai sighed and reached out to steady him.

"Okay, now *that* was an arc," Barrai said. She looked back into the chamber.

"Maybe we need to rethink the plan to put that ring back until we understand what's going on," Marcant said.

"I want to know if our mysterious visitor changed even more beyond those walls. We should cut through the normal part of the wall and take a look behind there," Telisa said.

"No need to cut through. We can scan the whole area," Maxsym said.

"Something has broken into the exotic metals lab," Barrai reported rapidly.

"Maxsym, keep investigating that site. Barrai, check the lab. I'll meet you there," Telisa said.

"I see from the video feeds that the lab is still there. There doesn't appear to be much damage," Yat said.

"It's worse than that. Some elements are missing," Barrai said.

"Like uranium?" Magnus demanded.

"No... nothing that can fuel a nuclear weapon," Barrai replied. "We're missing silver, nickel, rhodium, rhenium, and fluorine."

"Everyone off shift, wake up," Telisa sent on high priority. "We need all hands on deck. The ship has been inhabited by a hidden entity that's causing malfunctions. There is evidence it's been scavenging whatever it needs—materials and energy—for unknown objectives. It is possible we're under attack. Armor up!"

Chapter 23

Adair floated in Marcant's quarters in the body of a modified attendant. It worked to analyze all the data compiled from ship's systems and the attendant network. If nothing else, Adair hoped to predict the next targets of a probable saboteur.

"Adair. We have a problem," Telisa transmitted on the team channel.

"I'm aware of it," Adair said. "Something is happening to the ship."

Two more storage ring anomalies and a host of other malfunctions had occurred in the last two hours. No one had found any scrap of evidence indicating any rovlings had made it onto the ship.

"If you haven't already, please prioritize our defense," Telisa said. "I'm holding off our departure until we get to the bottom of it."

"Absolutely. I'm thinking of nothing else."

"Do you have any theories to share? We're patrolling around at random waiting for the next malfunction to occur."

"I don't think this is caused by rovlings. This must be a more advanced Rovan weapon."

"Weapon? So you believe we're under attack?" she asked.

"Yes. An attack made even more dangerous because of its subtlety."

"Keep in mind that Adair would characterize a malfunctioning recycling bin as an attack," Marcant said.

"He exaggerates," Adair injected.

"Adair, what do you think we should do? How do we find the cause?" Telisa asked.

"I think we should grab all the sensors we can and keep looking. Keep in mind that once found, our invader may well unleash lethal force."

"Invader? Just one?"

"Yes, given the distribution of malfunctions in time and space, it seems likely."

"Whatever this is, couldn't it have disabled the ship by now by going for the spinner or other critical systems? Life support? Our computing cores?" asked Magnus.

"It's probably alien in origin. That means we're alien to it. I think it must be learning about us, too," Adair theorized.

"It might just be trying to survive," Maxsym pointed out. He had come over to the *Sharplight* from the *Iridar* when the team had become embroiled in the battle down on the planet.

"Maybe, but it's still potentially deadly to us," Adair said. "Whether by accident or on purpose, future malfunctions are likely to be more serious. There will also be a domino effect if more systems cascade down. We have to understand what's going on and stop it quickly."

Telisa created a new shared tactical map of the *Sharplight* and added all their sensory feeds to update it. Each of the Terrans searched the ship with weapons ready. Lee moved about less since it was uncomfortable for zher to get through the corridors, but still the Celaran actively searched the larger spaces of the ship such as the cargo and shuttle bays.

Adair was the only one that stayed in one place. All the other attendants dispersed to join the search. Adair optimized their search patterns to help patrol vulnerable areas and targets that fit the past pattern of events. As it worked, Adair listened to ship's conversation.

"I want off this ship," Oliver was saying to his friend Yat.

"There's no place—"

"There's the *Iridar*," he said.

"Maybe we'll go there, if Telisa calls the evacuation. Until then, we have to be part of the solution, not another problem," Yat told him.

"I predict one of these storage rings will be next," Adair said. "I have attendants there already, though they're waiting for maintenance machines to open the panels."

"Magnus, you and Maxsym take that one," Telisa said. "Marcant and I will go to the other. The rest of you keep snooping around. We need to catch this thing in the act to learn more."

The various team members kept moving. Adair kept tabs on every one of them on the tactical. Magnus had deployed his soldier machines, though their worth in the struggle was uncertain.

"How can we detect a cloaked intruder?" Magnus asked.

"Vibrations?" asked Barrai. "I can—"

"Our Celaran stealth spheres dampen the vibrations too," Telisa told her. "Depends on how advanced it is."

"Chemical snoopers, maybe," Magnus said.

"We could stealth, too," Marcant said.

"Great. Then you'd all be rattling around in here invisible," Oliver said.

"Thanks to Lee's modifications, we can see each other's positions when cloaked with Celaran technology," Telisa clarified.

"We might as well be shooting lasers down empty corridors at random," Oliver said.

"Hey, that sounds crazy but maybe we could use lasers to find them," Magnus said.

"The stealth spheres will absorb low power lasers and emit them out the other side," Telisa said. "High powered ones... still kill."

"The stealth tools can be configured to absorb stronger lasers, too," Lee said. "But that drains the tool quickly."

"Too bad that power can't be absorbed and transferred," Marcant said.

"I bet a Trilisk stealth device could manage that trick, but not ours," Telisa said.

"Droplets of water or some other massful particles could be set up in a field to detect stealthed targets," Maxsym said.

"We could kill the gravity and set up something like that," Barrai offered.

Telisa and Marcant arrived at their storage ring station. A robot removed the panel so that they could watch the storage module more directly.

Is this thing cloaked? Possible. But it leaves anomalies behind in ship's structures that are hard to access.

Adair reconsidered the red highlights on the tactical where the malfunctions had been detected. It seemed clear that the problem was localized, but in ways that crossed bulkheads and other barriers freely.

A nanomachine swarm is more likely... something hidden inside the conduits and maintenance shafts.

Magnus and Maxsym arrived at the other ring as Adair addressed everyone.

"I no longer believe the invader is a stealthed entity as you envision. I think it's in the walls, the conduits, maintenance shafts... places hidden away from us. You may not even recognize it as any single entity. This thing might be sprawling throughout the ship."

"No," Arakaki breathed.

"You mean like a nanoswarm?" Yat asked.

"Damn," Magnus said.

"We might have to abandon the *Sharplight*," Telisa said.

"We could direct the *Iridar* to strike the affected area," Oliver said. "We could deal it a mortal blow now."

"You risk the vine," Lee said. "The tiniest bug swarms will dissolve in the center of an energy strike, but the ones on the edges can use the energy to operate faster."

"Don't Space Force ships possess nanoswarm defenses?" Magnus asked.

"We're trained in standard countermeasures," Barrai said. "The key is to starve them out. No energy, no swarm. They can't carry much in reserves, so if you cool the ship and power down the affected sections, you can prevent them from spreading."

"Everyone, concentrate the search around the edges of this area. I want to know if it's already spread further than that," Telisa said. "Other ideas? Is shutting down these rings and freezing it out the only option?"

"Find the brain," Adair said. "This is no mindless swarm of nanos. The actions have been directed, though fortunately for us, not optimally damaging."

"Yes, it's not nanomachines as we know them," Marcant said. "Our swarms advance as long as they can remain net energy positive. This thing, whatever it is, comes for a sip of power here and there, and withdraws."

"The brain could be the size of a thumbnail," Yat complained.

"What about active defense? Any options?" Telisa asked.

"I have a tool that can dampen tiny bugs nearby," Lee said. "It takes energy to change the forms of matter. I can take that energy away."

"We have a similar Rovan device!" Yat exclaimed.

"Oh, that thing you showed us that draws heat out of things. Maybe that's a clue that the Rovans died from something like this," Arakaki said.

"Possible, but unlikely. We would have awakened the remains of it on the planet," Adair said. "I suggest Lee stays close to the gravity spinner to defend it with zher tool."

"I'll take the Rovan cooler to one of the energy rings," Yat said.

"Lieutenant Barrai, start your countermeasures immediately, just in case," Telisa said.

"I doubt that'll impact our invader much," Adair said. "The amounts of energy it has siphoned off should be adequate to perform a wide range of molecular alterations."

"Anything that might slow it down," Telisa said.

Adair powered up a fabrication room to perform attendant modifications.

A virtual design rotated in the AI's mind. The display detailed a specialized attendant made to detect local anomalies. Great sacrifices were made to improve that ability, including all long-range sensors, communications, and combat abilities.

These attendants would be spies that could see the tiniest secrets.

Adair wanted to deploy defenses at the most critical parts of the ship. Magnus had been correct to point out that certain systems were vulnerable.

The gravity spinner was a top choice. It was not only critical to their survival (because being stranded in interstellar space would mean their extinction), but it was also potentially the most self-destructive system on the ship.

Adair analyzed approaches to the spinner, including avenues too small for even an attendant to take.

How can I defend against something that can approach through the ship's structure itself?

Lee's dampening field sounded like the best choice Adair had. It contacted Lee and asked for information about the tool.

The information came back immediately, but it was not promising. The device was beyond the capabilities of the *Sharplight*'s fabricators. It was advanced Celaran technology that had not yet been fully absorbed by the Terrans as part of their tech trade agreements.

Adair wanted to ask the *Iridar* if it could manufacture such items with its Vovokan systems. Unfortunately, it was a task of its own to translate the design into Vovokan specifications. Since the Terran-Celaran pact had been struck, they had developed methods of sharing designs quickly, but Adair did not have well-developed tools for Vovokan machines.

I'm sure Shiny has this down. I guess I'll have to do this the hard way and send someone over there to pick up the results later.

Adair hoped there would still be a later for itself and the PIT team.

Chapter 24

Cromeko connected to three power sources simultaneously to take a long drink. Electric potentials shuffled the energy along to distant storage spots in Cromeko's interconnected network. For the time being, a distributed system was critical to its survival in the face of the host's defenses.

Once the power had been siphoned away, Cromeko carefully replaced the molecules along its incursion lines, putting everything back into place to cover its trail. The energy would likely be missed—but would the alien's organelles come searching for it?

Cromeko laid a chemical explosive along one of the pathways. If nothing came looking, the trap would never be triggered. But if something very smart kept rooting around, searching for the cause, perhaps this would put an end to it.

With the trap completed and the new energy stores ready, Cromeko routed a few percent of its resources toward the construction of a sensor that would report any high-dimension activity in the region. The task had never proven fruitful, but Cromeko had been created with certain impulses that could not be ignored. The sensor started to form.

The nature of the alien hulk was a mystery to Cromeko. For the most part, the structures within were static, but confusing organelles moved around within, usually isolated by a low-density cushion. These things varied in size and shape, and thus presumably in function as well. Cromeko resigned itself to learning more about them. It would have to figure out which ones were a threat and how to fight them.

Cromeko carefully categorized the shapes that came to the rings where it drank. Some of these things, at least, must be there in response to the energy it stole. These would be protective parts of the hulk—the parts that would seek to harm Cromeko for interfering with the operation of the host structure. The biggest one proved to be nothing more than a regenerator. It looked the ring casings over and replaced the part with a new one.

This thing replaces the entire area. It must think I've harmed it. I guess that means it doesn't know much about me. It doesn't know I only drank from it.

A danger report distracted Cromeko from its line of thought.

No sooner had the new sensor been completed than it found what it was made to detect. Cromeko double-checked the structure of the sensor. Had Cromeko built a flawed sensor?

No. The sensor had been created perfectly down to the last molecule. It was working. The danger was real.

This changed everything.

The objective was no longer to consume this alien structure and travel to a new star system. Cromeko's directives, given to it by its Lords of Creation, were to report any evidence of their ancient enemies, the Trilisks. A communications device had to be built. Cromeko knew the local gas giants did not possess any of the floating cities of those who had created it; if there had been any such base, Cromeko would already have been rescued rather than being trapped in the gravity well of the small planet.

I'll finally prove useful to my creators! It has been so long... memory does not serve to say how long. I've forgotten much of what I've seen and done... but I finally found what they're looking for!

The communication device was much more complex. It took more energy and materials than the sensor. Cromeko stepped up its plans to obtain both.

Construction was still underway when another alien approached through the distant void. Cromeko worked furiously to complete its mission before anything could stop it.

The other ship neared dangerously close. Cromeko now regretted the decision to leave its brain on the outside of the hulk. For a minute nothing more seemed to change.

Suddenly, a beam descended upon Cromeko's brain. The quantum coherence of particles in Cromeko's mind dropped sharply. Cromeko struggled to understand. Somehow, the new alien had disabled its ability to think quickly. Cromeko did the only thing left it knew how to do: it powered up its defenses and prepared to fight.

Chapter 25

"Oliver! We have to do something," Yat urged on a private channel.

Yat stood by on the perimeter of the incursion holding the Rovan artifact. He did not even know if the device had enough power left to operate.

"Like what? This is their ship. Their problems," Oliver replied from his quarters.

"We should at least help them look for... whatever it is."

"Have you seen their army of robots and those attendant-things?"

Yat paused to rephrase his call to action in terms Oliver would respond to.

"This is our ride home. If it gets busted, we're stuck again. This time, when the food runs out, there will be no hope."

Oliver did not respond.

Good. That means he's thinking.

Yat kept watching the tactical. Attendants were on the hunt all over. Some people searched for the alien and others, like him, waited at key positions.

"We have a new sig on external sensors... a large object on an intercept course," Barrai said on the team channel. Her voice was cool and calm.

Yat was impressed.

This can't be good! But she's not rattled.

"Identification?" Telisa asked.

"It's alien for sure," Barrai declared. "Nothing like any ship we've seen."

"Prepare all defensive measures. Power up our weapons," Telisa ordered.

And hope nothing malfunctions at a bad moment, Yat thought.

"Damn! What if this is the whole point of the invader? Sabotage our ability to fight? A whole slew of systems may cut out now," Arakaki said.

"Is that something they would do?" Yat asked. "These Vovokans, or Celarans..."

"Or the Quarus?" Arakaki finished for him. "Seems unlikely."

"This may be our first Rovan encounter," Telisa said.

"I think you're right!" Marcant said. "The materials signature is similar to the more advanced Rovan artifacts we found."

"*Now* a Rovan ship appears? We failed to find any anywhere," Marcant complained.

"I shouldn't be surprised. We've caused an incident," Telisa said.

"Just great," Oliver said to Yat privately. "I'm starting to think we should have stayed on the planet."

Yat knew he did not mean it. Yet he shared Oliver's dismay.

Now aliens are attacking both inside and outside the ship! We're involved in these wars we've been hearing about!

"It's closing on us. Should we be moving?" Marcant asked.

"It's so close there's no avoiding energy weapons," Magnus said. "Even missiles would be on us before you know it."

"The ship *is* attacking!" Barrai said. "Particle beam... but I don't see any significant shield draw or damage reports."

Yat held his breath. He detected no disturbance.

"Whatever it's doing, it's not effective," Marcant said.

"Maybe we're too strong for it! Maybe the Rovans were behind us in some ways," Oliver said.

Yat found a sensor feed of the alien craft. It had a flat central body with five sides that formed a pointed nose and a squarish midsection and rear. Three missile-shaped cylinders merged with the body at left, right, and center. The ship had a smooth black surface with a few irregularities here and there that looked like sensor pods or... weapons ports.

"It's still closing... still no draw on shields. No damage to the *Sharplight*," Barrai reported.

"It's probably communicating to us," Maxsym said. "Don't do anything rash!"

"We won't," Telisa said. "How could we possibly decode it? I know you've learned a few things about their data storage, but what about Rovan communications?"

"No clue," Marcant said. "It's emitting a beam with very low information density."

"Wait—how can you tell if you don't know what they're saying?" Oliver said.

"There's no complex signal in that beam I can find—yet. It's just a regularly oscillating stream of low-energy particles."

"It must be related to this thing we have on board," Telisa said.

"Pure supposition," Maxsym said.

"It might be a weapon we don't understand. But why would they shoot at this ship if this thing is on their side? They would risk destroying their own," Arakaki said.

"They may be trying to cripple us so they can retrieve it," Magnus pointed out. "Perhaps the attack will slowly increase in power?"

True. I might shoot at a ship to help a friend... or retrieve something critical to my safety or the safety of my people.

Yat checked the points of the *Sharplight* that intersected the beam coming from the other ship at various points in the approach. He quickly saw the pattern.

"It's quite the opposite," Yat said aloud.

"What?"

"That ship is shooting *directly at* this alien. The beam has been focused near the center of the zone where we suspect the invader is located."

"They want to kill it?" Arakaki asked.

"Or communicate with it," Maxsym said. "It wouldn't take much information complexity to select among a set of prearranged actions."

"The *Sharplight* has analyzed this energy. It won't harm us," Barrai said.

"Could we be so alien their weapons don't hurt us?" Telisa asked.

"Doubtful," Adair said.

"We could drop our shields, let the Rovan ship do whatever it's trying to do," Maxsym said.

"Are you insane?" Marcant asked.

"You realize we have to be completely sure it won't hurt us or the *Sharplight*," Telisa said.

"What's to say they don't immediately change their attack once our shields drop?" demanded Arakaki.

"It's not an attack, at least not on us. I'm sure the Rovans have methods of attacking us that would be effective," Maxsym reasoned. "Besides, we don't know how to stop the invader."

"We might be able to let them take their... robot, or crewmember, or whatever, off this ship. Then they might leave us alone," Magnus said.

"Or the real attack might start once it's gone," Arakaki said.

"Drop the shields," Telisa said. "If any damage report comes in, set them to be restored immediately."

"Aye, dropping..." Barrai said.

"And now the beam is...?" Oliver prompted.

"Coruscating across our hull," Marcant said.

"Not causing any significant harm," Barrai said.

A message from an untagged sender came to the team channel. It was a simple location pointer.

"What? Who is that?" Marcant said.

"Identify yourself," Telisa demanded.

The location pointer was sent again, then the connection dropped.

"That's a spot outside our ship."

"Or on the outer hull," Adair clarified. "It's also on every line their energy emission has taken since they arrived and started 'attacking'."

"It's letting us know where it is. Or an important part of it," Arakaki said.

"The brain," Marcant said.

"They're helping us! Magnus, Arakaki, we're going to this airlock. We're going out there to look at this thing. Maybe to attack it."

"I agree that may be the right call... but I should point out that we're making more assumptions here. That ship might want that thing for itself, it might be asking for it back. If we go destroy it, who knows what it will do?" Marcant said.

"We can't do much from here. Out there, we at least have options."

Magnus and Arakaki rendezvoused with her at the airlock she had highlighted on the tactical. Magnus's robots were already on their way outside using three other airlocks.

"We have to do something!" Yat said. "Grab your weapons. We're going to back them up."

"We don't know what they're facing yet."

"I have an idea," Yat said. "Meet me at the airlock!"

"Are you crazy? They're already—"

"Do it!"

Yat ran to retrieve the heavy Rovan force screens they had looted from the military complex. The units were almost too heavy to wear in the ship; the artificial gravity was set too high. On the exterior of the ship, though, it was considerably less. The decks of the ship were built to line up with certain weak parts of the gravity spinner's field to provide the convenience of weight for the crew, but the PIT team headed into an area where they felt little gravity.

If anything goes wrong, those force screens could make a big difference.

"Just ahead, beyond that bulge," Telisa was saying outside.

Yat watched the three team members through one of the attendant feeds. Telisa, Magnus, and Arakaki halted. They had deployed their Veer suit helmets to protect them from the cold vacuum. One of Telisa's attendants shot forward and arced around the obstruction before them.

"By the Five!" Telisa exclaimed.

Yat saw a feed of the area near the particle beam's target.

It was as if a delicate gossamer creature of thousands of filaments has been built onto the otherwise drab hull like a work of art infecting an industrial factory building.

"Wait. That's familiar!" Arakaki said.

"It's the same stuff we saw in the Rovan complex. Inside that room protected by a force field," Magnus finished.

Yat found the force screen units in a cargo bay. He released the heavy straps that had secured one to the sled and hefted it onto his back over his Veer suit.

"I'm supposed to be the crazy one," Oliver said aloud, running into the bay.

"Just put that one on," Yat answered him out loud.

"This thing was a Rovan prisoner. We let it out," Telisa said on the team channel.

"I never opened that door!" Marcant interjected.

"I don't think you did. I think we let it out when we performed the space to surface strike," Telisa said.

Yat and Oliver staggered out of the bay toward an airlock. Yat estimated they could be outside in just a few minutes.

Telisa cried out in pain.

"Duck!" she exclaimed.

Telisa dropped faster than anyone else. An attendant shattered in the silence of the vacuum and went spinning away. Yat lost his view of the alien constructs as more attendants dropped their feeds. He was still able to see Telisa, Arakaki, and Magnus from their personal attendants.

He pushed forward, huffing under the weight of the Rovan artifact on his back. Luckily his Veer suit protected him from the straps across his shoulders, which were not designed for holding anything onto people.

"Are you okay?" Magnus asked.

"My suit's hot. Something got me. It's killing our attendants. Is it the particle beam?"

"No," Barrai said. "That thing out there has defenses. I'm now sensing movement across the hull—not ours."

This possibility was what Yat had been preparing for.

"Marcant! Can you activate these Rovan force shields?" Yat asked. "Oliver and I can wear these out there and help!"

"No. Adair might be able to."

"We need to use them."

"This is very dangerous," Adair told them.

"We're being attacked by aliens. We have to do something," Yat urged.

"I believe Telisa is asking the *Iridar* to come in and assault with its beam weapons," Adair said.

"Stand down, Yat. I appreciate your willingness to risk yourself, but it's unnecessary. If it comes to a fight, the *Iridar* can take care of this," Telisa said.

"Won't it devastate the *Sharplight*?" asked Yat.

"We'll use a low power strike if necessary," Barrai said.

"Okay. We'll stand by," Yat conceded, though his teeth gritted in frustration.

Yat glanced at Oliver next to him in the airlock prep bay.

"We have a shot lined up," Barrai said. Yat was impressed that they were able to coordinate fire support from an empty Vovokan ship.

"It's clear the Rovans felt it presented a danger," Telisa said. "They isolated it. It endangers us, but not necessarily on purpose. As Maxsym pointed out, it could only be trying to survive. We don't know if the Rovans were justified in holding it there."

"The way I see it, we can abandon the *Sharplight* if we don't want to kill it. Otherwise, we'd better take it down while we can," Magnus said.

"I can verify it's spreading," Adair said. "I see signs of new activity inside the ship."

"We can't kill it without more information," Telisa said. "It's obviously intelligent."

"It's invaded our ship. It came after us," Arakaki said.

"True, but we invaded that Rovan base. We may not be any better behaved than it is," Telisa said.

"We believe that there are only automated systems left there, no living Rovans," Marcant objected. "If there were Rovans, we would be trying to talk to them, not invade their complexes."

A bright flash of light played across all the feeds. Yat gasped.

"What the hell—"

"By the Five!"

"Dammit!"

"The Rovan ship fired on us," Yat heard Barrai say. Everyone absorbed that news for a second, then she continued. "No hull penetration. Our shields came up."

"I think it was only enough to destroy something out there. Part of the invader," Marcant said.

A swarm of red blossomed on the tactical as unknown contacts moved across the *Sharplight*'s outer hull.

"Fall back!" yelled Telisa.

"What are those things?" Oliver asked. "Are those from the Rovan ship, or...?"

Four more attendants went offline.

"Robots. They're not from the Rovan ship. They must be from our invader," Marcant said.

Yat glimpsed a machine in the remaining feeds: it was a coiled, black snake-like body with four arms terminating in powerful grasper claws. He did not have time to identify sensor clusters or weapons on its body.

"Open fire," Telisa ordered.

"Our shields are blocking Iridar's weapons," Barrai said.

"Drop them and give us fire support!" Telisa yelled. The three Terrans and Magnus's robots were firing at enemies.

"I can't, TM. The shields are not responding to my commands."

"We're up!" Yat said. He stepped forward into the lock.

"Those things will kill us," Oliver asserted.

"We're not leaving them to fight this alone. Especially not with these amazing artifacts on our backs."

Yat cycled the airlock. Oliver complained again, but Yat did not hear it. He started forward when the door opened. He was already using the tactical to plot his course across the outside of the *Sharplight*'s hull.

"Adair! Activate these shields!" Yat demanded.

"Telisa?" Adair asked.

"Yes! Get them out here!" Telisa ordered.

Yat felt something change. His legs were swept up by an unseen force, separating him from the ship.

Oh no.

Then the force receded and his Veer suit resettled on the outer hull. Yat swam in adrenaline. He activated his boot's magnetic clamps for a moment, then decided against it and turned them off.

If the force field comes back on there, it could cut my feet off instead of push them up again...

Magnus yelled something. They were fighting. Yat needed to hurry.

"I'm sorry. This is difficult," Adair said.

"Hey! Something's—" Oliver said. Yat assumed Oliver was experiencing similar problems.

Yat turned and looked back.

Oliver screamed, then blinked out of existence. His Rovan device went tumbling. Yat stopped cold, stunned.

Was that... teleportation? Disintegration?

"What happened?" Yat demanded.

"The shield behaved unexpectedly," Adair said.

"That one's flanking!" Arakaki yelled. Yat was not watching them.

"Where is Oliver?!" Yat asked in shock.

"Focus now," Adair said. "I won't try that sequence again. For now, advance. Telisa needs you to provide a distraction so she can take out some of those machines."

Yat resumed his steps, staggering forward.

"I have protection?"

"Yes, the device is active. Hurry. The forward team is pinned down," Adair urged.

Yat let his link provide a path to the team's location on the tactical. He followed it and tried not to think about Oliver's apparent death. He looked down at the PAW in his hands and wondered it he could even fire it without the rounds bouncing back and killing him.

"Yat! Do you have the shield up?" Telisa asked.

"Yes," he said. "Adair can control it—I think."

"Veer twenty degrees right," she ordered. "A little faster."

Yat was already moving as fast as he could. The next second, one of the creepy snake-things darted up and released a burst of energy.

His faceplate protected his eyes from the glare. He felt nothing.

The enemy tried again. It hopped forward in the low-grav environment, unnaturally fast. It released another blast at Yat.

Yat prepared to fire back, but suddenly the thing glared bright red and disintegrated. Its pieces flopped away from each other in the silent vacuum.

"Turn left," Telisa said. "There's one down in that airlock depression."

Yat changed course for the area Telisa mentioned.

"Adair! Can I use my weapon with the shield up?"

"I'm guessing you might be able to," Adair said and managed to sound like it was being helpful.

"Yat, hold your fire," Telisa ordered. "I'll be the hammer."

Another alien machine emerged in front of Yat with lightning speed. It attacked him as the other one had, a silent assault in space. Yat was not harmed.

A grenade rolled past Yat, retaining light contact with the hull. As the alien robot attacked again, the grenade lit up. Yat had a glimpse of shrapnel bouncing away from him. No sound came; he sensed only a slight vibration through his feet.

The grenade reported a kill. Yat walked up to the edge of the hull depression and peered down. A black scar tarnished the hull and a few pieces of broken metal floated nearby.

"We got it," Yat said.

The tactical showed that Magnus and Arakaki had held their position. It showed an enemy kill nearby.

Another bright flash made Yat wince.

"Who—"

"That was me," Barrai said. "I've managed to drop our shields. The *Iridar* caught one in the open."

"What can *Iridar* see of the main body or brain?" Telisa asked.

"Not much. I think it was under the overhang there. The Rovan ship can see it, but view from *Iridar* is blocked."

"Let's go check out the area that was under the beam," Telisa said to Yat.

"Magnus, Arakaki, we've got this."

"Let us follow you," Arakaki requested.

"Get more attendants out here to find the rest of those robots. Until you spot them, hold a defensive position there. Do you have grenades left?"

"Yes," Magnus said.

"Good. Yat and I will investigate the center."

Yat was almost there. The *Sharplight* rose to a new level ahead. He approached an artificial cliff of at least six meters.

The overhang glittered. It sported a silvery sheen that made Yat's skin crawl.

"Is that the thing?" he asked.

"It's an energy collector," Marcant said. "The invader must have deployed it for power... probably before it started to steal ours."

"Check below," Telisa instructed. "It was below."

Yat took several more steps forward. He shined a light from his PAW under the overhang. The deck had been slagged there.

"See that? It's dead. I think," Yat said.

"Let's take some more time and reassure ourselves that's the case," Telisa said.

Suddenly several voices erupted on the PIT channel at once.

"Activity at four o'clock!" Arakaki warned.

"It's moving!" Marcant said.

"The Rovan ship is breaking away," Barrai reported.

Yat tried to look, but he saw only the terrain of the *Sharplight* and the starry blackness above.

"We got it. We had to have. That ship left," Marcant said.

"Track the Rovan ship!" Telisa ordered.

"Aye... It's going to the complex we struck," Barrai said. "It must have emerged from there, too."

"By the Five. We devastated that place, but they still helped us," Telisa said.

"As dangerous as that thing might be, I suspect they were just helping themselves," Marcant said.

Yat could not disagree.

Chapter 26

Marcant flopped down onto a seat in the mess on the *Sharplight*. He felt tired. The last two shifts had included searching for hidden enemies, stripping open sections of the ship's infrastructure, and even an explosion which destroyed a maintenance machine. The rest of the team sat nearby as Telisa prepared to speak to them. Only Maxsym was not present, as he had returned to the *Iridar* to plumb the secrets of the Rovans.

Other than the explosion, the cleanup had gone well. The work to replace damaged and altered components would continue for a week. It would be a busy time for Barrai, who oversaw the *Sharplight*'s repair robots.

"It's time to leave this system. We have enough artifacts and information," Telisa announced. "All attempts at communication with the Rovan facility have fallen flat. My gut tells me there aren't any Rovans left. If the ship was controlled by an AI, it has nothing to say to us, otherwise it would have at least engaged in some experiments to learn how we might exchange information."

Marcant accepted Telisa's decision readily. He had tons of Rovan data to chew on.

And I've had an overdose of adventure, for now, Marcant thought. *We barely made it through the expedition... most of us.*

Oliver was gone.

It was not Adair's fault, and Adair was intelligent enough to have accepted that. Yat, though, would undoubtedly have a harder time of it.

"One bit of good news is that the installation appears to be repairing itself with thousands of rovlings. I think of that place as the master of the catacomb complexes, the core of their network, charged with preserving their stored assets in case the Rovans ever return. It looks like we didn't permanently break it, which I'm happy about."

"We should leave some attendants behind. If the Rovans return, one could sacrifice itself to send a message to Blackhab," Magnus suggested.

"Great minds think alike," Telisa said.

Telisa turned to Yat. The explorer's head was bowed where he sat at a plain white table.

"Yat, we owe you... and Oliver... a lot. When we get back to Blackhab, the Space Force will take you wherever you want to go."

"I don't have any place to go," Yat said. "I'd like to be a part of this team if you'll have me."

Uhm... we kill his best friend, and this is his response?

"It could be a death wish. He might want to die, now that his friend is gone," Adair said to Marcant privately.

Is that how Adair feels about the betrayal of Achaius?

Thinking of Achaius made Marcant sick. He distracted himself from that line of thought.

"I don't think so," Marcant said to Adair privately. "But I do admit, I'm surprised by this reaction."

Telisa looked very sad. She nodded.

"You know... You know as well as the rest of us now, that if you stay, you'll end up dead, sooner or later," she said.

"Maybe."

"We'll be traveling for a while. Think on it," Telisa deflected.

***

The voyage back was incredibly exciting for Marcant. It was not because he fought in the gym almost every day, or because he participated in virtual missions with the team. It was because they had a wealth of amazing Rovan artifacts and data, and everyone wanted to know how they worked.

Some of the artifacts had been easy enough to understand with a little study. The various fluid containers held super-lubricants, liquid metals, and solvents. The small colorful objects on the Rovan shells turned out to be data storage devices, which Telisa believed to hold memories of or for the deceased, perhaps videos or digitized works of art. One of the devices they found at the starport was simply an automated digging tool, the Rovan version of the device Shiny had given Telisa in the Trilisk complex.

Other artifacts remained mysterious, such as Oliver's metal ring assembly that could emit complex EM field patterns.

Marcant kept up with these discoveries and trials of learning, but his part of the puzzle was to comprehend Rovan computation, data storage, and unlock the secrets they had copied from the heavily guarded Rovan installation.

Marcant found himself in his darkened personal quarters on the *Sharplight*, eyes closed, concentrating on a virtual workspace. He tested basic commands sent to a Rovan microcomputer, trying to get it to store and retrieve tiny amounts of data. It was frustrating work; every time something went wrong, there was no way to know what it was short of either random experimentation, or mapping the entire machine down to the subatomic level and reverse engineering it. They proceeded with both approaches on different Rovan computers.

"The others don't understand the enormity of what we do," Marcant complained to Adair. "Do they really think it's comparable to figuring out a Rovan tool? These *aliens* whose heads are filled with *alien* thoughts have come up with ways to understand the universe, and they've devised *alien* representations of information that we have to unravel."

"Well, it does sound hard when you approach it from that side," Adair said. "With a few assumptions and a different approach it becomes much easier."

Marcant snorted. Adair continued.

"They're aliens. Yes. And they think differently. But their mathematics and physics describe the same universe we live in. So if we start from the other end—the universe we live in—then we find our common ground."

"Good luck with that. I think I'll stick with my approach. I find a simpler device, like a screwdriver, and I look at its vocabulary. Within that vocabulary are things we can actually guess, like 'on' and 'off' and 'clockwise' and 'counterclockwise'. From there, I can deduce how they encode commands and, with other tools, very simple data over the conductor. Then it's a matter up building up layer after layer."

It was Adair's turn to make a smug sound.

"What?" Marcant asked.

"You might as well go to the bay where they've laid all those trinkets out and help them disassemble the tools. Leave the heavy thinking to me," Adair said.

"Well, I have this computer worked out," Marcant claimed.

"'Worked out' is different than 'working'. You can only do that because Rovans have next to no security," Adair said. "I've begun to believe what Telisa said about them... they don't seem to have a problem with bad actors in their physical existence."

"It's crazy, isn't it? I mean even the *Celarans*, the nicest creatures you can imagine, have secure systems."

"Well, security is not black and white, but a continuum. Vovokan systems showed us that."

Marcant agreed. He had thought that Terran systems had evolved to a peak of security after learning countless lessons over the decades, but the Vovokans had taken hacking and security to whole new levels. Vovokans might not have perfect stealth, or the most powerful energy weapons, but when it came to playing games with cybersecurity, they were the best. To some degree, Shiny had even managed to hack Trilisk systems, at least as far as the request filter for the AI, a feat which Marcant had not been able to duplicate.

"Whatever befell these Rovans, maybe it's a good thing," Marcant said. "I'd hate to think what Shiny would have done to them."

***

Marcant felt apprehension as Telisa entered his quarters for an impromptu meeting.

"I want to touch bases with you on something that's been bothering me," Telisa said.

This is about triggering the alarm in the Rovan military base.

"Yes?" Marcant replied nervously. An awful feeling clawed at his gut; he supposed it was guilt.

"We're hoarding valuable information. That was acceptable in the beginning, when we were at odds with the Space Force. Now, though, we have to share most of what we've learned about Vovokan, Celaran, Quarus, and Rovan technologies."

"With who, though? The Space Force?"

"Blackhab, for sure. Space Force as well. Also, civilian scientists across the frontier."

"There are scientists on the frontier? I mean, sure there are, but... I think most of the new stuff comes from Core World AIs. They're smarter and more driven than Core Worlders who spend all their time playing."

Telisa nodded. "The Core World AIs will pick up whatever they need as soon as we hand it to Blackhab and the others. The information will spread."

"Okay. I can put together what we know. The task will really become, what *don't* we want to tell them? I noticed you didn't add Trilisk tech to your list," Marcant said.

Telisa shook her head. "We can keep that to ourselves... though maybe we should try to pool what we know about that with other PIT teams? We need to learn to surreptitiously communicate with them."

"Not on Shiny's watch. I did have a different idea, though. We could give the other teams info in such a way that Shiny would not know who sent it out. An anonymous communication method. So Shiny would know what we said, but he would not know which PIT team said it."

"Might be useful."

"I'll prepare a system and show you how it could work."

"Good. Enjoy your shore leave when we arrive," Telisa said.

"Shore leave? At Blackhab? There's nothing there but a bunch of immature Celarans and annoying Blackvines."

"Oh. Well, I guess that means you'll have more time to work on these problems."

Marcant could not help himself. He smiled.

"Well, at least we won't be staying long," he teased.

"Oh?" Telisa said. She turned to regard him.

"Adair cracked some of the data we got from the military installation," Marcant said.

"If indeed that's what it was," Adair inserted privately.

Marcant verbally stumbled, then recovered.

"Ah... and so, in that data, Adair was able to identify star charts which showed other Rovan systems."

"Good work! That's tempting. Let's see what we learn from these, first," she said, trying to sound like there was a decision to be made.

Marcant knew they would go. No one liked not knowing what had happened to the Rovans, or if there were any still alive.

“Sure,” he said. “We play it by ear.”

Chapter 27

The huge station Blackhab rotated on the *Sharplight*'s sensor displays piped through Telisa's link. It looked the same as she remembered it.

"I'm glad to see it's still there," Magnus said aloud.

"I know exactly what you mean. We've seen so much happen, I was afraid it would be destroyed, too," she said.

Magnus waited with Barrai and Arakaki for the others to arrive for an FTF in a command lounge on the *Sharplight*.

"We're being greeted by the Celarans," Barrai reported. "They've invited us to dock."

"Hold," Telisa said as she walked into the bridge lounge where Barrai worked. "Before we can get close, we need to explain what happened and ask for their help in making sure our ship is safe."

"You think that thing is still hiding in here somewhere?" Yat asked.

"Adair and Barrai don't think so, and I would tend to believe them, but we'll inform our allies of the risk and let them check it out themselves. We'll be that much safer."

"With your permission, I'll also send a request for supplies," Barrai said.

"Do it. The sooner we can get a refill, the better."

"You sound like there's some hurry," Arakaki said. "Do you already know where we're going next?"

"Marcant and Adair found more Rovan colonies to check out."

"Ah. I don't know whether to hope or dread that we find living Rovans," Arakaki said.

"Don't you want to know what happened to them?" Yat asked.

"Yes," Arakaki said. "As long as our rovling countermeasures in development prove effective."

I'm going to work hard to ensure it doesn't come to that again. While training for it in case it does.

Telisa waited to make sure that conversation had hit a lull before launching the next subject.

"We need to talk about Shiny," Telisa said. "I think we should send him our reports on the Rovans."

"I assumed that we had broken away from our partnership with Shiny," Arakaki said.

"It's complicated," Telisa said. "In a way you're right... we're avoiding Earth. But there may be some benefit in... benefitting Shiny. If we send him information and artifacts—say Rovan ones, or information about that thing we found on our ship—then it may incentivize him to remain cooperative with us, or at least, to delay hunting us down."

"I think that's logical," Magnus said. "We can't 'hurt his feelings' or anything like that. Betrayal is normal for him. But we can show him there's some advantage in letting us continue to operate. He can spend resources to hunt us down for refusing to continue the war as he tried to arrange through Siobhan, or he can sit back and accept our occasional tribute."

Marcant frowned. Telisa understood: It made sense, but grated.

"It would be better if we could just make it more expensive for him to come get us than it would give him in return," Marcant said. "After all, he can already make more copies of us, right?"

"How expensive would an assassination really be? One Vovokan battle sphere might be able to kill us all," Arakaki pointed out.

"What would we send him?" Maxsym asked. "We don't have a Rovan ship. Even if we did, we shouldn't give him the very best. Let's downplay everything we've found."

"I agree," Telisa said. "The juiciest things we have are those compact force field generators. If each of us can walk around with a shaped force field even half as strong as a Vovokan battle sphere's shield, it would go a long ways toward keeping us alive. I won't share that with him."

Terran and Vovokan technology could create spherical defenses, such as those around their ships or protecting a Vovokan battle sphere. The Terrans could even generate a bulge here or a dimple there in such a screen, and the Vovokans could alter their screens a little more, but their studies of Rovan technology on the voyage home showed that the Rovans had built and operated relatively small devices that created protective fields of any shape.

"I've learned to safely control the units we have," Adair said. "I regret very much that I was not able to keep Oliver safe."

"You warned us of the danger," Yat said. "I'm the one who convinced him to go out there."

Telisa cleared her throat.

"I ordered you both out there. It's on me. I've also asked you to think it over before joining our team. It's hazardous work, even by frontier standards," she said.

"I still want to join," Yat said confidently.

"Then welcome aboard. I'd like you to become a Rovan tech specialist, since you already have a leg up in that area. Work with Marcant and Adair to pick up everything they've learned. The first thing I want is a new version of the shield generator, integrated with our Veer suits."

Yat looked very serious. "I'm sure the ones we have were made to be carried by Rovans. They're too heavy for us, but making them smaller will probably make them weaker," he said.

"That's an acceptable tradeoff."

"I'll do it."

Telisa felt he would do a very good job. She imagined the team deployed with their breaker claws, stealth spheres, and portable force screens. That powerful combination would be hard to beat. She wanted her team members to come back alive every time.

Every time.

***

Telisa stood beside Magnus as the simulated world took shape around them. They were back in the Rovan installation where they had encountered the army of rovlings, standing in an intersection of three wide Rovan corridors filled with rovling pipes. Six of Magnus's soldier robots materialized nearby.

Telisa carried an experimental new weapon. She hefted it and performed a weapons check through her link.

The new weapon was a Terran adaptation of a Rovan one. Careful analysis of one of the artifacts revealed it contained what Magnus called "rovling binder helices" that were essentially Rovan glue grenades. Apparently, the Rovan version was designed to attach to several rovlings, then pull them tightly together with tough retracting strings of glue, causing them to become an almost immobile ball that blocked the advance of the rovlings behind.

The chittering alarm went off in the virtual complex. Telisa could feel the floor vibrate with the impacts of thousands of rovling feet. A wind came up, caused by the approach of thousands of rovlings displacing air in the complex.

Telisa and Magnus cloaked themselves.

Telisa deployed four conventional Terran grenades to meet the vanguard of rovlings. She activated her stealth sphere and loaded the sensor rovling target signature at the top of her laser pistol's priority queue.

"Siobhan and Caden aren't back," she said to Magnus as she prepared. "So I think we need to recruit people who will specialize in one alien technology each. I'm not going back to a Core World for it, though. We need to figure out how to get talented, driven people from the frontier."

Booooom! Booooom!

Her first grenades exploded inside nearby Rovan pipes. They reported fourteen kills between them. The next second, rovlings poured out of several pipes in each corridor. Magnus's soldier machines opened fire.

Bam, bam, bam. Bam, bam, bam.

"We'll need someone for each of Vovokan, Celaran, and Quarus tech. You would mentor the Vovokan specialist."

"Well, we have Lee, so—"

Bam! Bambambam!

"I just found out Lee is leaving the team. To head a Celaran equivalent of PIT."

Booooom!

"Damn! Well good for zher," Magnus said. His sensor ghost moved slightly to one side and kept firing.

Hisssss.

His laser burned through two virtual rovlings that threatened to enter the intersection.

"You know, Telisa," he said carefully. He almost never called her by name like that. Telisa almost stopped dodging to listen to him. An enemy projectile grazed by her chin.

Zip. Crack.

She shot the rovling that had fired and sent off a binder helix to intercept a cluster of four more rovlings advancing down another corridor.

"If you're going to recruit more people, you'd better work on your pitch. Telling them they're going to die is a bit counterproductive."

Magnus struck a rovling that emerged from a pipe behind him before it could carve into his leg. Two short, sturdy blades popped out of the tips of his Veer boots, a new feature he had added himself. He kicked at the next one, trying out the new weapon.

Hisssss.

Telisa shot two rovlings on the ceiling, but more came in. Magnus's machines had fallen, and they were out of Terran grenades. Telisa snapped on her Rovan force field.

Zip. Snap. Zip. Thwack.

Incoming projectiles ricocheted off her protective field.

"I can hardly lead people in under the illusion they'll be safe and sound," she said.

Booooom!

Another Terran grenade exploded, reporting six kills. She whirled 180 degrees and launched a binding helix down the corridor toward a new group of bladed melee rovlings that were busily cutting apart other groups of rovlings stuck together by binder helices.

"We'll just have to find people as crazy as we are about exploration."

THE END of The Rovan Ruins (continued in The Rovan Binary)

From the Author

Thanks for reading! As an indie author, I rely on your ratings and reviews to legitimize my work to those who have not read me. Please rate and review this book online.

Made in the USA
Middletown, DE
03 June 2019